TWO GOOD MEN

BOOKS BY S. E. REDFEARN

AS S. E. REDFEARN
Two Good Men

AS SUZANNE REDFEARN
Where Butterflies Wander
Moment in Time
Hadley & Grace
In an Instant
No Ordinary Life
Hush Little Baby

TWO
GOOD
MEN

S. E. REDFEARN

BLACK STONE
PUBLISHING

Printed in the United States of America

Fiction / Thrillers / Suspense

Blackstone Publishing
31 Mistletoe Rd.
Ashland, OR 97520

www.BlackstonePublishing.com

For
My family

I learned that courage was not the absence of fear, but the triumph over it.

—NELSON MANDELA

1

Dick stares at the two birthday cards on his desk in front of him, still unable to decide: *Taylor Swift or the teddy bear?* The Taylor card sings, but he can't recall if Kiley idolizes or despises the singer. He spent an hour in the Hallmark store trying to find the perfect card to welcome his daughter into teenagedom. Finally, the salesclerk took pity on him. She asked Kiley's age, then handed him the Taylor Swift card. The woman frowned at his teddy bear choice. Dick bought both.

He smiles at the teddy bear card. It reminds him of the stuffed bear Kiley slept with when she was a toddler, a brown raggedy animal, half an ear gone and only one black button eye.

It's hard to believe so much time has passed.

His alarm beeps, and he puts the cards back in his briefcase, grabs his cigarettes, and walks from the cubicle. With a nod to Graham, who is at his workbench in the lab, he continues to the stairs, then climbs the three flights to the roof of Pentco Pharmaceuticals.

Squinting against the brightness, he walks to the parapet, lights a cigarette, and takes a deep drag. The soothing nicotine fills his lungs, giving him his third heady buzz of the day. As the smoke drifts, he looks at the brilliant blue sky stretched to the Santa Ana Mountains in the distance and thinks God must hold a special place in His twisted, sadistic heart especially for him. For a month, he's waited for the steely gray clouds to clear, and now, here it is, a day beautiful as the maker can make, and there's not a damn thing he can do about it.

He glances over the parapet at the concrete below then back at the mountains and sighs. *Man plans, and God laughs,* his dad used to say.

The thought occurred to him on a morning similar to this but the sun obscured. There was nothing particularly memorable about the moment except for the certainty. Nothing to look forward to, and the best of his life behind him. He might have done it right then but didn't like the idea of leaving on such a gloomy day. He wanted baseball weather, blue skies and sun. But like a cruel joke, the past month set records for consecutive days of overcast skies and rain, Southern California dark and stormy as Seattle.

He lifts his face and sneers at the blinding blue heavens, then lowers it back to the sidewalk. Give or take, it's about thirty feet. A thin hedge runs beside the strip of concrete, the bushes trimmed each Tuesday by a pair of brothers, Eduardo and Armando. The landscape team has been with the company longer than Dick. He remembers meeting them his first day, his boss at the time introducing him as the new hotshot chemist who was going to find a cure for allergies.

He scoffs and flicks the ashes of his cigarette over the edge, watching as they float like snow to the ground. His own fall, accounting for acceleration, will take less than a second. Which means, in less time than it takes to inhale a breath, the toil of thirty-nine years will be over.

He studies the spot he expects to land and considers again

the awful possibility of failing, of waking up to people oohing and ahhing and tsking over him. The odds are slim, the physics of survival nearly impossible, but bad luck has always had a way of finding him.

With a last glance at the stunning blue sky, he crushes the cigarette beneath his toe and returns to the stairs, a hard wish in his heart that the weather holds until Monday.

2

It's strange having to knock.

"You're early," Caroline says, clearly displeased. "I'll take that."

His ex-wife relieves him of his boxed burden—pink Heelys, size seven, bought from the sporting goods store for $79.95. Kiley knows it's what she's getting from him. She dictated what she wanted to Caroline, who then dictated it to Dick. He'd wrapped them anyway.

Taped to the top is the card. He settled on the teddy bear— too unsure to give her the other one. The front of the card reads, "To my daughter on her birthday." Inside, "You're a beautiful sight and stuffed just right." He signed it, "Love, Dad."

He follows Caroline through his living room and his kitchen to his backyard. Kiley is on the trampoline with Jim. Dick smiles and waves, uncertain as he always is around his kids, a strange feeling made stranger by knowing other men don't feel this way. His kids are the most important thing in the world to him, the thing he works for and would die for, yet constantly they baffle and terrify him. He's felt it since they were born, enamored and panicked at once.

Kiley ignores him, while Jim gives a slight nod.

"Hello, Dick. Can I get you a drink?" The meaty palm of Pete, Caroline's new husband, extends toward him. Pete is the same height as Dick, an inch or two over six feet, but that's where the similarities end. Pete is thick; Dick is thin. Pete is ruddy and covered in hair—head, face, forearms, tufts sticking out of his collar at his chest. Dick is fair and still unable to grow a full beard. Pete is a plumber. Dick is a chemist.

"Thanks, Pete, but I think I still remember where the beers are."

In the kitchen, he finds Caroline pouring small carrots from a plastic bag onto a plate. She looks good, her dark hair freshly dyed and her face made up with eyeliner and lipstick. She's kept off most of the weight she lost for her wedding two months ago and looks happier than she did when they were married.

He grabs a Heineken from the fridge and, ignoring her peeved look, retrieves the bottle opener from the top drawer beside the sink. He pops off the cap, then, knowing it will irritate her even more, sets the cap and opener on the spotless counter.

She opens her mouth to snap at him but, saved by the bell, the door chime interrupts. He smirks, and she sneers, then hurries off to greet the guests.

Dick takes a long swig and returns outside.

Three beers and one cold slice of Domino's pizza later, the party is over. The gifts have been opened and the wrapping paper and empty boxes cast aside. Kneeling, he retrieves his unopened card from beneath the wrought-iron patio set he and Caroline picked out a decade ago.

"Happy birthday, sweetheart," he says, handing Kiley the lavender envelope and giving her a peck on her dark curls.

She groans and shifts away. He leaves her and crosses the yard to Jim, who is again on the trampoline. "Hey, buddy, I'm going to take off. I just wanted to say goodbye."

"Then say it," Jim says, playing up his insolence for his friends.

Dick stands awkwardly a moment before giving a thin smile along with half a wave. He doesn't bother saying goodbye to anyone else.

———

He gets to his apartment a little after eight, sighs at the television, then marches back out the door. The rest of the evening is spent drinking beer and watching the Angels play the Padres at the bar down the street.

Near midnight, almost drunk enough to be numb, he returns. He pulls his phone from his pocket to change for bed, surprised to see the voicemail symbol lit up.

"Dick, how could you?" Caroline's voice squawks.

He shakes his head and slumps to sit on the mattress.

"What kind of a cruel card is that to give your daughter?" *Cruel?*

"'Stuffed just right'!" she shrieks. "Kiley hasn't stopped crying since you left. It's not her fault she's overweight. I wouldn't blame her if she never forgave you. I certainly wouldn't—"

Dick taps the screen, cutting off the rant, then drops his elbows to his knees and his face to his hands. He rubs his sockets as if trying to erase the day, then without bothering the change, crawls beneath the covers and falls into drunken sleep, visions of teddy bears and gray concrete swirling in his mind.

3

His head fuzzy from his hangover, Dick sets the groceries on the counter, makes himself a peanut butter and jelly sandwich, and pours himself a ginger ale. Then he settles on the couch to watch the second game of the Angels-Padres series.

His phone buzzes, signaling a new voicemail. He considers ignoring it, certain it's Caroline continuing her beratement. But then, mostly out of boredom, he pulls it from his pocket to see there are actually three messages, all from his sister.

He taps the first one, left an hour ago when he was at the grocery store.

"Dickie, call me," Dee says.

He moves on to the next, left fifteen minutes ago on his drive home.

"Where are you?" she says, her voice tight.

His pulse ticks up a notch as he taps the one left a moment ago.

"Jesse and I are going to Janelle's. Call me when you get this."

Janelle is his sister's best friend.

He hits the callback button, and Dee picks up on the first ring.

"He's back," she says without a greeting.

He blinks at the words, which make no sense, though he understands perfectly what she is saying.

"Otis is back," she says, confirming it.

Twelve years ago, Dee's neighbor, Otis Parsons, was sentenced to twenty years for raping Ed Collins, the eleven-year-old brother of Joe Collins, Dee's boyfriend at the time.

"Did you hear me?" Dee asks, and he realizes he hasn't responded.

"Huh? Yeah. How?"

"Does it matter?" she says, her fear reverberating through the phone.

He supposes it doesn't, but he has always struggled with things that don't make sense. Twenty years is still eight years away.

"I don't know what to do," Dee says.

"Did you call the police?"

"I did. As soon as I realized he was back, I called Sheriff Barton."

"And?"

"And he said there's nothing he can do. Otis served his time and can live where he wants."

"But he *didn't* serve his time."

"Dickie, *stop!*"

"Okay," he says, squeezing his eyes tight and forcing himself past it. "Is Jesse okay?"

"Freaked out by my freak-out, but other than that, yeah, he's okay. He's inside playing Monopoly with Janelle."

Dick imagines his nephew and Janelle sitting in Janelle's cluttered living room—Janelle giggling as she collects properties based on their colors, and Jesse generously trying not to bankrupt her, telling her it's okay if she doesn't pay the rent when she lands on his properties and trading her Boardwalk for Baltic Avenue so she'll have the pretty blue match to Park Place. Janelle loves having fun but couldn't care less about winning.

"He's going to make good on his threat," Dee says at the same time Dick thinks it, his heart clenching tight like a fist.

Twelve years ago, it was Dee's testimony that put Otis behind bars. And a year later, when Jesse was born, Otis wrote her from prison congratulating her on the birth and saying how happy he was that she'd had a BOY and how he couldn't wait to MEET him.

Dee gave the letter to Sheriff Barton, and a copy was put in Otis's file, but since there was no actual threat, there was nothing more that could be done. At the time, Dee wasn't overly concerned. By the time Otis got out, Jesse would be grown.

But Jesse isn't grown. Jesse is eleven, the same age Ed was when Otis raped him.

"Are you there?" Dee says.

"Yeah. Just give me a second."

His brain whirs wildly to come up with an idea of what they should do, and finally, with no great epiphany, he says the only thing he can think of: "I'll come tomorrow, and we'll figure it out."

"Thanks," Dee says with a sigh of relief. "I knew I could count on you."

Her faith in him makes him want to hurl the phone across the room.

"See you tomorrow," he says and hangs up.

He sets the phone on the table beside his untouched lunch, closes his eyes, and takes several long, slow breaths. When the whooshing in his brain stops, he moves to the folding card table he uses as a dining set, pulls a yellow pad from his briefcase, and begins the way he always does when given an assignment:

Statement of Problem: Otis has returned.

Implications: Otis, a deviant who molests boys and with a vendetta against Dee, poses a direct threat to Jesse.

Hypothetical solutions:

- *Protect against the threat. (i.e. guard dog, security system, gun)*
- *Remove Dee and Jesse from the threat. (i.e. Dee and Jesse move)*
- *Remove the threat. (i.e. Otis returns to prison)*

He crosses out the first solution, knowing no dog, security system, or gun would be foolproof enough to guarantee Jesse's safety.

Then for a long minute, he stares at the second—*Dee and Jesse move*—his blood growing hot at the unfairness. Four generations of Rayneses have lived in the Raynes' home, and Dee and Jesse have grown their lives there.

Moving on to the third solution, he retrieves his phone from the coffee table, searches through his contacts, and hits the call button.

"Barton here," Sheriff Barton says, his gruff voice exactly the same as the last time Dick spoke to him, which was at his dad's funeral a decade ago. The whole town was there, his dad well loved.

"Quiet greatness," Sheriff Barton had said as he shook Dick's hand, and truer words have never been spoken. Dick's dad was small in stature and humble, but he always helped a neighbor and never wavered from what was right.

"Hello, Sheriff. It's Dick Raynes. Sorry to be bothering you on a Saturday."

"No bother, son. I assume you're calling about this business with Otis?"

"Yes, sir."

"Damn shame him getting out early and coming back."

"More than a shame," Dick says. "Terrifying considering the circumstances and the threat he made against Dee."

"I can't disagree."

Dick hears activity in the background and realizes the sheriff is at the community center playing Bingo. "B5, B as in boy, 5." More mumbling. "N3 . . ."

"Unfortunately, like I told your sister, there ain't much I can do. The law's pretty plain when it comes to the rights of released felons. Unless he does something wrong—"

"He raped two boys!"

"Unless he does something *new* wrong, I have no choice but to leave him be. I've put extra patrols in your neighborhood, but that's about all I can do."

"Sheriff, I don't think you understand—"

"Son, don't tell me what I do or don't understand"—his voice flares, betraying his true emotions—"your family wasn't the only ones who knew and loved those boys. I coached Joe. He was a good kid and a hell of an athlete. So was Ed. If there was something more I could be doing, I promise you, I'd be doing it. I'll do what I can to keep an eye out for Dee and Jesse, but like I said, as far as the law's concerned, my hands are tied."

"Well, if you can't help, who can?"

Silence.

"Sir?"

"My prayers are with you."

The phone clicks off, and Dick stops pacing and stares at the black screen, pulse pounding. In the apartment next door, the ballgame is on, and the neighbor's team must be losing because muffled grumblings followed by a more discernible outburst reverberate through the wall.

Returning to the table, Dick takes out his laptop, logs onto the internet, and types "Megan's Law" into the search field.

He was in college getting his undergraduate degree when the legislation passed. Because of Otis, he took an interest in the law. Named after a seven-year-old girl who had been raped

and strangled by a twice-convicted child molester, the law requires sex offenders to register with local authorities whenever
they relocate. If they fail to do so and the crime they were convicted of was a felony, the violation is a felony.

California is a three-strikes state, which means not reg-
istering would send Otis away for life. A prayer in his heart,
he punches in the zip code for Independence, California, and
a map of Inyo County appears along with twenty-eight blue
squares and three red circles, signifying nonviolent and high-
risk sex offenders. Dick clicks on the red dot located by itself
in the middle of the county, and his hope deflates. From the
upper right corner of his screen, Otis looks out. While older
than the last time Dick saw him, the pale eyes, long nose, and
small-toothed smile are exactly as he remembers.

Beside the mugshot is a description:

> Otis Parsons; born 5/10/75; 5'10"; 155 pounds; brown
> hair; blue eyes; Caucasian; no known body piercings or
> markings; accused of (208d) kidnapping person with
> intent to commit rape, (286c) sodomy with person
> under fourteen years or with force, (f289a) sexual pen-
> etration with foreign object by force, (261.2/261.3)
> rape with force and threat, (288) crimes against chil-
> dren/lewd or lascivious, (207) kidnapping/to commit
> 261, 286, 288, 289.

Dick closes the computer and drops his face to his hands.
Otis registered, which means he is completely out of ideas.

4

Unable to sleep, Dick rose an hour before the sun and got on the road, and the trip, so far, has been a journey of self-loathing interspersed with jazz from KKJZ and attacks of mind-numbing anxiety. It is St. Patrick's Day, and Dick wonders if the luck of the Irish is limited to those of green-beer-and-cabbage descent. He could use a bit of four-leaf-clover luck right now, and though not superstitious, he wears the only item in his wardrobe with green, a golf shirt with thin mint stripes that Kiley gave him for Father's Day two years ago.

The tank is half full, but he fills up in Adelanto anyway, two hours into the four-and-a-half-hour drive. He smokes another cigarette, his third of the day, and stares at the glowing window of the minimart. He should eat something but knows he won't be able to keep it down. A nervous stomach, his mother used to say, a nice way of saying, even as a boy, he was a coward.

Be a man! he thinks as he climbs back into his Volvo. *Be a man! Be a man! BE! A! MAN!* The mantra plays each time he is asked to do some requisite act of manliness of which he should be capable but finds himself grossly incompetent: killing the rat dying a slow death in the sticky rat trap in the garage; telling

Jim's idiot baseball coach to go to hell; letting Caroline know she can't screw the plumber in their bed, in their house, while they're still married; facing the Pentco board and convincing them to give him another chance to figure out Freeway, his anti-allergen medicine that could help millions.

His fingers start to tingle, and he pulls to the side of the road and puts his head between his knees. He is very familiar with panic attacks, having suffered them since high school. He needs to calm his breathing before he hyperventilates. Grabbing a McDonald's bag from one of last week's lunches, he places it over his nose and mouth and inhales the stale smell of grease and fries, his shame overwhelming.

It takes several minutes for his breath to settle, and he pulls back onto the road.

———

A little before eleven, he arrives at Janelle's, and, despite the circumstances, the sight of the sunshine-yellow Victorian brings a smile. The house is like a bright little lemon drop plopped in the middle of a drab landscape of dull clapboard boxes and desert.

The screen door slams open, and Jesse bounds out. Though he looks like Dee—fine-featured with large, expressive eyes— his raven hair, tan skin, and deep-colored cheeks are his dad's.

"Hey, Uncle Dickie."

Dick hugs him longer than necessary.

Dee walks from the house, and he hugs her just as hard.

"Thanks for coming," she says, pulling away and giving a brave smile.

"Hey, Dickie!" Janelle hollers from the kitchen window, her curly blond hair catching the sun. "Come on in. I made sandwiches."

Dick follows his sister and nephew inside.

He busses Janelle on the cheek, and before he can pull away, she catches his face between her hands and plants a sloppy kiss on his forehead. Dick's certain she does things like that to fluster him . . . which works every time. His cheeks burn, and his eyes dart every which way to avoid looking somewhere they shouldn't.

Janelle was the first girl Dick ever kissed, and because of that, he's probably had more fantasies about her than any other woman on the planet, and he thinks she knows that and finds it endlessly entertaining.

She hands Dick a plate with a grilled cheese sandwich, potato chips, and a dill pickle. He carries it to the dining room and joins Jesse and Dee at the table.

"Hobby shop?" Jesse asks, his face lit up.

Dick reflects his nephew's grin back and nods. He and Jesse have been building model airplanes since Jesse could walk.

"The new Corsair is out," Dick says.

"Cool," Jesse says. "But I still need to finish the biplane."

Dick feels a pang of guilt as he thinks about the biplane they started three months ago, the thought reminding him of how long it's been since he last visited.

"I think I'll pass on the hobby shop," Dee says. "I have some things to do back at the house."

———

A few hours later, Dick drives with Jesse and their hobby shop purchases into the neighborhood of his childhood home, two parallel streets with a dozen small, tidy houses built in the thirties for the workers of the borax mines.

In Otis's driveway is a shiny black sedan, and Dick's eyes ricochet from its glossy paint to his sister's blue Subaru two driveways away as panic floods his veins. How could he have been so stupid as to let her come back here alone? He slams on the accelerator, whips into the driveway, and races into the house.

Dee looks up from the sofa, where she is curled with feet tucked beneath her, a bag of chips in her lap, and the TV blinking in front of her.

"Uncle Dickie?" Jesse says, walking in behind him, a question in his voice.

"I need to use the restroom," Dick says quickly to cover up his "freak-out," as Dee would call it, and hurries down the hall. Sitting on the toilet, he shakes his head, feeling like an idiot. He is not equipped for this. Already, he messed up. Otis is two doors away, and he let Dee come here alone. And now, the three of them are here, which is quite frankly no less unsettling.

Through the door, Dee laughs at something on the television, and he is struck by a jolt of déjà vu. His mom used to laugh like that. She'd sit in that exact spot, her feet tucked beneath her like Dee's are now, and laugh. He shakes the feeling away. The house holds ghosts, and each time he returns, he needs to fight past the dizzying vertigo that inevitably knocks him off balance.

Blowing out a breath, he pushes to his feet and returns to the living room.

"How'd it go?" Dee asks, sitting up and stretching her arms over her head.

"Great!" Jesse says, appearing from the kitchen with a half-peeled banana. Then he launches into a long explanation about the parts they bought and how he's going to paint the biplane.

Dee listens patiently, and Dick marvels as he always does at what an amazing mom she is, especially considering she never had anyone to teach her.

Finished with his explanation, Jesse bounds out the sliding glass door to the patio, and Dee's eyes follow with concern.

Standing, she says, "I need to get ready for work. Don't let him stay up. He has school tomorrow, so he needs to be in bed by nine."

———

From the open sliding glass door, Dee says, "I'm going to take your car so I don't have to move it."

Dick nods from the patio table where he and Jesse are working on their planes. She hurries away in her waitress uniform, still as pretty as she was in high school. Dick had hoped after Jesse's dad left that she might find someone, but it's been eleven years, and it's always just been her and Jesse.

He returns to the Corsair as Jesse paints Swiss crosses on the wings of his biplane. Being with Jesse is not like being with most kids. Since he was a toddler, he's been content with silence, which is good for Dick since he's never certain what to say. Dick's own kids are like most kids; they like noise—the television, music, games, bickering, exclaiming, complaining. Sitting still for hours, working on model airplanes from bygone eras, Kiley and Jim would lose interest before the parts were out of the bag. Dick has always been curious about genetics. He and Dee come from the same parents but are so different. Yet Jesse, her son, shares something with him undeniable and unique.

The left wing of his plane is slightly off-kilter, and Dick is debating whether to disassemble it or force it straight when the back gate opens. He looks up to see Otis walking through, and his blood goes cold.

"Dickie?" Otis says, his voice pitching in surprise. He stops a couple steps inside the gate. "I thought you left."

Past Dick's panic, a single synapse connects. Dee took Dick's car, so Otis thought it was Dee who was home. Alone. With Jesse.

Dick's eyes move from Otis's face to the right pocket of Otis's navy-blue windbreaker, his hand fisted around something long enough to cause the hand to partially stick out. Dick's fingers tighten around the fuselage of the plane in his hand as he stands. Straightening to his full height, he manages a tense, "Nope. Still here."

Otis tilts his head as if sizing Dick up, and Dick feels as if he's making the decision right then as to what he is going to do.

Forcing his eyes to remain steady on Otis's and to not roam back to the windbreaker, which the night is far too warm for, he says, "You need to leave."

"You heard him," Jesse snarls, and Dick realizes his nephew has stood as well.

Otis's eyes move from Dick to Jesse, and Dick watches as a sick smile crosses his face.

A flood of adrenaline to surges through him, and he repeats, "Leave."

The smile twitches, and Otis gives a half-salute as he says, "Have a nice night, boys," then pivots and leaves the way he came.

Dick nearly shoves Jesse inside, yanks the sliding glass door closed, and latches it, heart pounding.

"Uncle Dickie?" Jesse says, voice wavering, his mettle of the moment before evaporated.

"It's okay," Dick says, forcing his face into what he hopes is some semblance of reassurance before turning to face him. "He's gone."

"But what about tomorrow?" Jesse asks, knowing, as Dick does, the half-salute held the silent promise of "see you around."

Dick works to keep his face blank. "Tomorrow, I will figure something out. I'm not leaving until I know you and your mom are safe."

It's a lie, a guarantee he can't possibly make. Only minutes ago, Otis waltzed into their yard, and Dick was entirely unprepared.

But Jesse is an eleven-year-old boy, and desperately he wants to believe. Santa doesn't exist, but the world is still good. Bad things happen, but not to him. His uncle is here, so it's going to be okay.

"I'm going to bed," Jesse says and shuffles toward his room.

Dick looks at the clock on the mantel, realizes it's nearly ten, an hour past when Dee told him Jesse needed to be in bed, and he hates himself a little more.

When Jesse's bedroom door clicks closed, he pulls out his phone to call Sheriff Barton. He stares at it, his hand clenched around the device so tight his knuckles are white. Nothing Otis did was against the law. He walked into their yard. Dick asked him to leave. And he did.

He shoves the phone back in his pocket, then walks to each window and door in the house to check that they are latched. Each is secure. Each could easily be broken into.

In Dee's room, the room that used to be his parents, he looks over the bureau, but his dad's rifle is gone. Continuing into the garage, he rummages through the amassment of stuff until finally he unearths what he is looking for: *Lucille*—forty-two inches of hardwood cut from the heart of a hickory that fell at the hatchery where his dad worked most of his life. The bat was a gift for his tenth birthday, and her name was carved into the barrel by Dick that same day, named for his mom's love of *I Love Lucy*. It's still too heavy for baseball.

Carrying it into the house, he lies on the sofa, and with its comforting spirits beside him, he waits.

5

Dick rests his hand on Jesse's shoulder as they wait for the school bus, and he feels Jesse's stress. Finally the bus arrives, and when Jesse is safely on board, Dick returns to his car, calls in sick to work, then drives to the library in Bishop.

Dick may not be any kind of hero, but his reasoning power is better than most, and as the great Francis Bacon once said, "Knowledge is power." Bacon has always been an inspiration to Dick. He was the forefather of the scientific method and believed most problems could be solved by systematic inductive reasoning and deduction.

Dick spends the morning surfing the web and studying microfiche, reading every scrap of news he can dig up on Otis, his crimes, and his sentences. Most of what he reads he already knows. He knew about Otis's two convictions, his sentences, and his recent parole. What he didn't know was revealed in a small article printed on page twelve of the *San Francisco Chronicle* six years ago. The short editorial is barely three inches long and alleges that appropriate measures had not been taken to ensure inmates' medical conditions were addressed while incarcerated. Otis was mentioned because he suffered a near fatal seizure from an allergic reaction to peanut oil carelessly used in one of the meals.

———

Dick arrives back on Campton Street in plenty of time to be there when Jesse gets off the bus. They walk back to the house to find Dee waiting, her Subaru loaded with suitcases and their most precious belongings.

Dick helps her load a few more things in the back of his Volvo, and Jesse climbs into the passenger seat. Dick follows Dee to the hatchery, where they will stay until they come up with a more permanent solution. The hatchery is on the outskirts of town, is protected by electric fencing, and has plenty of guns along with men who know how to use them. Greg Larson, the owner, lives on the property with his two adult sons. He was Dick's dad's friend, and Dick trusts him to watch out for Dee and Jesse until he figures out a plan.

Jesse sits, hands balled in fists on his lap, still only a boy yet old enough to feel a sense of honor to protect his mother and his home. Dick feels the same but also has a lifetime of experience to know action movies aren't real and that, most of the time, the good guys don't win.

When he turns onto the highway, Jesse asks, "Who was Joe?"

The question is unexpected, and Dick takes a second before answering carefully, "That's probably a question for your mom."

"She won't talk about it."

Dick nods. Some memories are simply too hard.

"There's a picture of him in her drawer, and last night, I heard her say his name."

Dick heard it as well, a cry through the door that startled him. It's no surprise Joe would visit her dreams now that Otis is back.

"He was your mom's boyfriend a long time ago," Dick says. "They started going out in middle school and were together until your mom was seventeen."

"Then he died?"

"Yes. He was killed."

"By Mr. Parsons?" It's strange to hear Jesse call Otis "Mr. Parsons," but Dick doesn't correct him.

"Indirectly. But, yes, he died because of Mr. Parsons."

"And that's why Mr. Parsons went to prison?"

Dick's head pulses with the start of a headache, and desperately he wants a cigarette, but Dee would kill him if he lit up with Jesse in the car. He sucks at not saying the wrong thing, and this conversation is fraught with opportunity to do just that. He's not sure what Dee has told Jesse about why Otis is so dangerous, and he's not sure how much an eleven-year-old boy knows about sex or the horrible crimes Otis was convicted of, but he's pretty sure it's not his place to tell him. Though at the same time, he feels terrible for Jesse, knowing if it were him, he'd want to know what's going on.

So after a long moment, he says, "It doesn't really matter why Otis . . . Mr. Parsons . . . ended up in prison, only that it's where he belongs. And well, you asked about Joe, and what I can tell you is Joe was the opposite of Mr. Parsons. He was good, as good as they come, and he died doing what was right. Mr. Parsons didn't kill him, but he might as well have. It was just another example of bad winning over good, which happens, happens more than it should."

Jesse glances over, his face serious, then he returns to looking out the window.

Dick turns onto the gravel drive that leads to the hatchery and, five minutes later, parks beside Dee in front of the old groundskeeper's cottage.

Dee tousles Jesse's hair when he steps from the car then nods toward the trout ponds. "Go on," she says. "See if you can catch us some dinner."

Jesse slumps away, and Dick watches as he flops on his belly on the bank and toys with the fish with a stick.

"I forgot how beautiful this place is," Dick says.

The afternoon light has painted the scene gold, and the glinting ponds reflect the trees, clouds, and sky.

Dee doesn't admire it with him. Eyes on the ground and arms folded across her chest, she says, "How long do you think we'll need to stay here?"

"I'm not sure. Until we come up with a plan."

"He's not going to stop," she says. "He's never going to stop."

Dick works hard not to nod, not wanting to add to her distress. After last night, it's clear Otis intends to carry through on his threat. Men like Otis don't change. They don't suddenly get better and wake up one day rehabilitated. They are sick, and not curable kind of sick. Dick deals with illness every day. His job is to come up with formulas that remedy anomalies of biology, flaws in the system, and he knows better than most, some diseases simply can't be cured.

"I'll figure it out," he says, the words weak but the only ones he can think of. "In the meantime, at least you and Jesse will be safe."

Dee toes the dirt. "I've been thinking a lot lately about Joe. And Ed."

Dick never met Ed. When he left for college, Joe's brother was a toddler. Joe was only nine, and Dee a little girl of eight. It seems so incredibly long ago.

"How it was my fault," she says.

"Dee—"

She shakes her head, stopping him. "Not my fault, like I

intended for it to happen, but my fault because that's how life is sometimes, you do something small that, at the time, seems like nothing, and it turns out to be the thing that changes everything."

She unearths a pebble, then grinds it back into the ground with her shoe.

"The day it happened, Ed had been hanging out with us like he always did, and I asked him to say he wanted to go for a walk so Joe and I could be alone."

Dick blushes. Despite his sister being twenty-nine, the thought of her having sex still embarrasses him. Dee would have been seventeen and Joe eighteen, not that young when you consider they'd been together since they were twelve and thirteen, but the thought is still distinctly uncomfortable.

"He was supposed to come back in an hour," she says. "And Joe was pissed when he didn't show up. They needed to get home for dinner or his mom was going to be mad, and Joe knew he'd be the one she blamed."

She inhales deeply and blows out the breath.

"Ed wasn't the wandering-off type. It's why he was so annoying. He was always underfoot. Which was why, after a while, when he still didn't show up, we started to get worried."

Dick's nerves bristle, and he wishes she would stop. While he knows what happened, hearing Dee talk about it brings it into focus, memory a trick that easily distorts time and facts and allows things from the past to feel distant and removed.

"Joe went to look for him in his truck while I stayed at the house," she goes on. "I was on the stoop, and it was maybe ten minutes later that I saw him stumble from Otis's."

She glances up at Jesse, then returns her eyes to the dirt.

"He staggered down the steps and collapsed, and I ran to him." She shakes her head again. "I knew something was wrong, but I was so stupid. I thought maybe he was sick, that he'd thrown up or something."

"Dee—"

"I tried to help him up, but it was like his body wasn't working, his muscles misfiring or his brain not connecting."

Tears leak from her eyes, and Dick clenches and unclenches his fists. All of this was after Meghan's Law, yet no one in Independence knew Otis had already gone to prison for child molestation. Otis left home around the time Dick went to college, and Otis's mom told everyone it was because he'd gotten married and had moved to Reno. Eight years later, he returned with the explanation that the marriage hadn't worked out. No one had any idea that he'd spent five years in Ely State Prison and another three living in Nevada serving out his probation. The day he raped Ed, he'd been home two and a half months, two weeks shy of the ninety-day window he had to register in California as a sex offender.

"That's when Dad pulled up," Dee says. "He saw us and helped me get Ed home."

Dick imagines his dad climbing from his work truck and lifting Ed to his feet then supporting him back to the house. While he was a small man, he was incredibly strong when it was needed.

"I still didn't get it," Dee goes on. "I still thought he was sick, like he'd had a seizure or had some sort of really bad flu."

Dick looks hard at the ground, acid in his mouth.

"When Joe showed up, he took one look at Ed, heard where I found him, and . . ."

The words trail off, swallowed by a quiet sob. She doesn't need to finish. Dick knows the rest. Joe stormed into their parents' bedroom, pulled the .22 from its rack, and charged for the door. Dick's dad tried to stop him, but Joe was big as a linebacker and barreled past. Dee ran after him, and Dick's dad turned his efforts to holding her back.

Joe was pounding on Otis's door when Doug, Dee's ex and Jesse's father, pulled onto the street. He was the deputy on duty that night and was responding to Dee's call about Ed going missing. He saw Joe with the rifle and ordered him to drop it.

Joe didn't listen.

Doug yelled again as Otis opened the door.

It was halfway open when Doug fired.

Dick heard the story from his dad in a conversation that led to one of the greatest regrets of his life. His dad told him Dee wasn't doing well and asked Dick to come home. But Dick was a new father, had just started at Pentco, and was working round the clock on Freeway. He said he would try but then didn't, and six months later, Dee had dropped out of school and was pregnant with Doug's child.

A striped cat saunters by, and Dee squats down and holds out her hand to greet it, tears still on her cheeks.

"I'm going to figure this out," Dick says.

Dee lifts her face, offers an anemic smile that holds little faith, then with a sigh, pushes to her feet, grabs a suitcase from the back of her car, and shuffles toward the cottage.

6

Dee puts the last of her clothes into the large pine armoire and sits on the bed. She runs her hand over the antique ringed quilt, her conversation with Dick on her mind. It all happened so long ago yet feels so close. Though Joe's been gone over twelve years, he's never far from her thoughts, and last night, he wove in and out of her dreams—eternally young and haunting. She felt his touch, his lips, his breath, then startled awake as the gunshot blast reverberated in her mind. She cried out, then pulled the sheets to her mouth to muffle the sound of her sobs.

How many times has she relived that moment? Joe on Otis's stoop, his head on her lap as the life ran out of him. Her skirt was hunter green with small white dots. Her shirt, her favorite at the time, was pale pink. Joe wore his Rams T-shirt and jeans. The rifle, her dad's, was still in his hand.

It's in the cellar now, along with a tin of bullets. These past two days, she's thought a lot about climbing down to get it and finishing what Joe started, knocking on Otis's door, then backing up to make room for the barrel, and when he answered, pulling the trigger. *Bang!* The jarring sound of her nightmares becoming the thing of dreams.

Otis served twelve years for what he did to Ed. She wonders how long she would serve for killing him.

What stops her of course is Jesse—her forever light no matter how deep the darkness. Strange how her greatest tragedy led to her greatest gift, and that it was Joe's killer who gave it to her. Twisted and disturbing, it aches when she thinks of it. But she also knows there's no explaining some things and, deep down, believes Joe had a hand in it, that he saw her suffering and found a way to nudge destiny to help her move on.

At first, Doug only stopped by to check on her, guilt compelling him to see if she was okay or needed anything. He hadn't meant to shoot Joe but, when he saw Otis's door opening, reflexively pulled the trigger. He was twenty-three and had been a deputy less than a month. He thought he was responding to a missing kid call and wasn't prepared for what he drove into.

Dee lied and said she didn't blame him. He lied and told her none of it was her fault. They drank a lot. They wallowed. He quit his job. She dropped out of school. They clung to each other like life rings, and six months after Joe died, she discovered she was pregnant.

The next day, she told Doug it was over. She didn't tell him about the baby, but instead told him it would be better for her if he moved back to Texas, where he was from. It was time for them to get on with their lives. Already, Jesse was her moon, her sun, and her stars, the only thing that mattered, and she knew what she had with Doug wasn't real or healthy.

Opening her eyes, she stares at the dust mites dancing in the late afternoon light. And now, twelve years later, the nightmare has returned. Only this time, it is Jesse who is in danger, and if something happens to him, she knows she won't recover.

Bang! How easy it would be.

Her thoughts drift to Dick. He doesn't look good. His skin

is pale, and his body stooped. He's smoking too much and not eating well. Caroline and the divorce did a number on him, and she's worried he's spending too much time alone. She should have made more of an effort to visit or to invite him to spend more time here with her and Jesse.

Ten years is a big gap between siblings, yet they are close. Her mom died the day she was born, so growing up, it was just her, Dick, and their dad. And until Dick went to college, he was the one who mostly raised her. He was the one who did the shopping and cooking, was the one who bathed her, helped her with her homework, and made sure she brushed her teeth. "Give your teeth a treat. Up and down and all around, keep them clean and neat!"

She used the same rhyme with Jesse when he was little. Dick did with her all the things their mom had done with him, and he took the responsibility seriously.

Until he left.

She knows she shouldn't blame him for that. He had a right to make a life for himself. But it didn't stop her from feeling abandoned. He only came home a few days each year at Christmas and rarely called. Part of it was money. Long-distance calls were expensive, so were plane tickets. But it was more than that. It was like he had escaped. He was in college and finally among people who were smart like him. A butterfly burst from his cocoon, Independence no longer fit.

Even after Joe died, he stayed away. He called, and knowing it's what he wanted to hear, she lied and told him she was fine. He missed coming home for Christmas that year, and he missed Jesse's birth.

The next time she saw him was almost a year later at their dad's funeral.

She rubs her knuckles against her chest to rub out the hurt.

He's here now. And that's what matters. And he is going to fix this.

The problem is this isn't a mathematical equation and devils like Otis don't fight fair, and she's worried Dick—her earnest, good brother—doesn't stand a chance.

7

Dick is so engrossed in what he's reading he startles when Graham says, "Hey, Dick, got a minute?"

"Uh, sure," Dick says, swiveling his body to block the screen. His deep dive into sexual predators and their behaviors is probably best kept to himself. What started as research to try and understand Otis has led him down a rabbit hole of dark perversion both fascinating and repulsive.

His friend pulls off his glasses and wipes them with the tail of his shirt, his farsighted eyes squinting. "I think I figured something out."

"That's good. Right?" Dick asks.

For thirteen years, Graham has been working in the science of genomics, the chemical alteration of an individual's DNA to cure disease. Specifically, he's been looking at it in regard to the genetic disposition for obesity. He jokingly refers to himself as the Jenny Craig of genomics and jests he'll be the first volunteer to try his discovery once he figures it out. At five six, he tips the scales at close to three hundred pounds, and the number continues to grow.

"I think so," Graham says. "Though I'm not entirely sure."

Dick nods. It's the life of a research scientist. For years, you struggle for a breakthrough, and finally, when it comes, it's all so uncertain.

"I could use a sounding board. Beer after work?"

His friend's request is not something he can say no to, so despite his preoccupation, he nods. Truthfully, a beer might do him good, give him the dose of liquid courage he needs.

He watches Graham as he returns to the lab where his team is hard at work. At one time, the tables had been reversed. Dick was the star on the precipice of success, and Graham was one of the pool scientists. But that was a long time ago.

If Graham figures this out, he will be famous . . . and rich. Any Pentco scientist who makes a significant discovery gets half a percent of the profits that come from it. A cure for obesity— Dick can't imagine how much that could be worth.

———

Pro Sports Grill is a megapixel haven of sports entertainment located a few minutes from Pentco. The Angels are playing the Dodgers, so Dick asks the hostess for a seat in the bar where he can keep an eye on the game. It's only five thirty, but already the bar is busy, baseball fans excited about the local team rivalry.

"You, okay?" Graham asks when they're settled on their stools. "You look like crap."

"Thanks."

"No, seriously. I might actually be the good-looking one tonight."

The server sets down their beers, and Dick, ignoring his friend's insulting concern, takes a sip and says, "Tell me what you've got."

With a deep breath, Graham begins, the science so complex

few people in the world could understand it. Basically, the gist is, through genetic editing, Graham intends to alter the hereditary DNA that contributes to obesity, potentially not only providing treatment but also prevention. In other words, infants with genetic markers for becoming overweight could be treated as newborns and never struggle with obesity at all. But baseline editing of the sort Graham is proposing has never been done in humans, and making the transition from mice to people is full of potential pitfalls. Dick listens intently as Graham lays out his theory, staying quiet as he catalogs questions and thoughts for consideration.

"Which is why I think it could work," Graham finishes with a flourish of his hand almost like the thump of a gavel. Case closed.

Dick leans back processing what's been said. Graham is brilliant, so smart it causes Dick to question his own intelligence. Though when Dick was at the top of his game, he also had hubris and swagger. He rubs his chin, then leans forward and methodically sets out to disprove everything Graham said, picking the theory apart piece by piece—the premise, the results, his methods. Graham volleys back, and as they talk, new questions and arguments arise along with new ideas and ways to test them. They're in the zone, Graham scrawling notes and Dick's brain spinning so fast that, for the first time since Dee called about Otis's return, he is thinking about something else.

Finally, three beers later, the two of them sigh and slump in their seats, weary and worn as if they've just walked off a battlefield.

After a moment, Dick says, "Scary stuff, getting this close."

"Yup. It's definitely over if this fat man sinks." Graham puts his finger to his temple and pulls an imaginary trigger, then flops his head to the side with his tongue hanging out.

"Kidding," Graham says when he sees Dick isn't smiling.

Dick's own catastrophic failure a dozen years ago is an albatross he still carries around his neck. Dick tries to lighten his expression and takes another sip of beer.

The leadoff hitter for the Dodgers hits a walk-off home run to win the game, and the bar crowd boos and cheers.

Graham lays a twenty on the table. "The battle of the bulge awaits," he says and lifts his chubby fist in salute of the charge. He pivots away, leaving Dick alone.

Dick remains at the bar, sipping his beer and staring at the postgame interview while not hearing a word, his mind spinning with his conversation with Graham, Otis, Dee, and Jesse. When his beer is gone, he sets another twenty on the table, returns to Pentco, and climbs to the roof.

He smokes and, for the millionth time, considers the situation and the choice in front of him. Voices below cause him to look down, and he watches as two Pentco employees walk to their cars. He recognizes one of them, Sam, a guy from accounting—three kids and a pretty wife. He hosted a barbeque last year to celebrate his fortieth birthday, and over a hundred people showed up, everyone laughing, complimenting him, and slapping him on the back as they wished him a happy birthday. An average guy, but somehow, he did it right.

Dick used to dream of that and, for a while, pretended he had it with Caroline.

He watches Sam climb into his car and drive away, the taillights of his shiny BMW fading.

When they disappear from sight, Dick blows out a final stream of smoke, crushes the cigarette beneath his toe, and looks at the concrete below. *Nothing to lose.* So he might as well, for the first time in his life, finally do something right.

8

The rental car is a compact navy blue sedan. On the seat beside Dick are two printouts of a temporary California license plate. Outside Adelanto, he pulls into a rest stop, parks, and exchanges the rental car plates with the paper ones, then he smokes a cigarette and watches the sunrise. The world turns orange, then gold, and the silhouettes of Joshua trees come to life as the sand swirls in the breeze and transforms from shadow to dust.

When the day is fully light, he climbs back in the car to continue the drive. The air conditioner of the small car whirs at full power but does little to squelch the now stifling heat, the temperature gauge hovering at ninety-eight.

He pulls onto Campton Street, and as Dick expected, Otis's car is gone. Dee said he has a job at the auto parts store in Lone Pine, and yesterday Dick called the store to confirm he would be working.

Dick parks at the end of the street, pulls on a Yankees cap given to him as a joke by a coworker, a chest guard and shoulder pads umpires wear for protection, an XXL red-and-black checked flannel shirt he bought at Walmart last night, and a pair of latex gloves. For extra measure, he pops the lenses out of his aviator sunglasses and puts on the rims. Before he's stepped from the car, he's already drenched in sweat.

With a glance at his watch to check the time, he heads into the desert behind the houses. His feet crunch through the brittle top crust to the dusty sand below, the footprints blurring with the prevailing winds before he's taken his next step. He focuses on his breathing—deliberately inhaling through his nose and exhaling through his mouth, knowing it's the best way to stave off a panic attack.

Something moves in the window of Mrs. Bronson's house, and his heart jumps. Lowering his head, he hurries past. The course set in motion, there is no turning back.

Half a minute later, he reaches Otis's sliding glass doors. His costumed reflection stares back—his skinny face atop a lumberjack's body almost comical if he weren't scared out of his mind. The door is identical to the one on Dee's house, so ill-designed for security it might as well not have a lock at all. He wipes his brow with his gloved hand, then lifts the door from its track to release the latch.

He slides it open and slips inside.

The space is frozen in time, and seeing it spirals Dick back to his childhood—same couch, table, and television as when Otis's mother was alive. Same musty smell and darkness.

Beside the kitchen is a photo wall of Otis's ancestors. Like the Raynes family, the Parsons have lived on Campton Street since the borax factory opened over ninety years ago. One of the photos is the same one that hangs in Dee's hallway—Dick's grandfather and a group of other rugged men posed in long john shirts, baggy trousers, and boots. They hold picks and shovels and lean against a borax wagon. Unlike the Raynes portrait wall, there are no military photos, very few smiles, and the history stops short of the current generation, with not a single photo of Otis.

Dick walks into the kitchen and studies the sparse contents of the refrigerator—half a carton of eggs, three Coors, ketchup, mustard, a jar of pickles, a gallon of milk, and half a carton of OJ. Pickles would be the best camouflage, but it's uncertain the next time Otis will eat a pickle. So instead, Dick chooses the orange juice. He pours the vial of honey-colored liquid into it, shakes the carton, and returns it to its place.

Next, he searches the cupboards and drawers and finds what he's looking for in the drawer beside the sink. He slips the EpiPen into his pocket, then rummages through the rest of the house and finds two more, one in the medicine cabinet and another in the side table beside Otis's bed.

Returning to the front room, he scans around him to be sure there's nothing he missed. It feels too easy. Unable to come up with anything left undone, he leaves the way he came.

The sliding glass door can't be locked from the outside, so he leaves it unlatched and hurries back through the desert.

He arrives back at the car twenty-eight minutes after he left. Less than half an hour, that's how long it took to change his life.

9

According to the divorce papers, Dick has shared custody of the kids. The weekends are supposed to be his. At first, Caroline insisted they comply because she wanted time with Pete, but it became such a battle that eventually she relented. Dick didn't force the issue. The few weekends Kiley and Jim were forced to be with him were dismal, two days of silent disdain from Kiley and visible boredom from Jim interspersed with bursts of vile sibling warfare. He's not sure where he failed as a father, but it's obvious, somewhere along the line, he became a nuisance his kids want nothing to do with. Maybe he worked too much. Maybe Caroline poisoned them against him. All he knows is it wasn't only his marriage he lost when Caroline chose to end things, it was his place in the family.

But at least he still has baseball.

"Hey, buddy, ready to go?"

Jim shrugs, but his crisp uniform and freshly oiled glove suggest he's been preparing for the game for hours. He throws his bat bag in the back of the Volvo and climbs into the backseat.

"Did you see Mike last night?" Dick asks.

A slight nod in the rearview mirror, but he says nothing.

"That was 1480," Dick says, baiting him.

Jim bites, "No, it was 1481. He got a hit Monday."

"Oh, that's right. Forgot about that one. So you think he'll break 1500?"

"If the suckers pitch to him. The cowards don't even give him a chance half the time."

Dick doesn't like the language and thinks the comment sounds a lot like Pete but keeps the thought to himself. At least Jim's talking to him. Or he was. Jim has turned back to the window, and Dick feels his stress. It's been a rough season.

Dick rubs his own stiff vertebrae, hoping to work out the tension bunched in his neck. It's been three days since he drove to Independence and did what he did. Three days without a word. It's strange knowing he's done something so radical and that not a single person knows, his life humming along as if nothing has happened at all. He understands now why people confess. The desire to tell someone is nearly irrepressible. He can't sleep, can barely eat, and every other minute, it feels as if his brain is going to explode.

He was back at work later that morning, and now, he is driving his son to his Little League game. Each evening, he's called Dee under the pretense of checking in to see how she's doing, and each day, she's reported the same: she's fine, so is Jesse, and they haven't seen Otis.

He parks in the shade and safely out of foul-ball territory.

Jim climbs out and, as he lifts his bat bag from the back, says, "I hit one last game."

"Yep. And it was an RBI," Dick says. "Great situational hitting."

"You think he noticed?"

Dick sighs and turns to him. "All you can do is play your game. The rest isn't up to you."

"Yeah, whatever." He skulks away, and Dick follows, wishing

he was better at these sorts of things, able to offer words of wisdom or golden nuggets of encouragement.

The problem is Jim's coach is a jerk as well as an idiot, and there really isn't anything you can do about people like that—ignorance and arrogance a horrible combination and incredibly difficult to deal with.

As always, they are the first to arrive. Jim stretches as Dick stripes the field. Officially, Dick is the assistant coach. Every year since Jim was six, Dick has stepped up to help. He's never tried to be the manager, knowing he'd never be chosen among the testosterone-packed, all-star dads who vie for those positions. But he's a good assistant and has always earned the respect of whatever manager he's worked with. Until this year, when they had the great misfortune of ending up on Andy Simms's team.

Twenty minutes before game time, Andy shows up, and Dick, who had been warming up the boys, leaves the field, passing Andy without a word. When the season started, Dick would stay in the dugout during the games to help with the lineup, keep the stats, and make sure the batters were ready. But that was before Dick tried to make things right. Three weeks ago, after the team won, Dick approached Andy as he was packing the equipment bag.

"Good game, Coach, nice to take that one," he said, trying to assume the gruff manner of guy talk.

Andy grunted. Even after a victory, he didn't seem happy.

"Listen, Andy, I was hoping to talk to you about Jim."

Andy stopped stuffing the bag and stood. He glowered down at Dick, which should have been the first sign that maybe Dick should reconsider, but at the time, Dick was certain, once he explained things, it would make so much sense that Andy would be grateful for the feedback.

"The thing about a player like Jim is they're easy to overlook," he said. "Because they're not the ones hitting the grand slams or racing around the bases, their contributions aren't as obvious, but if you look at his stats, you'll see his OBP is—"

"Are you questioning the way I'm managing my team?" Andy said, interrupting.

"Not questioning," Dick said, his voice grown tight as he realized the conversation wasn't being received the way he had hoped. "Simply trying to point out the possibility that some of Jim's potential might be being overlooked—"

"We won, didn't we?" Andy said.

"Well, yes." Dick bit back the retort that they'd lost the three games prior. "But I've been running the numbers on all the players, and I think if we—"

"You know, *Dick*," Andy said with too much emphasis on the name, "at the moment, I think I have all the help I need on the field during the games."

Dick blanched, unsure what he was saying. He thought they'd been talking about Jim.

"From here on out, it's probably best if you stay in the bleachers."

He shrugged the hundred-pound bag onto his shoulder as if it weighed no more than a knapsack and walked away, leaving Dick staring after him.

And so now, three weeks later, Dick climbs into the stands and takes his seat with the other parents, then watches as the team gets clobbered by a team with half the talent but a far better coach.

In the bottom of the fifth of the six-inning game, Andy has no choice but to let Jim have his required at bat. With two outs, Andy puts him in, and silently, Dick rages. Jim had been so excited when the season started, and now, the bat practically drags as he walks to the plate.

Jim digs his feet in, narrows his eyes at the pitcher, and Dick holds his breath as the pitcher lets the first pitch fly—high and outside, the exact first pitch he's been throwing all game. Jim doesn't flinch, just watches it go by. The next is low and in, which puts him up in the count.

Look for one down the middle. This is it. You've got it.

Just as Dick thinks it, his heart sinks as he watches Andy give the take sign.

A perfect strike sails across the plate.

It's okay, buddy. You're still up. He's going to throw you another. Be ready.

Steam practically blows from Dick's ears as Andy gives Jim the take sign again and as another juicy strike goes past. Before Dick can rein in the emotions, the pitcher hurls the next pitch, high and outside, exactly like the first pitch, and Jim swings with all his might and hits only air.

———

"Tough loss," Dick says as they pull up to the house after a silent ride home.

Jim shrugs, climbs from the car, and shuffles inside.

Dick pulls Jim's bat bag from the trunk and walks it toward the door as Caroline appears.

"Why's Jim upset?" Her tone is accusatory.

"Rough game. The coach is a jerk."

"Really? Pete likes him. They've done work together."

Dick bites his tongue. Makes sense. *Birds of a feather . . .*

"Yeah, well, maybe now, Jim will finally give it up. Pete likes hockey."

Dick sets the bag on the porch and walks away. He stopped fighting with Caroline years ago.

He gets back in his car and, for the millionth time since Wednesday, looks at his phone. Still no call from Dee.

He can't take it anymore. Tomorrow, he will return to Independence.

10

Dick's right foot wants to ease up as he drives past Otis's house, but he forces the speedometer to hold at twenty-five. Campton Street is unchanged from four days ago. The heat is still oppressive, causing ripples to rise from the asphalt. Bundles of scrub still randomly blow about with no particular destination. The American flag outside the Brady house is raised. It will be lowered when the sun goes down. Mrs. Bronson sits on her porch as she always does in the early afternoon, knitting blue yarn, what she knits and for who a perpetual mystery. And Otis's black car is parked in its usual spot in his driveway, a fine dust settled on its glossy black enamel, thick enough for someone to have scrawled, "WASH ME" on the back window. Four newspapers are strewn on the walk, and patches of brown grass scar the yellowing lawn.

Dick's hand clenches the steering wheel, and a lump closes his throat as he continues past and parks in Dee's driveway.

Jaw locked forward, stiltedly he walks to the door. His fingers fumble with the key, and finally he manages to get it in the lock and pushes inside. Sliding down the wood to the floor, he drops his head to his knees. Though he believed it could be true, the weight of what he's done hadn't fully hit him. *Otis is dead. Gone. No longer part of this world.* And he's the one who caused it.

He pulls a deep shuddering breath through his nose, as a sickly swirl of relief and guilt roils in his gut—his relationship with Otis complicated. Few remember the man he was before he turned into the vile person he became. But Dick does. There was a time when he even considered Otis a friend and when he and his dad owed Otis a great deal.

When Dick's mom got sick, Otis, as a neighborly kindness, would bring the groceries. Once a week, he came by with bags of the things Dick's mom had carefully listed on the lined pad she kept in the drawer of the side table beside the couch. And when she could no longer stand for long periods, he stayed to help Dick put them away.

The cancer Dick's mom had was an aggressive form of brain cancer. With treatment, she might have lived five years, but the fetus would have needed to be aborted. Without it, the hope was she would make it long enough for Dee to survive. For his mom, it wasn't a choice.

A week before baseball season started, Otis asked Dick if he wanted to watch the opening game on his mom's new television. Dick was excited. He liked Otis, and it was a whole lot more fun watching baseball with a fellow fan than alone.

He showed up wearing the Giants T-shirt he'd gotten from his mom for his birthday two months earlier. Otis opened the door to let him in, and past him, Dick could see the flickering screen on the new television, the colors more vivid than life.

"Dickie!" his mom called from their house as he stepped toward it.

He pretended not to hear.

"I think Gausman's starting for the Giants," Otis said.

Gausman was one of Dick's favorites, a hard-throwing righty with a nasty slider. Dick stepped past him, and Otis started to close the door, but Dickie's hand shot out to stop it.

"What?" Otis said.

Dick stepped back and cocked his head, his ears straining.

The national anthem was being sung on the television, but other than that, the world was quiet.

She hadn't called again. His mother always repeated herself. She said things twice. *Dickie, turn off the radio. Dickie, you need to turn that off.*

He stepped back outside and turned toward his house, a moment that will live forever.

Otis, recognizing something was wrong, stepped outside as well, walking onto the stoop at the exact moment Dick took off running.

They reached his mom together, both of them dropping to their knees beside her collapsed body. Her thin maternity dress was hiked up around her legs, and her eyes were rolled back in her head, a sliver of white showing between the lids.

"Dickie, get Mrs. Bronson," Otis said as he rolled Dick's mom onto her back, then pinched his mom's nose and blew a breath into her mouth.

Dick stood frozen.

"Now!" Otis barked, and Dick took off for the house next door.

When Dick returned with Mrs. Bronson, Otis was still breathing life into his mom, sweat dripping down his stubbled face and soaked through his shirt.

He panted and swore between sets, "Breathe. Damn it, Mrs. Raynes, breathe."

Mrs. Bronson held Dick against her bony ribs, her knotted hands on his shoulders.

The ambulance arrived a few minutes later and took his mom away. Otis led Dick to his truck, and they followed.

Dee came into the world via C-section, while their mother lived suspended between worlds by a ventilator.

Otis never left Dick's side. Even after Dick's dad got to the hospital, he stayed. He went to the cafeteria and got Dick food and, when it was late, got a pillow and blanket from the nurse so Dick could lie down.

Dick doesn't remember Otis saying much, but he remembers clear as day what his dad said when he finally came into the waiting room. His normally proud shoulders were stooped and his ruddy face colorless. Dick sat up groggy, and Otis stood and accepted his dad's outstretched hand.

"Otis." Dick's dad's voice, always soft, was barely a rasp. "Thank you. You saved her."

Otis's face lit up. "She's going to be okay?"

Dick's dad's eyes dropped. "Not her. You saved the baby."

Dee turned twenty-nine last month, and Dick doubts anyone, other than him, even knows the story. He swipes the tears that have escaped from his face and forces himself to his feet. His mother's final act was saving him from a fate he has nightmares about. And, in a twisted cosmic turn, she also saved her unborn daughter who, seventeen years later, would be the one to send Otis to prison.

He drives out of Independence and, at the first rest area, stops and uses the payphone.

"9-1-1, what's your emergency?"

"There's a dead man at 2262 Campton Street in Independence."

The operator starts to ask a question, but he's already placing the receiver in its cradle.

11

Dick stumbles into his apartment a little after seven and pulls out his phone, not surprised when he sees the voicemail icon lit up.

"Dickie, you're not going to believe it!" Dee says excitedly. "He's dead! Otis is dead! The cops found him. Call me. Someone was listening. My prayers have been answered."

Dick continues to his room and collapses on the bed, a sliver of pride haloing his grief. His sister and nephew are safe.

He feels like he's just closed his eyes when his phone startles him awake, and he squints into the blinding morning brightness then at the clock on his nightstand to realize he's slept nearly fourteen hours.

The phone rings again, and he grabs it, but then, remembering the day before, hesitates. Otis is dead, and he is the one responsible. He stares at the unfamiliar number as it rings a third time, then taps the answer button and lifts the phone to his ear.

"Hello? Hello, is anybody there?" squawks the caller, and Dick realizes he forgot to say hello.

"Yeah, I'm here. Sorry about that."

"Is this Richard Raynes?"

Closing his eyes, Dick tries to figure out where he went wrong. A fingerprint? Someone saw him sneak into Otis's house? Otis scrawled Dick's name before he died?

"This is Dr. Richard Raynes," he says, irrationally thinking the use of his title will somehow affirm his upstanding citizenry and clear him of suspicion of murder.

Murder. The thought sobers him.

"This is Paul Chester, president of Irvine's Little League."

His body sighs in relief.

"I understand you're the assistant coach for the Cubs."

"That's right," Dick answers, though he's not sure that's still true.

"Well, after what happened Saturday, Mr. Simms has been removed from managing, and we were hoping you wouldn't mind stepping up and taking over for the remainder of the season. I know it's a lot to ask, but we'd sure appreciate it."

Dick has no idea what incident the man is referring to. Jim was so upset after the game they left quickly. But he's so overwhelmed with relief he'd agree to just about anything that doesn't involve confessing to murder.

"Of course. That would be wonderful. Yes. It would be an honor. I'd be happy to." Realizing he's blathering, he forces his mouth shut.

———

He arrives at Pentco at ten fifteen, over two hours late and, as he walks to his cubicle, feels his boss's eyes following through her office window. Already on thin ice, he decides this might be a good time to appease the gods, or in this case, the middle-aged pencil-pusher who recently took over the reins of the lab.

He sets down his briefcase, grabs the project folder for his current assignment, and carries it to her office.

With a light rap on her open door, he pokes his head in and says, "Good morning."

Joanne looks up to peer over her reading glasses then sets down the report she was studying and runs him over with her eyes, her expression sighing as she says, "Morning, Richard."

"Morning. I finished the report on Nite-air." He steps inside and places the folder on the desk in front of her.

Nite-air is a new medicine Pentco is adding to their cash-cow line of allergy products. Its added benefit is that it also helps the user sleep. Dick completed the formula a month after the project was assigned but, not wanting another, has milked it along for three.

Joanne takes off her glasses, which he doesn't want her to do because, whenever she does that, she sighs and leans back in her chair, which causes her jacket to fall open and the white silk of her blouse to pull against the lace of her bra, which is always several shades darker, and which happens to be one of Dick's weaknesses. He focuses on her red-painted lips, the deep crimson a good distraction.

"This took longer than I thought it would," she says, her slouch perfectly timed with her sigh. *Indigo. Or perhaps purple?* Dick snaps his eyes back to her red mouth.

"A problem with the beta blockers," he says.

Joanne is not a chemist, so he could say just about anything and she'd have no choice but to believe him.

Leaning forward again, she clasps her hands in front of her, the nails the same color as her lips, and asks, "Is everything okay, Richard?"

Dick feels the blush in his skin.

"Yup," he says. "Can I go now?" He realizes after he says it he sounds like a five-year-old asking for a hall pass.

Joanne frowns then reaches sideways toward a stack of folders on her desk. "Before you do, I have your next assignment."

The folder she unearths is exactly like the one he just returned. "Alert-air," she says. She slides it toward him. "Same idea, but rather than helping the user sleep—"

"It helps them stay awake," he finishes and tries to contain the sigh but does a poor job of it, the words nearly coming out a groan. Trying to recover, he says, "Great. I'll get right on it."

He reaches for the folder, but she pulls it back and laces her hands on top of it, and the thought crosses his mind to grab it and make a run for it.

"Richard, it's pretty clear this work doesn't interest you."

He says nothing, a lump forming hard in his throat, fairly certain this is the moment she fires him. Which perhaps he deserves, and a week ago, he wouldn't have cared about, possibly even welcomed. But now, surprisingly, he cares very much. His first baseball practice with his team is tomorrow afternoon, and if he loses his job, he's not sure, with his history, he'd be able to get another.

"I've looked at your file," she goes on, "and read your final report on Freeway."

The flush of embarrassment returns. Freeway is his greatest failure. For his doctoral thesis, Dick chose to explore the new field of leukotriene-antagonists, otherwise known as oral anti-allergens. When he began his research, oral allergy drugs paled in comparison to inhaled steroids. The primary problems were that ingested medicines metabolized too quickly, and the absorption varied depending on how full the stomach was at the time of consumption. Dick worked on a solution of adding a binding agent which controlled the rate of release. The thesis was good and showed promise for a new treatment for an ailment that afflicted hundreds of millions of people. The drug companies saw dollar signs, and Dick received several offers from top pharmaceutical companies. Pentco's offer was competitive, and Caroline wanted to move to California, so theirs was the offer he accepted.

His research progressed, though slower than anticipated. The problem was finding a binder that didn't compromise the effectiveness of the anti-allergen. His boss at the time, an accountant type with a nervous paranoia about his job, gave Dick a hard deadline of two years. Caroline was also losing patience. Money was tight, and they had a new baby on the way. Feeling the pressure, he rushed the conclusions, which turned out to be a catastrophic mistake. Two months after submitting for FDA approval, he needed to retract the application. His clinical trial subjects were showing a buildup of poly(A) proteins in their blood, a dangerous side effect that could prove fatal. The fiasco cost Pentco millions, and the plug was pulled on the project. Dick was reassigned from lead research chemist to staff chemist and has been working on mundane rehash assignments since.

"Based on what I read," Joanne says, "it sounds like you had a theory about what went wrong as well as an idea of how to fix it?"

Unable to look at her, he nods. He knows exactly what went wrong, and for ten years, every other minute has been spent considering the solution. The problem wasn't the medicine but the binder, a minor player he hadn't given enough thought to.

Joanne pushes the Alert-air folder aside. "Fine," she says. "Take a week to work up a proposal, then let's talk."

Dick doesn't move.

"Is there something else?" she asks.

Dumbly he shakes his head and turns, then reconsidering, turns back and, voice tight with emotion, says, "Thank you."

12

Agent Steve Patterson wakes up snarling. It was another fitful sleep. The nightmare returned. Always he wakes to the explosion:

The end of the corridor in sight—a steel door with an industrial lever—he runs faster, needing to reach it, but—Alice in Wonderland strange—the rectangle recedes. Then it is in front of him and opening, and he is being sucked in or blown through—hard to know—cyclonic forces pulling and pushing. Followed by airless orbit. He struggles to right himself as images flash on the surface of an endless gray silo. Danny. As a baby. Then as a man. A woman with a gun. His wife in her wedding dress. Dizzy. Nauseous. He tumbles. Then always, an explosion, deafening loud, that ruptures the noiselessness, a flash of blinding light, and he wakes.

A mortality dream, a friend told him when Steve described it. Time running out and Steve dying before he's resolved some unsettled issue. Steve laughed at the interpretation, so obvious it was about as perceptive as a fortuneteller divining romance in a jilted lover's future.

Despite it being five in the morning, he pushes from the bed to start his day. Steve is the product of a military family and military career, and in his world, time is never wasted and a lazy man has no honor.

Half an hour later, he is in his office sipping coffee as he looks out his window at Pennsylvania Avenue, the normally bustling street serene in the predawn. When his coffee is done, he turns back to his desk to review the day's status report. One new incident. A recently released repeat pedophile was found dead from what appears to be natural causes in California.

He sets the paper aside. It's still the middle of the night on the west coast. In a few hours, he'll call the local sheriff and confirm the details.

With no other new cases, he returns to his latest crusade. Donald Memphs has been living on the grounds of Connally Penitentiary in Texas for the past two months. He's a free man but can't find a place to live. Nobody wants him near them, NIMBY, not-in-my-back-yard, at its finest. A remote retirement community a few hours from Houston looks promising, but Steve knows it only appears that way because the residents have yet to be notified. As soon as they get wind that Donald Memphs, a notorious serial pedophile, is considering moving into their community, the protests will begin—marches, banners, pickets, and photos of his victims plastered everywhere. A group of concerned citizens will gather. They will discover a registered sex offender cannot live anywhere where children assemble. And suddenly there will be a weekly grandchild playgroup that will preclude Memphs from moving anywhere near them.

It's Steve's job to be Memphs's advocate, which means finding him a place to live. The problem is Memphs raped and mutilated a fifteen-year-old girl and left her in the desert to die, and most people in the world know it. The reason he got out was because, miraculously, the girl survived. Her testimony put

Memphs in prison, but because she lived, the maximum sentence was fifteen years.

With a sigh that resembles a groan, he sets to work crafting a letter to the community board informing them of Memphs's right to live among them. He peppers it with bullshit words such as *rehabilitation* and *reformation* and *paid penance* so Memphs won't sound like the monster he is. When the letter is done, he moves on to writing a similar letter to the community's city council. And finally, he writes a less cordial letter to the police, reminding them of their duty to protect Memphs regardless of their opinion about it.

This is the toughest part of his job, advocating for men who don't deserve it. But there is no choice. It's what allows the system to work, hard choices tolerated to protect the greater good. Memphs served his time and needs to be allowed to live somewhere so every other released felon gets to live somewhere as well. Redemption and second chances, it's what the country is founded on.

It's near noon when he finishes, and he considers breaking for lunch, his rump numb from sitting so long, but decides to take care of the dead-ped file first. He pulls the status report back in front of him: Otis Parsons, forty-nine, two-time loser from Independence, California. Cause of death: asphyxiation from anaphylaxis due to an allergic reaction to peanuts.

He punches in the number at the top of the fax for the Inyo County sheriff.

"Barton here."

Steve introduces himself.

"How can I help you, agent?" the sheriff asks. He has a gruff, no-nonsense voice, and Steve pictures a seasoned veteran of tough country stock.

"I'm looking into the death of Otis Parsons."

"Looking from pretty far away I'd say. We don't get the FBI in these parts much."

"Yes, sir. I'd appreciate a rundown on his death."

"Man died from an allergy attack. I believe it was peanuts."

"Any problems with Parsons since he returned?"

"A few folk not too happy about his homecoming and some grumblings from parents worried about their young ones, but that was about it."

"Anything suspicious about his death?"

"Wasn't at the scene myself, but I don't believe so. EMTs responded to a call and found him dead. And ripe. Didn't turn up for almost a week. Might have been a little less on account of the heat we've been having."

"Who called?"

"Don't rightly know. Hold on an itch." Steve hears the sheriff's muffled voice like his hand is over the speaker. "Beck, you get a name on the fella who called in for Otis?"

He comes back on the line. "Caller didn't stay on the line long enough to give us much more than he knew Otis was dead."

"How'd he know?"

"Didn't say, just gave the address and said someone was dead."

The hair on Steve's neck bristles. He thanks the sheriff, then calls Bishop Hospital, where the body was taken, and leaves a message for the doctor on duty the night Parsons was brought in.

13

Jim surprises Dick when he says he'll play on the team with Dick as the manager. Dick had been certain his son would be the first one to quit. Amazingly, all twelve players show up for practice . . . and so does Andy Simms.

Dick's setting cones in the outfield for a drill when Andy walks up. "Afternoon, *Dick*," he says. "Looks like I'm going to need you on the field after all." He gives a my-bad shrug. "So I'll handle the practices and give you the game plan, and you can run it at the games." Without waiting for a response, he strides toward the players who are stretching near the dugout.

Dick sets down the last cone and hurries after him.

"Huddle up," Andy says.

Jim glances at Dick, shakes his head, then shuffles toward the parking lot. The other boys form a loose circle around Andy.

"Jim, wait," Dick says, and Jim stops but doesn't turn.

Dick's voice cracks as he says, "Andy, a moment please."

Andy glances up from where he's on a knee talking to the boys, and for a brief, terrifying second, Dick thinks he might ignore him. "Dick, we're kind of busy here."

The players stare, everyone except Chase, Andy's son, who looks hard at the dirt.

Dick looks at Chase, then at Jim, then at the other boys, and the most extraordinary thing happens—rage, soft and warm like the sun, washes over him, and in a voice surprisingly calm, he says, "Andy, you need to leave."

Andy stands, and his eyes narrow on Dick's.

"Practice ends in an hour," Dick says. "You can pick Chase up then."

"You're not honestly listening to those idiots on the board?" Andy says with a guffaw. "I lost my temper. I mean, hell, who doesn't? We all get a little heated sometimes."

Dick remains quiet, but his eyes remain steady on the bigger man's, watching the flicker of his eyes and the thump of the artery in the side of his neck, and he realizes how important this is to him.

"We'll see you in an hour," Dick says.

Andy's fists ball. "Are you kidding? After all the time I've put into this team!" He steps close and glowers, but Dick doesn't move. "This team needs me! Without me, these boys can't find their flies."

A dozen retaliations play in Dick's mind, but he says nothing. There's no need; eleven faces, including Andy's son's, have turned dark.

"Fine. See how you do without me." He storms off the field, passing Jim, who is returning to join the team.

14

It takes several more messages before the doctor on call the night Parsons was brought in calls Steve back. She confirms what was in the report. Parsons died from a laryngospasm—he suffocated from a hyperallergic reaction to peanuts. The reaction would have been almost instantaneous. Something containing peanuts was ingested, and his throat swelled closed.

Steve jots: *peanuts, scene?* in his notebook.

"Do you think Mr. Parsons knew of his allergy?" he asks.

"Wouldn't have made it to forty-nine if he didn't. Anyone with an allergy as sensitive as Mr. Parsons would have been very aware of their vulnerability."

Steve writes: *previous attacks?*

"I need to remember to tell Lynn," the doctor mumbles.

"Excuse me?"

"Nothing, just reminding myself of something I need to do because of Mr. Parsons. Are we done here?"

Steve rolls his eyes and sighs silently through his nose. "Mind sharing?" he asks.

"Sharing what?"

"What you need to remember to do because of Mr. Parsons."

"It's really not relevant."

"I'd like to know anyway."

"Fine. I'm fairly certain the last thing Mr. Parsons ingested was orange juice. Typical of the kind of reaction he suffered, some of the contents of what he was eating at the time of the attack didn't make it past his swollen esophagus and were therefore still in his mouth."

"Orange juice contains peanuts?"

"Not typically, but peanuts, peanut oil, and peanut extracts are used in a lot of foods as an organic additive because they're full of protein and vitamins and low in carbohydrates. Flavored drinks, yogurts, cereal—people like Mr. Parsons need to be very careful."

"So you think the orange juice caused his attack?"

"Isn't that what I said?"

No. You said you needed to tell Lynn something. "And?" he says.

"And nothing. My niece is also allergic to peanuts, and I was just reminding myself to tell my sister to be careful about the orange juice she buys."

Bold letters in the notebook: ***PEANUT POISONING! MY ASS!*** He underlines it three times, his nerves buzzing.

He calls back the Inyo County sheriff.

"Barton here."

"Afternoon, Sheriff. It's Agent Patterson."

Silence for a beat, which causes the buzz to grow, wondering if the sheriff knows more than he's letting on. "What can I do you for?"

"I'm calling again about Parsons."

"Man's dead. What more is there?"

"I believe his death might not be as open-and-shut as it seems."

Another slightly too long pause. "Sir, I've been fair to you asking questions, but what that man died of is, pure and simple, God's will. And considering what he's done with his life, I can't say I'm sorry. Must be more important things for the FBI to be doing than poking around the death of a man not worthy of a prayer over his grave."

Steve nods. He gets it. Judging by Parson's record, his death doesn't deserve to be mourned. But that doesn't change the fact that a crime might have been committed. The law only works if it's enforced for everyone. It's the reason Steve created this division within the bureau, and when nobody wanted to head it up, it's the reason he stepped down from his position as assistant director to do it himself.

"I understand your feelings, Sheriff, but it's my job to investigate crimes against sex offenders, and unfortunately, I think that could be what we're looking at. I'm not trying to step on toes, but I need you to seal off the scene until I can get out there with my team."

Steve listens to the sheriff breathing.

"Tell you what," he says finally, "how about I save you a trip? Let me take a look around, and if anything turns up that looks fishy, I'll give you a call."

"Sorry, Sheriff, I'm afraid that's not how it works. Seal off the scene. I'll be there in the morning."

15

A strong dry wind swallows Steve as he deplanes, and he regrets not wearing lighter clothes. When he left D.C., it was wet and cold. D.C.'s always either wet and cold or sticky and hot. One week a year, usually in April, the cherry blossoms bloom and the weather is nice.

Steve rolls down the windows of his rental car and lets the furnace air rush over him. His stomach growls as he drives through the town of Bishop and past several restaurants, but adrenaline propels him forward.

Forty minutes later, he smiles as he passes his destination's marquee: "Welcome to Independence, Elevation 3925 ft., Population 574." His West Point graduating class had more students than the entire population of Independence.

The two-lane highway splices through the tiny town, a small, desolate place with more abandoned buildings than occupied ones. The businesses that remain—a gas station, a diner, a motel, and a jerky stand—sag in various states of dilapidation.

He turns into a neighborhood of boxy clapboard houses, then makes the second right onto Campton Street. A sheriff's car is parked in front of a toothpaste-colored home, and leaning against it is a stout older man wearing a tan uniform and a frown.

"Sheriff," Steve says, extending his hand.

"Agent."

Both flex their hands as they shake.

Steve gestures to the shattered front window beside the front door, shards of glass still in its frame. "Before or after?"

"After," the sheriff says. "Door was bolted, so the EMTs needed to break in."

The two men crouch beneath the yellow tape that extends across the entrance, and both wince as the stench of death hits them, a pungent smell akin to manure mixed with rotten cabbage, an odor Steve's never gotten used to, no matter how many times he's faced it. According to the report, the body was found three days ago, but it had been decomposing in the heat for several days, so the stink still lingers.

Breathing sparingly, he scans the front room, which is small, dark, and typical—a tweed sofa, likely older than him, a cracked leather recliner, a scarred coffee table, and an old television on a wood stand. There's a small kitchen to the left and, across from him, a sliding glass door that leads to a fenced backyard.

The sheriff gestures to the kitchen. "Body was found beside the table."

Steve steps closer. There's not much to see—a glass of orange juice with a few flies floating in it, an open carton of Minute Maid, and a plate with a crust of toast. One of two wood chairs is pulled out and askew. Other than that, the kitchen is in perfect order, not a dish in the sink or a crumb on the floor. Parsons kept a meticulously clean house.

Steve walks a wide birth around the table, then leans in to examine the ingredients listed on the orange juice: 100% orange juice from concentrate contains pure filtered water, premium concentrated orange juice.

"Agent Patterson?"

Steve turns to see two young men in the front room. Typical FBI recruits, both have military-cropped hair, muscular frames, and one carries a forensics kit. Steve comes from a different generation, still military, but less gym molded and more life molded.

Steve tells them what he wants covered in the kitchen, then leaves them to do their jobs as he checks out the rest of the house—two bedrooms and a small bathroom with a shower and no tub. He opens each drawer and cupboard, along with the mirrored medicine cabinet. No EpiPens?

Returning to the front room, he looks out the sliding glass door. The yard is dirt and weeds, and beyond it is the desert. It would be the logical way to break into one of these houses, out of view and with nothing around for miles. As he reaches to unlatch the door, he realizes it's already unlocked and pulls his hand away. Men like Parsons don't leave doors unlocked.

He calls one of the technicians over and asks him to dust the slider for prints, then, leaving through the front door, circles around to the back.

He looks over the fence. Even in the light breeze, the sand swirls like a living, breathing thing, and whatever prints there might have been have long since been erased.

He moves to the sliding glass door, which is old and on a track system that allows the one that slides to be lifted on and off. He's looking at the frame when he sees it, a smudge in the dust in the spot you would grab hold to lift it.

"No prints," the technician says through the glass.

Steve nods, he already deduced that based on the smear, the swath too clean and sharp to have been made by a bare hand. He feels the sweat beneath his shirt and plays the crime through in his head. The perp walked across the desert to the backyard, lifted the door off its track, spiked the orange juice, and left. He wore gloves so as not to leave prints but made a single mistake. It was hot, so he wiped his brow before lifting the door.

He smiles at the smudge. "Got you," he says quietly. Then raising his voice so the technician can hear through the glass. "I need you to swab this spot of the frame for sweat DNA."

The sheriff steps into the backyard, and Steve turns to him. "I'm reclassifying Mr. Parsons's death as a homicide."

The sheriff blows out a hard breath, clearly not happy about the news. Leveling his eyes on Steve's, he says, "Otis was a bad man, bad as they come, and he caused a lot of misery in these parts."

"I understand, but we still have a job to do."

16

Steve's hungry, but before he breaks for lunch, there's one more thing he wants to knock off his list. In the file the sheriff faxed over before Steve left D.C. was a complaint from a neighbor, a woman by the name of Denise Raynes, who lives two houses down.

His knock is answered by a boy with straight dark hair to his chin. "Can I help you?" he asks politely, smiling and revealing a row of braces banded in intermittent colors of green and blue.

"I'm looking for Denise Raynes."

Turning, the boy hollers into the house, "MOM . . . some guy wants to talk to you."

From the hall that leads to the bedrooms, a woman in faded jeans and a white T-shirt appears.

"Hello," she says as the boy disappears down the hall.

Denise Raynes is not what Steve expected. First, she's young. The complaint said she had an eleven-year-old son, so he expected someone middle-aged, and this woman can't be older than thirty. Second, she's pretty, far too pretty to be living in the middle of a desert with nothing around but sand and scrub.

She smiles, and her brows lift, and Steve realizes he's acting like a buffoon.

"Denise Raynes?" he asks.

"Yes."

"I'm Agent Steve Patterson." He takes a business card from his jacket.

She reads it carefully.

"I'd like to ask you a few questions regarding Otis Parsons."

It's very slight, but at the mention of Parsons's name, she stiffens.

"Would you like to come in?" She opens the door wider.

"Thank you."

"Can I get you something to drink?"

He loves small-town hospitality. In D.C. nobody offers anybody anything ever.

"Lemonade?" she asks.

"Yes. Thank you."

She disappears into the kitchen, and Steve settles on a large white side chair across from a denim blue couch. It's hard to believe this house is a replica of the Parsons home. Like one of those before-and-after transformations, everything that was old and sad and dark has been made light and bright and new.

Through the archway, he watches as Mrs. Raynes moves from the fridge to the cupboard, then as she pulls out a rack with dishes and contemplates which to choose.

"I hope you like oatmeal cookies," she says when she returns and sets a tray on the coffee table with two glasses of lemonade and a plate of cookies.

His mouth waters, and his stomach rumbles as he takes one.

"These are delicious," he says around the first bite, the cookie one of the best he's ever had, chock full of cinnamon and nutmeg, raisins and nuts.

"I got the recipe from a friend. She's the queen of baking."

She has settled onto the couch, her bare feet curled beneath her, and again Steve is taken by her youth, her gold hair pulled into a high ponytail and a monkey face on her T-shirt.

"Mrs. Raynes—" he starts.

"Miss, actually," she says. "I'm not married. But please, call me Denise."

"Denise," he starts again, "you're aware Mr. Parsons has passed away?"

She nods.

"And are you aware how he died?"

"Some sort of seizure," she says, her voice even and her face poker-straight, though Steve feels the effort it takes.

"You called the sheriff about him?"

"I was concerned for my son."

"Because of Mr. Parsons's past?"

Her expression tightens. "Because of *our* past. I testified against him at his trial."

Steve wonders how he missed that, then realizes it's because it wasn't included in the information the sheriff faxed over, an intentional omission for sure.

"He vowed revenge," Denise goes on, "and I was worried he was going to make good on the threat and use my son to do it."

Steve glances down the hall where Denise's son disappeared moments before, and Denise notices.

"Do you have children?" she asks.

His heart reflexively clenches, and he needs to work to keep the reaction in check. "I did," he says, his voice almost normal. "A son."

Her eyes pulse once in sympathy before growing soft with compassion. "I'm sorry."

"It was a long time ago." He reaches for another cookie to break the connection, condolence still difficult to accept graciously, even after six years.

"Doesn't matter how much time passes," she says. "Those we lose linger in our souls."

The words pierce, the void of Danny's absence as hollow as the day he was killed.

"So you were worried about your son?" he says, bringing the conversation back to his reason he's here.

"Terrified."

"And what did you do?"

She shrugs and looks down at her hands in her lap. "What could we do? We left. Otis had made it clear he was going to hurt Jesse, so we moved into the groundkeeper's cottage at the fish hatchery where my dad used to work."

"You left?" Steve says, the idea of this sweet woman and her son being forced to leave this lovely home upsetting, while at the same time, the news ratchets up the motive for why someone might have wanted to kill him.

"How long were you there?" he asks. "At the hatchery?"

"A week. Until he died, and it was safe to come back."

"And what would you have done if he hadn't died?"

She shakes her head. "I don't know. Seriously, I don't." He hears the distress in her voice. "I prayed every night for an answer." She lifts her green eyes to his. "And it seems God was listening."

Steve doesn't know about the Almighty taking heed of her plea, but he fully believes someone did.

"So you were relieved when you found out he was dead?" he asks.

Her gaze unflinching, defiantly she says, "More than relieved. Happy. Ecstatic. I celebrated. I grabbed my son, and we danced around the room."

He nods in understanding, swallows the last of his cookie, then asks almost casually, "And did you have anything to do with his death?"

She rears back. "No. Of course not." She blinks several times. "He died of a seizure."

"Actually, he died from an allergic reaction to peanuts."

It's very subtle, her eyes flickering down and away then returning to his.

"Did you know he was allergic to peanuts?" he asks.

"No. No, I didn't," she answers too quickly.

"This is just standard procedure," Steve says with a half shrug. "Because Mr. Parsons was recently released, we want to make sure there wasn't any foul play."

He looks for another tell, but her face shows only deep thoughtfulness as she says, "If there was, you should give the person a medal. We need more heroes in this world."

17

Dee leans against the door as tears of gratitude fill her eyes. She slides down the wood to the floor and laughs as she shakes her head in disbelief. A wolf in sheep's clothing. Nobody understands her brother, but she does. He promised he would figure something out, then found a way to keep his word.

Peanuts. She laughs again. *He killed him with peanuts.*

Jesse sticks his head from his room. "You okay?"

"I'm great!" she says, sounding like Tony the Tiger in a Frosted Flakes commercial.

She wonders for a brief second if she should be worried about the investigation but dismisses the thought. The agent said it was just standard procedure. Otis died of an allergic reaction, and no one, other than her, would ever suspect it was Dick.

Pushing to her feet, she skips to Jesse and drops a kiss on his head before continuing to her room.

Heart dancing, she calls.

"Dickie, it's Dee. Come this weekend. I've got a surprise for you."

There's no way she can repay him, but she is going to try, and she knows exactly how she is going to do it.

18

After a quick roast beef sandwich at Trudy's Roadside Diner, served by none other than Trudy, Steve returns to Campton Street to interview Parsons's other neighbors. It's so hot it feels as if every ounce of water has been leached from his body, and he wonders how anyone manages to live here.

The answer he receives from each neighbor is the same: nobody saw anything, and nobody cares.

He's almost back to Parsons's house when he gets his first possible lead.

Mrs. Bronson lives in the house between Parsons and Denise. Well into her eighties, she has raisin skin, a bent spine, and piercing blue eyes. "I told you. I saw a large hunter walking behind the house Wednesday morning." She thumbs her hand toward the desert.

"Yes," Steve says. "But what makes you believe he was a hunter? Did he have a gun, a deer slung over his shoulders?"

"No need for sass, young man."

Steve conceals his smirk. The woman reminds him of his grandmother, and it wouldn't surprise him if she twisted his ear if he sasses her again. "Sorry," he says.

Her frown straightens. "He just looked like a hunter. He was big and wearing a red-and-black checkered shirt and was skulking." She hunches her thin shoulders in imitation.

The rest of the description is useless—blue hat, possibly tan pants, glasses.

Steve thanks her and leaves. The timeline works. Parsons worked Wednesday but didn't show up for his shift the following day.

He starts back toward his rental car, then changes his mind.

"Hello again," Denise says. "Miss me already?"

"Sorry to bother you, Miss Raynes. I was just wondering if I might be able to use your bathroom?"

"Only if you stop calling me Miss Raynes." She rolls her eyes and opens the door wider.

He gives a small bow. "Denise."

In the bathroom, he counts to twenty, flushes the toilet, runs the water, and returns to the living room.

"Find what you were looking for?" she asks with a knowing grin.

His skin warms. "It's just a suspicion I had," then adds quickly, "not about you."

Her brows arch.

Not seeing the harm, he says, "Mr. Parsons's house is the same as yours, but his bathroom seemed small. I wanted to confirm the size." He offers a contrite shrug. "Sorry."

She giggles. "It's okay. It's your job to be sneaky."

"Well, thank you." He gives an imaginary tip of a hat before continuing toward the door. Before reaching it, he turns back. "I was wondering if there's somewhere other than Trudy's to eat around here?" The roast beef sandwich he ate at lunch sits like a rock in his gut.

She laughs again. "I'm surprised Trudy isn't on your

most-wanted list for attempted murder against hundreds of innocent people."

"I might consider adding her after the lunch she nearly killed me with."

"You could try the truck stop in Lone Pine, though the food's not much better."

He starts to nod when she adds, "Or you could stay and join us for dinner?"

He tilts his head.

"You seem like a decent fellow, fighting for justice and all, so I'd feel kind of bad if I didn't try to intervene to save your life."

"Are you sure?" he says, his mouth watering as he thinks about the delicious cookies from earlier. It's been a long time since he's had a home-cooked meal.

Charlotte was a wonderful cook, and he used to tease her that he married her for her food. The truth is he married her for a million reasons, including her food. Then he ruined it. And now, three years later, she is cooking for someone else, and he is eating takeout most nights.

"I don't want to intrude," he says.

"We'd love the company. Follow me, and I'll put you to work."

He traipses after her, feeling a little like a stray puppy who's been adopted, and he believes, if he did in fact have a tail, it would be wagging.

"Chop," Denise says, handing him a cutting board, a head of lettuce, three carrots, and an onion.

As he makes the salad, Denise makes fried chicken, roasted potatoes, and green beans, and the smells dizzy him and spiral him back in time to another life, one complete with a wife and son and frequent meals just like this.

"Jesse! Dinner!" Denise hollers, completing the chimera,

and he wonders if all moms are inherently born with the same singsong notes for calling their young to food.

Jesse bounds in. "Hey," he says to Steve.

"Did you wash your hands?"

Jesse groans, then disappears back down the hall.

When he returns, Dee says, "Now, properly introduce yourself."

"Hi," he says obediently. "I'm Jesse."

"Steve," Steve says and extends his hand.

The boy does a good job with his handshake, and Steve wonders who taught him.

The dinner is delicious as it smells, and the conversation is comfortable and easy. Jesse is bright and curious and asks a lot of questions about Steve's job.

"How'd you end up being in the FBI?" Jesse asks.

"I started out in the army. It's what the men in my family do. And when I got out, the FBI recruited me."

"You ever shoot anyone?" Jesse asks, eyes hopeful.

"Jesse!" Denise says.

Steve smiles at her. "It's okay. I've been asked that before. Truthfully, I don't know."

"You don't know?" Jesse says.

"As an agent, I've never discharged my weapon, but when I served in Iraq, there were a few times when we were engaged. And war's weird that way. Most of the time you have no idea who you're shooting at or who's shooting at you. You're just following orders and hoping the other side's losing. It's only after the battle's over that it sinks in that some of your trigger pulls might have been responsible for the dead or dying you're then trying to save."

Denise stands abruptly and carries her plate to the sink.

Steve follows with his own plate. "Sorry," he mumbles, realizing he stepped way over the line of polite dinner conversation.

She nods curtly and turns back to the table with a painted-on smile. "Homework," she says to Jesse, and Jesse groans and slinks from the room.

"Really," Steve says, feeling like a first-rate idiot. "I shouldn't have said that."

"It's fine," Denise says, though clearly it's not. "I'm just not a big fan of guns." She scrubs extra hard at the plate in her hand.

"Me neither," Steve says. "These days I prefer to kill people with my charm." He hits her with a big toothy grin.

She huff-laughs, and he sighs with relief. Though he barely knows her, he never wants to be responsible for dimming her remarkable brightness again, not even for a second, and wishes he could think of something else funny to say.

Setting the plate in the dishrack, she picks up their wine glasses from the table along with the half-empty bottle of Chardonnay and carries them to the living room.

"You used to play football?" she says as Steve sits in the chair and she sits on the couch.

"What gave me away?"

"You don't reach so well with your right. I used to date a football player."

Steve flushes. "Second-string offensive lineman for West Point."

"Does it hurt?"

"Only when I reach." He smirks, and she smiles.

"Where'd you go to school?" he asks.

"I didn't. My life sort of got derailed when I was seventeen, then I had Jesse at eighteen and never fully got back on track."

Steve calculates. Jesse's eleven, which makes her twenty-nine, twenty years his junior and only a year older than Danny would have been.

Time a trick, for a moment, he'd forgotten his own age and thought she might be flirting.

As if to further confuse him, she reaches over and touches his knee as her other hand moves to her lips. "Shhh," she says.

He freezes.

"Do you hear them?"

Steve arches his eyebrows, the only sound he hears the crazy pounding of his heart, the tips of her fingers warm through the cotton of his pants.

"Listen."

He strains his ears, and she flitters her nails on his kneecap. "You don't hear that?"

Past the siren of his pulse is a faint noise that sounds like Alvin and the Chipmunks in fast-forward.

He nods, and she smiles. She has a wonderful smile, her lower lip riding up slightly over the bottom of her upper teeth.

She leans back, and he breathes.

"I used to be scared of them," she says. "As a little girl, when the bats would come out, I'd hide under my covers. But now, each night, I listen for them."

Jesse reemerges. He wears navy boxers emblazoned with baseballs and a white T-shirt.

"Ready," he announces.

Steve remembers Danny at that age, independent but not so grown up as to give up being tucked into bed and kissed goodnight.

Denise stands, and so does Steve, realizing he's probably overstayed his welcome. "Thank you, Denise." He extends his hand to Jesse. "And thank you, young man."

Jesse shakes it. "You're welcome."

"Don't run out now," Denise says. "This will only take a second."

She disappears before he can respond. He listens to them

talking and giggling behind the door, and then their mutual "I love yous." And a second later, she is back.

"Denise, I really should go. I still have some work to finish—"

"At Otis's?"

"That and some other things."

"I want to come with you."

He tilts his head. "Come with me? Where?"

"To Otis's." Her jaw slides out.

"Why?"

"I want to see it."

"Why?" he repeats.

Her boldness falters, her chin trembling as her eyes drop to the floor between them. "To know that he's gone."

"He is," Steve says gently.

"I need to know. To see his empty, vacant house and know."

"Denise—"

She shakes her head. "For twelve years, every time I've walked by that house, it has haunted me, and I want to know it's no longer something to be afraid of."

"It's not. It's just a house."

"Maybe to you. To me it's every nightmare I've ever had."

The words strike a chord, his own nights haunted by the same recurring dream of running toward Danny and arriving too late.

"That probably sounds silly to you," she says.

Not silly, he thinks, but perhaps naïve, things not always what they seem and some things better left unknown.

19

Steve's unsure about this. He is leading a possible, though unlikely, suspect to the crime scene of an open investigation. But
he understands better than most the need to confront your
demons. Parsons's house is just that, a house, and if it helps
Denise see that, it will be worth it.

The night sky is black, and a billion stars shine down from
above, the lack of light here in the desert creating the remarkable brilliance. Denise walks beside him, bare feet padding softly
on the road.

When they reach Parsons's walk, he stops.

"There's a smell," he warns.

Her eyes are fixed on the door, and again he wonders if this
is a bad idea. They're still outside, and already she looks rattled.

"Denise—"

"There's a smell," she says, cutting him off. "Got it."

She continues toward the stoop, and he follows, wanting
to protect her but knowing it's already too late, the damage
caused by this place and the man who lived here inflicted long
before this moment.

He lifts the police tape for her to duck under, then follows her beneath it and opens the door. She steps through and stops just inside. The odor is half what it was this morning, a day with the doors open reducing it to a smell no worse than rotten food in a fridge.

She scans right to left, and her eyes momentarily pause on the table in the kitchen. The juice glass and Minute Maid container are gone, and the chair that was askew has been straightened. Expressionless, she takes it in, and then continues to the hall.

She glances into the first bedroom, stops at the bathroom to study it a second, then continues to the main bedroom. Steve follows a foot behind. She walks into the room and stops at the foot of Parsons's bed. The drab gray spread is pulled taut, and two dingy white pillows are propped against the headrest. Her right hand goes to her mouth, the knuckles against her lips, and her left arm hugs her waist as her body begins to quake.

Steve sets his hands on her shoulders to steer her away, but she resists. Her head shakes as she shrugs him off, then, with a deep shuddering breath, she turns and steps toward the closet.

"Denise—"

She shakes her head harder and takes another step.

"Denise, stop. It's just a closet."

But she knows, like he knows, it's not. The bathroom is too small.

She reaches for the knob, and he grabs hold of her wrist, stopping her. She tries to wrench free, but he continues to hold it tight. She cranes her head back, and her green eyes flash bright with tears.

"Trust me," he says, his voice low. "You don't want to see what's in there."

Her chin juts forward.

"Trust me," he repeats, his eyes holding hers.

Giving up the fight, she allows him to pull her into his arms, and her tears soak through his shirt and straight into his heart.

After a minute, she sniffles, and pulls away. She wipes her eyes with the back of her hands and says, "Do what you need to. I'll be outside."

He waits to be certain she's gone, then opens the closet door.

The hidden door is cleverly disguised as an air vent and is concealed by a large roller suitcase. He grumbles in irritation at whoever investigated Parsons a dozen years ago and missed it. Though, in truth, he almost missed it himself. He was nearly to his car before the thought occurred to him that houses from this era typically have tubs, which was when he realized the bathroom was too small.

He turns on his penlight, then crawls through the hole into a space about four feet square. He straightens, and the airless stench of stale semen and sweat makes him want to retch. Breathing sparingly through his teeth, he pulls the light chain, which sets the room aglow.

Steve considers himself tough. A veteran of two tours and a twenty-year FBI agent who has worked cases on every crime imaginable and witnessed the worst humans can inflict on each other. But nothing prepares a man for the kind of evil that surrounds him.

The photos are mostly beautiful—boys smiling and laughing, caught in unguarded moments of childhood—almost as if Parsons profoundly understood exactly what he was stealing. The before images evidence of a truly twisted individual who stalked his victims like prey before pouncing. The other photos, fewer and far more gruesome, are of the boys stripped naked, terror and confusion on their faces.

Steve focuses on the job. Using his phone, he documents the scene. Every inch of wall is plastered—polaroids, snapshots, and inkjet prints. Decades worth. Some so faded they're gossamer.

He does his best to count the victims, but there are photos on top of photos, and some are multiples of the same boy. At least a dozen are of Jesse, his images taking up a two-foot strip of honor in the middle of the main wall.

———

Denise sits on the stoop, and Steve lowers himself beside her. She takes his hand and holds it on her thigh as if it's the most natural thing in the world.

"Was it bad?" she asks.

"It's always bad," he says, his emotions close to the surface. "But, yeah, it was bad."

They sit silent after that, lost in their respective thoughts.

A moment later, when she shudders, he turns to see her touching the bricks beside her.

"Are you cold?" he asks, wanting to put his arm around her but unsure.

She looks at him surprised, as if she'd forgotten he was there. "Huh?"

"You shivered."

Her smile is sad. "It wasn't from the cold."

This time he doesn't hesitate. He wraps his arm around her, and she curls against him, her head nuzzled against his shoulder. She smells like shampoo and something citrus, lemon or orange.

Realizing he shouldn't be inhaling her scent or thinking about how wonderful she smells, he untangles himself and stands. "I should go." He holds out his hand to help her up.

She doesn't take it.

"Denise?"

"No," she says. "I want to sit here, and I'd like for you to sit here with me so I know I'm okay."

So he sits back down, and she leans against him again, and he wraps his arm back around her as her scent envelops him and he listens to the chirps and screams of the bats.

After a long time, she says, "Okay," then pushes to her feet, and, hand in hand, they walk back to her house.

When they reach her steps, she takes his other hand as well and looks up with her bewitching eyes. "I'd like you to stay," she says, startling him speechless.

She gives a sad smile. "I know you're leaving in the morning, but tonight, I'd rather not be alone."

He stares, unable to formulate a response.

His brain screams, *No! Absolutely not! Bad idea!* while an entire other part of his body enthusiastically wags its tail and does somersaults.

"I think it's best if I go," he says, leaning in and kissing her gently on the head.

"Why?" she says plainly when he pulls away.

"Because," he says, feeling frustrated with himself and with her. This is ridiculous. They just met. She's tangled up in his murder investigation, and she's far too young . . . and far too beautiful . . . for this to be happening. "It's been a long day, full of emotion, and I don't want to take advantage of that. I'm being chivalrous."

"Screw chivalrous," she says, then before he can say anything more, reaches up and pulls his mouth down on hers.

"Screw chivalrous," he mumbles through his lip-locked mouth, then sweeps her into his arms and carries her into the house.

20

Still in Steve's arms, Denise whispers, "I'll be back. I just need to get Jesse off to school."

Her warm body slips away, and for a second, Steve wonders if it's just the soft ending to a dream. He tries to return to unconsciousness and recapture the warmth, but she is gone.

He keeps his eyes closed and inhales through his nose—the sheets smell like flowers and soap, and from somewhere beyond the room, coffee brews. Reality demands he get up, but he resists. If this is a dream, he wants it to go on forever. If it's not, it means he needs to face what he's done.

He flops his arm over his eyes, then, with a groan, sits up and swings his legs over the edge of the mattress. He sucks in his gut that's a couple inches too soft, then releases it. Who's he kidding?

Pushing to his feet, he rolls out his stiff shoulder, his whole body satiated and weary in a way it hasn't been in years. A smile tickles his lips, astonished by what happened, perhaps even a little proud. Not just about the lovemaking, which was remarkably not as awkward as he would have thought, but by the conversation after. "Cuddle talk," Charlotte called it. Denise was so at ease it made him relax as well. Nothing serious, they talked about flavors of ice cream—they both like chocolate chip but only if it's with real vanilla ice cream and the best dark chocolate. Their childhoods, which were remarkably similar for how different they were. He grew up in the suburbs of Chicago with his two sisters and mostly just his mom since his dad was in the Navy. Denise grew up here in Independence with her dad and brother. Both their beginnings were surrounded with love and without fences or too many rules, though respect and manners were demanded.

When Denise returns, he is pulling on his pants. She leans against the doorframe in a blue chenille robe. "Would you like some coffee?"

Burdened with one-night-stand guilt, he avoids her eyes as he answers, "That would be great."

When she's gone, he sits back on the bed to pull on his shoes. He's bad at this. Since Charlotte left him three years ago, he's buried himself in his work and avoided women altogether. And this is the reason. In a single night, he's managed to get himself tangled up with a woman involved in his murder investigation and who lives on the other side of the country and who already has his heart wrapped so tight he's certain it's going to explode.

He can't do it. Can't handle any more heartbreak.

"You haven't made much progress," she says, handing him a steaming mug. His shirt is unbuttoned, his shoes at his feet. "I assume you take it black."

"How'd you know?"

"I've been working at a truck stop ten years. I'm a professional coffee drinker analyst."

He smiles and pats the bed for her to sit. As she does, she puts her arm around him and rests her head on his shoulder.

Staring into the black liquid, he begins, "Denise, last night—"

She interrupts, pulling away and putting her finger to his lips. "Last night was wonderful, and today, you have to go. It's okay."

She turns his face toward hers and gives him a peck on the lips.
"I'm going to make some breakfast. You can't save the world on
an empty stomach."

He watches her go, his stomach slick like oiled eels, knowing it's too late, already at the mercy of this magnificent creature
without a damn thing he can do about it.

———

After an awkward goodbye on his part and a composed one on
hers, he gets in his rental car to drive five hours to the San Francisco FBI field office. As he drives, he tries to focus on the case,
but Denise's smile and laugh keep getting in the way.

Near noon, he gets a call from the agent covering for him
while he's away. Memphs has disappeared. He left the grounds of
Connally Prison last night, and nobody's seen or heard from him
since. Steve hangs up and slams his palm on the steering wheel.
He was the one who convinced Memphs to stay put while he
worked out a relocation plan. Exactly for this reason. He didn't
want Memphs to disappear. Until thirty days have passed, they
can't even put out an APB. Which means Memphs has a month
to fly under the radar. He thinks of what he saw in Parsons's
hidey-hole last night, and acid fills his mouth—Memphs and
Parsons cut from the same wretched cloth.

Knowing there's nothing he can do about Memphs, he
pushes him to the back of his mind and returns to the case at
hand. Parsons. What he knows so far is that, Wednesday morning, sometime around nine, a large man wearing a blue hat and
a red-and-black checkered shirt passed behind Mrs. Bronson's
house. The man most likely wore gloves, entered through the
sliding-glass door, and doctored Parsons's orange juice with some
sort of peanut substance knowing Parsons was allergic. Parsons

was dead four days before the call came in reporting his death.

The small car's illegal U-turn across the desert divide kicks up a storm of dust. Steve slams on the accelerator as he calls the field office to let them know he's going to be late, then he calls Sheriff Barton. The green and white sign he passes reads, "Independence, 140 miles."

———

Four hours after leaving Independence, he is back. He parks beside Sheriff Barton's cruiser and walks to the payphone near the vending machines, a relic from a bygone era but one California still maintains at its rest areas.

"Sheriff."

"Agent."

This time, they do not shake hands. As soon as Steve found Parsons's disturbing photo collection, he called the local FBI field office so they could put a team on it to identify the victims and perhaps resolve some unsolved cases. He also called Sheriff Barton. The sheriff's first question was to ask if Steve was now going to stop his insipid investigation. When Steve told him no, the sheriff cussed him out and hung up.

The representative from the telephone company arrives a few minutes later, and they watch as he unlocks the coin box for the phone. Carefully, Steve pours the change into the cardboard boxes he picked up on his drive back to Independence, then using a capped pen, he moves the coins so they're flat on the bottom and not overlapping.

The sheriff and representative help him carry the boxes, three of them, to the car and set them in the trunk.

"Not right," Barton mutters, then marches back toward his car.

21

The San Francisco field office occupies half the thirteenth floor of the federal building and has a commanding view of the skyline and the Golden Gate Bridge. Steve checks in with the field team to see if there have been any more developments. The only prints at the scene belonged to Parsons, and as Steve suspected, the orange juice was the culprit. Analysis of the juice showed that an extrinsic substance had been added that contained peanut extract.

The only promising news was that the sweat DNA recovered from the sliding door didn't match Parsons, which means if Steve finds a suspect, it could place him at the scene within days of the murder.

He leaves the forensics office and, one box at a time, carries the three boxes of coins from his rental car to the latent lab. A kid with two dozen piercings and at least as many tattoos watches disinterestedly from a swivel chair at the log-in desk, and on Steve's final trip, he says, "That's a hell of a lot of coins."

Steve does his best to resist his stereotyped impression, which is indolent, Gen-Z sloth. "This needs to be made a priority. It's the only lead in an active homicide investigation."

"Homicide investigation of a perv," the kid says as he twists side to side in his chair.

Steve's blood grows warm. He already put up with Sheriff Barton's peevy attitude this morning and is in no mood for justifying his job or explaining the law to this punk.

"This needs to be made a priority," Steve repeats.

"I heard you, dude, but there are cases ahead of yours."

As the chair swivels back, Steve seizes the arms and leans into it with all his 220 pounds, at least twice that of the chair's occupant. His face close enough to smell the Juicy Fruit frozen in the kid's mouth, he repeats, "Homicide. Which means it takes precedence over everything not a homicide."

Releasing the chair, he reaches into the pocket of his sports coat and places his business card on the table.

"You can fax the results to my office. I expect them no later than Tuesday."

As he turns, he feels the tech glancing at the card and realizing his mistake. "Steve Patterson, Special Agent for Crimes against Sex Offenders, Emeritus: Assistant Director for Criminal Investigations." The kid just mouthed off to one of the highest-ranking "dudes" in the organization.

Steve returns to the offices, commandeers a vacant desk, and spins so he's looking out the window at the San Francisco Bay.

"So I finally get to see your ugly mug after all these years."

Steve pivots back around to see the craggy Irish face of Bob Finnerty.

"I understand you're putting us to work for the bad guys."

"Someone has to do it," Steve says as he stands and extends his hand.

The two men shake the way comrades of long-standing and tough times do after not having seen each other for a time.

"How's it going?" Bob asks.

"You'll be happy to hear, not well."

"I'd say I was sorry, but I wouldn't mean it."

"Thanks anyway."

"My agent just reported in from Parsons's place."

"And?"

"Fifty-four," Bob says.

Despite bracing for it, the number stuns.

"It appears your 'victim'"—Bob uses his meaty hands to make quote symbols around his face—"was a busy boy. Fifty-four victims, and we got him for two. Makes me feel like crap."

"We can only do the best we can."

"Which definitely isn't good enough." Bob shakes his head. "Fifty-four," he repeats. "So now are you going to drop this nonsense?"

"I still have a job to do."

The friendliness drops from Bob's face. "There are far worthier cases for you to spend your time on," he says before walking away.

Steve tries to return to his work, but his mind refuses to focus, his brain filled with the walls of photos and particularly of Jesse. Swiveling again to face the window, he pulls out his wallet, and digs deep into the crevice behind his credit cards to pull out an old portrait photograph to remind himself why he's doing this.

The background is the marbled gray school photographers love to shoot against. He smooths the tarnished edges and looks at the eighteen-year-old lifelessly staring back. Danny's eyes are Charlotte's—soft and brown, turned down at the corners—the wide toothy smile is his own.

Emotions spiraling, he dials, but when the machine picks up and Charlotte's voice asks him to leave a message, he hangs up. It's good that she's not home; he's relied on her too much. She's found a way to move on, while he hasn't. Last month, he heard she was getting married. It's not surprising. She's an amazing woman and still beautiful.

He dials another number.

"Hello?"

"Hey, good-looking," Steve says, feeling stupid and shy and a little desperate.

"I was wondering if you were going to call or if you were out of my life forever," Denise says, a smile in her voice, and he breathes.

"Do you have dinner plans?" he asks.

"I'm working tonight. But how about a late rendezvous at my place and a home-cooked breakfast instead?"

His groin hiccups, and he closes his eyes in gratitude, the thought of holding her in his arms like an antidote to the venom racing through his veins.

22

Steve waits on Denise's stoop. Denise told him Jesse was staying at a friend's, news that made him giddy. Last night, he
was so self-conscious for a million reasons, not the least of
which was that there was an eleven-year-old in the room next
door.

She pulls up a little after ten, and he loves that, before she
gets out of her car, she lets down her hair, tosses it, and checks
her teeth in the mirror. He tells himself not to be overanxious
and be a gentleman, but as soon as she lifts up on her toes to
kiss him, those ideas fall away, and he practically carries her into
the house and rips the clothes from her skin.

––––

"Excited to see me," she giggles when he rolls away breathless.

He would apologize, except he doesn't like to lie.

He takes her hand and brings her fingers to his lips, and she
curls into him. "I'm glad you called," she says and purrs against
him. "Why did you?"

"You're kidding, right?"

She pushes up on her elbow, and the sheet falls to her waist, revealing her perfect breasts.

"No," she says. "I mean I get that the sex is good." She beams proudly. "But I thought you were leaving. What changed your mind?"

He hesitates before saying, "I discovered something that put me behind a day."

It's very slight, but a shadow passes across her eyes. "Yeah? What?" she says, almost innocently, causing the air to pulse.

"Probably nothing." He sweeps a tendril from her face.

"You know, for an FBI agent, you're a terrible liar." She flops back to the mattress and draws circles on his chest with her nails, a tingling sensation that's intoxicating.

"You were right about Otis having a black heart," he says, feeling like he owes her something.

She nods her head against his shoulder, then, after a second, says, "So drop it. He's dead. If he died because it was his time or because somebody decided it was his time, who cares? What difference does it make?"

He sighs and takes hold of her hand to still it, the tingling no longer pleasurable. "I can't."

She sits up again, this time pulling the sheets with her so she's covered. "Why? You just said Otis was evil." Softening her tone, she says, "Explain. Help me understand."

He looks away as a lump forms in his throat. He never talks about Danny. He can't.

Gently she touches his cheek and turns his face. "Please."

He closes his eyes from her green ones, unable to take the earnestness, but then there, in his mind's eye, is Danny, eternally young, looking at him with Charlotte's wise eyes and offering a small nod of encouragement.

"I used to be married," he starts. "And I used to have a

son. Her name was Charlotte, and his was Daniel, Danny."
It takes a second for him to start again. "Charlotte and I had
been together since high school, and we got married straight
after graduation. We wanted to get married young because we
thought we were going to have a whole brood of kids." He
smiles at the memory. "She wanted ten. I wanted to go for the
full dozen."

Denise laughs.

"But it wasn't in the cards. Danny was a difficult birth, and
it made it so Charlotte couldn't have any more."

Her hand is resting on his heart, and he feels its comforting warmth.

"It turned out okay. Quality not quantity, we used to say."
He smiles again. Charlotte would also say, "Small but mighty."

"It wasn't until Danny graduated high school that things
began to unravel. Danny chose to go to UCLA. He was thinking of going into medicine and becoming a pediatrician. He
wasn't entirely sure, which was okay. We figured he had time
to figure it out."

He stops, and it's a full minute before he finds his compo-
sure to start again.

"Danny was gay." He opens his eyes to see Denise's reaction,
relieved when there is none. "Every weekend, dozens of gay kids
would gather at this one particular bar. Those who were over
twenty-one or who had fake IDs went in, and those who didn't
hung out on the sidewalk. Danny was a good-looking kid." He
sits up. "Do you want to see a picture?"

"Of course," Denise says, sitting up as well.

Steve pulls his pants from the floor, retrieves his wallet, and
shows her the photo.

"He looks like you."

Steve smiles. He thinks Danny looks like Charlotte, but he

used to love when people would say they looked alike. Denise continues to hold the picture as he leans back against the headboard and as she leans against him.

He caresses her shoulder, lost in the memory of his life before.

"And something happened?" she says.

He takes a slow breath, this part of the story always impossible. "He met someone."

"Okay."

"It turned out he was sixteen."

"Okay?" she repeats.

"Danny was nineteen."

She pushes off him, her brow furrowed and her face tilted, a cross of confusion and incredulity, like she sort of understands but that what she's thinking can't be right.

He gives the smallest nod as he says, "The boy's parents found out, and Danny was charged with statutory rape and child molestation."

Her eyes widen. "Are you kidding? They arrested him for having sex?"

"With a minor."

"But Danny was only nineteen?"

Steve closes his eyes again, his throat so tight with emotion he's not sure he can go on. Bad as the beginning of the story is, it turns unbearable.

"He went to jail?" she asks.

"Six months in prison," he manages.

"Prison for a nineteen-year-old for having consensual sex with a kid he met outside a bar?"

Steve doesn't go into the details of why the punishment was so harsh—the bad draw of judge, the overzealous dad of the victim, the unfortunate fact that Danny was a month more

than three years older than the other boy which made it a far
worse crime in the eyes of the law.

"The hard time nearly killed him," he says. "And when he
got out, he wasn't the same. We tried to help. Got him therapy,
tried not to push, gave him space."

Denise takes his hand, entwining her fingers in his. "Did
he go back to school?"

"Had no interest. Instead, he got a job at a record shop and
moved into a small studio apartment across town. We never saw
him, and he rarely returned our calls."

"I'm sorry," she says. "That must have been hard."

He shakes his head. The hard part is what comes next.
Damaged as Danny was, Steve knew eventually he'd get better.
He just needed time.

"Two weeks before his parole ended, a month before his
twenty-second birthday, he was murdered."

Denise gasps.

"He answered his door and was shot in the chest."

"Someone shot him?"

"A mother of three," Steve says. "A woman who had never
shot a gun in her life. Who didn't even own one until that day."

"I don't understand. Why?"

"Because two days before, her youngest daughter, who was
ten, had been pulled from the hallway of their building into the
stairwell and raped. The mom, crazed with anguish and rage,
discovered a child molester vaguely fitting the description given
by her traumatized kid lived in the adjacent building and concluded Danny was the rapist."

"No," Denise says. "Oh. That's awful."

"The actual rapist was a maintenance worker from Queens."
He blows out a breath. "The woman got off on a plea of temporary insanity and was required to go to counseling. The whole

thing was treated like a joke. The DA, knowing Danny was an accused sex offender, couldn't settle the case fast enough. It was as if killing him wasn't a crime and his life didn't matter at all, like he was less than human simply because he had a record."

"So that's why you do what you do?" Denise says.

He nods, swings his feet from the bed, and starts to redress. She sets her hand on his back. "Pain like that changes you."

He pulls on his pants, suddenly very tired. "Either changes you or destroys you, but it sure as hell doesn't leave you the same. And I know you don't agree, but Otis is part of the whole of what I need to defend. Innocent until proven guilty needs to apply to everyone, including Danny and Otis and every other criminal who's done their time."

He stands and starts for the door, but her voice stops him. "He had your smile."

He turns back to see her holding Danny's photo toward him.

"I'm glad you told me, and I understand how badly you still hurt."

Normally, he hates when people say things like that. Most people have no idea what it's like to have your soul ripped from your body. But Steve knows Denise lost the love of her life when she was seventeen, a boy she'd been in love with since she was a girl, so the words have weight.

"What happened to Danny is awful," she goes on. "And you're right to be angry and to want to stop it from happening again." As he takes the photo, her hands curl around his. "And people like your son deserve to be able move on with their lives and live without fear."

Her eyes hold nothing but compassion, and he finds himself falling into them.

"But people like Otis don't," she says.

He flinches and tries to pull his hand away, but she holds it tight, then steps closer so his hand is against her beating heart.

"And until our justice system can differentiate between the two, you won't convince me that condemning the guardian angels who serve the justice our system can't is worthwhile."

He nods as the glimmer of hope he held for this thing between them becoming something more is extinguished.

"But I think you are," she says.

His brow crinkles. "You think I'm what?"

"Worthwhile. And I'd like you to stay."

23

They won. The Cubs played their first game with Dick Raynes as the manager, and they won, beating the Red Sox by a narrow score of three to two.

Dick is walking on clouds. The win was amazing, but the look of pride on Jim's face is what resounds in his heart.

Dick arrives in Independence still pumped from the victory. Normally, Dee works Saturday nights, so he's planning on a night of pizza and movies with Jesse.

It turns out Dee has other plans. When he walks through the door, Dee, Jesse, and Janelle are standing in the living room, matching mischievous grins on their faces.

"What's up?" he says.

None of them say a word. Instead the grins grow, and that's when he notices the kitchen chair on the white sheet in front of the couch.

"Sit," Janelle orders.

He does as ordered, and like a surgeon directing a nurse, Janelle turns to Jesse and says, "Towel." Jesse hands her a teal bath towel, and Janelle wraps it around Dick's neck. "Water." Jesse hands her a spray bottle. "Might want to close your eyes," Janelle says to Dick.

Dick squeezes his eyes shut as his head is spritzed with water until it is dripping.

Dee and Jesse giggle and snicker as Janelle goes to work with scissors and comb, and Dick can't tell if it's all in good humor or at his expense. But they're having such a good time that, truthfully, he doesn't care.

Janelle continues to fly around him, snipping and snapping like Edward Scissorhands until he's quite certain he doesn't have any hair left. When she's done, they refuse him a mirror, and before he can ask what's going on, they are pushing him out the door and into Dee's Subaru.

"Where are we going?" he asks, which is answered with more conspiratorial giggles.

Janelle turns up the radio, and the three start singing along to a song about chicken fries and beer.

Two hours later, they arrive at the Antelope Valley Mall, and Dick is ushered into a store called Hollister. Janelle and Dee buzz around the racks while Dick and Jesse hang near the entrance. Fifteen minutes later, the girls give Jesse a thumbs-up, and he pushes Dick toward the changing rooms.

"We want to see each item," Janelle says, thrusting a bundle of clothes into his arms.

"And we will each give you a thumbs-up or down," Dee adds. "Two thumbs out of three is a keeper."

All he can do is smile. He hasn't seen Dee this happy since she was a kid, flittering around and giggling like the world is nothing but rainbows and light. And he's proud, knowing he had a hand in it.

He carries the clothes into the dressing room, sees his reflection in the mirror, and laughs. His hair is buzzed short on the sides, and the longer strands on top are gelled so they stick up like spikes. He runs his hands over the stiff tips and chuckles again. Since Dick was a kid, he's worn his hair the same, a side part swept to the left. Now there's no part, and hardly any hair. It's a good thing he's not going bald, or his scalp would show right through. He tilts his head this way and that, and his hair doesn't move. He looks a bit like a hedgehog but supposes it is hipper. Jim might approve. Maybe even Kiley.

He turns to the clothes, and with a resigned sigh, pulls on a pair of jeans and a shirt that looks like it's made from red polka-dotted boxers. He walks out to the judges, and fortunately, Dee and Jesse veto Janelle's enthusiastic thumbs-up on the shirt. The jeans receive unanimous approval.

He returns into the dressing room, feeling a little like a poodle in a dog show, but once again, the laughter outside the dressing room is all the motivation he needs to continue.

When he's done, they each carry two bags filled with an updated wardrobe—two pairs of jeans—one blue, one black—five casual shirts, four T-shirts, a sweatshirt, a jacket, a brown belt, a black belt, three pair of shorts, and one pair of swim trunks. He has specific instructions on how to wear it all and an explicit order from Janelle to throw everything in his current wardrobe away.

They continue on to Macy's and do a similar routine for work clothes. The dressing room is larger and the light less flattering, and as Dick waits for Dee to bring him different-sized slacks, he studies himself in the mirror. Beneath his T-shirt, his belly bulges, and he estimates he's well into his second trimester. His legs are bony and his arms flabby. His skin is sallow, and his teeth stained from cigarettes.

Disgusted, he redresses, and storms from the room.

"I don't want to try on any more clothes," he says. "Let's just buy what you think works."

"You okay?" Dee asks.

"Fine," he says, pulling out his credit card and painting on a smile, not wanting to dampen the mood.

"Ooh, Baskin-Robbins," Janelle says as they walk from the store.

Dee, Jesse, and Janelle each order a two-scoop cone. Dick orders a low-fat frozen yogurt.

Janelle looks at him from across the table as they eat their treats and tilts her head. "You're not bad-looking," she says as if seeing him for the first time.

He looks at her cockeyed, and Dee giggles. Jesse rolls his eyes.

Janelle is undeterred. "I'm serious. You have good features, a nice nose and strong chin. You still have most of your hair, which is more than I can say for most guys your age. You're what I would call intellectually handsome."

"In other words, not your type," Dee says, and they all laugh. Janelle is known for her taste in burly, tattooed rednecks.

"Well, the way I've been going, maybe I should change my type." She gives Dick a wink, and Dick gives an exaggerated wink back, and they all laugh again.

They walk from Baskin-Robbins, and Dick says, "One more stop." He turns into Foot Locker and says to his personal shoppers, "I need coaching and running clothes. I'll choose my own sneakers."

Dee and Janelle flitter away, and he and Jesse head to the shoe department. Dick picks out a pair of running shoes and a pair of black cross trainers, the kind he's seen the other coaches wearing.

It's ridiculous how many bags they are carrying when they walk toward the exit, all of them loaded down. They're almost to the doors when he notices Dee's eyes slide to the window display of a store called Express. He's already spent a month's salary, but unable to help himself, he says, "I think you girls deserve something as well."

Dee opens her mouth to protest as Janelle says, "Hell yeah." Grabbing Dee's arm, she pulls her into the store, and half an hour later, his American Express has bought a white miniskirt and zodiac-patterned halter top for Janelle and the simple, sexy black dress that was in the window for Dee. As they walk from the store, Dick wonders who she intends to wear it for.

———

It's late by the time the group gets back to Independence. Janelle kisses Dick on the cheek and, with an up-and-down appraisal, says, "You really do clean up well."

Dick blushes, and his heart swells with the same gratitude he felt when he was nineteen and home from college and Janelle took pity on him when she discovered he'd never been kissed and took him behind her dad's auto body shop and gave him a lesson to remember.

She hops in her truck and drives away, and Jesse gives a wave and shuffles into the house.

Dick turns to Dee. "Thanks for today. I don't know what I did to deserve all this, but I loved it."

Her gaze settles on his, and the gaiety stills. "For what you did, you deserve a whole lot more, but I wanted to do something."

His skin goes cold, wondering how she knows.

"I knew I could count on you."

Before he can respond, she turns, and he watches as she climbs the steps to the Raynes home to tuck her son safely into bed.

24

Steve's return to D.C. has been a mix of relief at being away from the source of the tizzy in his heart and painful aching to return to it. It's Monday, predawn, and the office is empty. He turns from the window to the stack of papers and files on his desk, his casework unattended since he left almost a week ago.

He smiles at the envelope on top, "Confidential, CJIS, San Francisco." The latent tech must have worked around the clock to get the fingerprint analysis on the coins done so quickly. Steve makes a note to email the kid on a job well done.

He scans the results. There are thirty-two hits, leaving seventy-three prints that don't match those in the FBI database. But halfway down the list, Steve knows it doesn't matter. He has his man, and the world stands still: Dr. Richard Raynes, Irvine, California.

He stares so long the name it blurs. He and Denise spoke on the phone last night. Since he left her house Friday morning, they've made a habit of calling each other before they go to bed—three wondrous nights of small talk, laughter, and jokes that hold the promise of someday becoming something more, the sweet private language of couplehood.

Saturday, he made oatmeal cookies using her recipe just so he could tell her about it. Sunday, he walked to the Tidal Basin because the night before she asked if the cherry blossoms were in bloom, and he wanted to be able to tell her. He had forgotten how beautiful the basin was, even with the trees only starting to bud.

He sets the sheet down and rubs his eyes. Denise mentioned her brother. She said he visited on Saturday and that they went shopping. But the way she described him—a science nerd who likes to build model airplanes with Jesse—it never occurred to him that he could be their defender.

He logs into the database and punches in Richard's name. His file is normal to the point of boring. He has a house, an ex-wife, two kids, and no felonies. He is registered in the database because his company sometimes does work for the government.

He Googles Richard's name and finds a single photo of a thin, erudite-looking man with eyes the exact color of Denise's, and looking at him, it's impossible to think of him killing someone. Yet Steve would bet his right arm that the sweat DNA on the sliding-glass door will come back a match to Dr. Richard Raynes. He had motive and opportunity. His prints were on the coins despite owning a cellphone, and he is a chemist.

He's still looking at the photo when another thought occurs: *Denise knew.*

He thinks of her reaction when he told her peanuts were the culprit and then about how she called Parsons's killer an "angel" and a "hero" and feels a flush of humiliation followed by a sharp stab of betrayal.

A sour taste fills his mouth as he wonders if everything that followed was an act, a ploy to keep him close to protect her brother. He shakes the thought away. While there's a chance it started that way, what they have now is real as the pulse of his heart. All he needs to do is think of her gentle goodbye and the way her lips lingered on his as if trying to memorize the feeling to know the feelings between them are real.

In the photo, Richard looks shy, uncomfortable with having his picture taken, an average guy who, until two weeks ago, was likely going about his average, law-abiding life. Then Parsons returned, and suddenly he was thrust into an impossible situation, his sister and nephew in danger.

He thinks of the photos of Jesse in Parsons's hidey-hole. What would he have done if it was Danny? Or one of his sisters' sons?

No question. He would have blown Parsons's head off. With no cunning at all, he'd have marched into Parson's house and ended it. Stupid, but it's what he would have done.

But Richard wasn't stupid. He was careful. He made the death look natural, and if anyone else were on the case, he would have gotten away with it. Hell, if not for Steve, the death wouldn't have even been investigated. An ex-ped dying of an allergic reaction wouldn't have lifted an eyebrow. But now, here Steve is, certain a crime has been committed and of the perpetrator, and for the first time in his professional life, he is unsure what to do about it. The prints, along with a DNA match to the sweat, combined with Mrs. Bronson's testimony, would almost certainly get a conviction. And that's without any further digging. If he calls Richard's work, he will likely discover he was late or a no-show that Wednesday. And he'd guess a GPS search of his phone would prove he was in Independence.

The bell tower down the street chimes, signaling it's seven o'clock and breaking him from his thoughts. He emails the research department and asks for everything they can dig up on Dr. Richard Raynes, then leaves the office and drives to Chincoteague.

Three hours later, he unmoors *Char*, sails her down the Potomac and into the Atlantic until he can no longer see land.

He drops the anchor, lowers the sails, and floats.

The afternoon sun roasts his skin, and the easy rise and fall of the swell lulls him into a trance.

Hours later, the squawking of seabirds searching for their dinners brings him back to the moment and the conundrum before him: Pursue the case and lose the single bright spark in his life, or let it go and break the solemn vow he made to Danny and himself?

Let it go, his heart urges.

But it's not that simple. Dr. Richard Raynes killed a man, and he did it in cold blood and with intention. It was premeditated, first-degree murder. This isn't only about Parsons. It's about the very thing our country is founded on and the thing he's spent his life defending. The law is the law, and those who enforce it don't get to pick and choose when or why it is followed. If they do, the whole thing falls apart.

A flock of skimmers wheel overhead, and their nasal yapping reminds him of the bats and Denise. Closing his eyes, he thinks about their conversation from last night. She asked him his favorite color, and he said green because as a kid he was a fan of Gumby.

"Who's Gumby?" she asked innocently, then laughed when he started to explain. "I know who Gumby is. You're not *that much* older than me."

But he is. He is twenty years older. And she is beautiful. And he is him.

And yet she loves him. Incredibly, this amazing, kind, stunning woman has given him a second chance at a dream he believed was gone forever. A dream that will be gone if he pursues the case. If Richard was convicted, which he would be, he would go to prison. For a very long time. Twenty-five years to life. Far longer than Parsons served for either of his crimes.

His eyes flicker behind his lids.

What would Danny want?

He would want him to be happy.

But Danny's not here. Which is the problem. If he lets this go, he will be going against everything he vowed to protect.

If he doesn't, he will lose her.

25

It's four in the morning, and despite his exhaustion, Dick can't sleep. He's had trouble since Dee called about Otis's return. At first, he couldn't sleep because he was stressed over what he needed to do, and now he can't sleep because of what he's tempted to do.

The problem is that numbers, like chemistry, are irrefutable. Given enough data, a proper analysis will reveal factual truth not colored by opinion, personal bias, or desire. And the reason his brain refuses to shut off is because of the exhaustive amount of data that exists on pedophiles to which, thanks to Otis, he has now been exposed. He cannot simply dismiss it out of hand, and he knows, if analyzed, it would result in conclusions that are incontrovertible, absolute, and terrifying. The pathologies he discovered are deeply troubling, and even though Otis is gone and the threat to his own family has been eradicated, thousands, possibly even tens of thousands, Otises still exist, along with tens of thousands, possibly even hundreds of thousands, innocent soon-to-be victims.

Rationally, he understands the threat has always been there. But now that he knows the statistics, it's impossible to put it out of his mind. Like trying to unsee the sun, no matter how hard he tries, he knows it is there. He knows its pattern, understands it is going to rise and set each day, and if he analyzed it closely enough, could figure out at exactly what moment. Each night, when he closes his eyes, he sees it—the numbers, the statistics, and the impossible-to-stomach truth that no one is going to do anything about it.

And so, he doesn't sleep.

Which is why, though it's still dark, he decides to get up and go for his run. He ties on his running shoes, puts a fresh nicotine patch on his bicep, and walks into darkness. He runs in the direction of his old life—Caroline and the kids. He won't make it. He's barely able to go two blocks without stopping, but he runs toward them just the same.

His feet pound the pavement as the numbers spin in his head. Thousands of repeat pedophiles are released each year. Within the first five years of their parole, violent sex offenders of children have a 43 percent likelihood of reconviction. Considering that only 32 percent of sex offenses are reported and that the conviction rate hovers around 75 percent, the actual percentage of re-offense is at least twice that, a whopping 86 percent. There are 98,910 sex registrants living in California, and that's only the 72 percent that registered, making the actual number over 137,000. Several hundred live here, in Irvine, the town where his kids live, where his baseball team lives, all of them at the mercy of a system that can't protect them.

Dick stops breathless and, hands on his knees, sucks oxygen into his lungs.

He looks up, pleased to see he's made it several houses farther than yesterday.

As he walks back toward his apartment, he admires the tidy, buttoned-up houses along the street, basketball hoops and bikes in the driveways, planter boxes filled with flowers, and signs that say, "Home Sweet Home," the people inside believing they've moved to a nice neighborhood and are therefore safe.

When he gets to his apartment, he opens his laptop and logs back onto the Internet, looking and analyzing the numbers that disprove them all.

26

Joanne leans against the doorway of Dick's cubical, her purse and jacket still in her arms and her red lipstick spread in a wide smile across her face. "Richard, I've got good news."

Dick could use some good news.

"I talked to the board, and they've agreed to give us some leeway in regard to Freeway and to let us see where it leads."

Dick blinks, stares, blinks again.

"You okay?"

He nods numbly, unsure he heard her right. For ten years, he's waited for a chance to address what went wrong with Freeway, and just like that, she's saying they're giving it to him?

"There's an oncology conference in Las Vegas in a couple weeks," she goes on, "and since your new theory involves chemotherapy binders, I thought you might want to attend."

He nods numbly again.

"Good. Then it's settled." She smiles wide again and turns to leave but then turns back. "By the way, I like the new look." She gestures up and down with her hand at his clothes and hair, and Dick feels a boyhood blush rise in his cheeks.

———

Three hours later, he lifts his head to find the lab deserted and realizes it's lunchtime. He smiles as he realizes how lost in his work he was, filled with the same passion and purpose he had when he was young.

He pulls out the low-fat yogurt and banana he brought from home.

As he eats, his eyes catch on the photo of his kids on his desk, a shot taken two summers ago when they were at Disneyland, a month before Caroline told him she wanted a divorce. He smiles, looking at Jim. Things are better between them since Dick began managing the team. He even called last night to discuss Saturday's lineup. It might have been the first time Dick didn't initiate a conversation with his son. He frowns, looking at Kiley. Since the birthday-card fiasco, she has refused to talk to him.

He sets the yogurt aside and pulls out his phone.

"Dick," Caroline says, already sounding irritated.

"I'd like to take Kiley to dinner on Friday."

"Why?"

"Because I haven't seen her, and I'd like to."

"She won't want to."

This would normally be the point where Caroline hangs up, but Dick stops her. "Caroline."

"What?"

"I want to take Kiley to dinner."

"You already said that."

"And I'm saying it again." He looks at the Freeway file on his desk and straightens in his chair. "I'm not asking your permission. I'm informing you that I will be coming by Friday after work to take my daughter to dinner."

Silence for a beat, and he's proud that, if nothing else, he's struck Caroline speechless.

"She can't. Kiley's on the South Beach Diet, so she can only eat specially prepared meals."

"She's on a diet?" he says. "She's thirteen."

"Yes, and she wants to get ahead of it. You know how my family gains weight."

He lets it go, knowing it will only lead to a war he won't win. "Fine. Tell me what she can eat, and I'll make sure we go someplace that can accommodate her."

"I . . . I don't know . . . I'll have to think about it."

"Well, text me when you figure it out. I'll be there at six."

He hangs up and stares at his phone, quite satisfied with himself.

"What are you grinning at?" Graham asks from the door of the cubicle.

"Nothing. It's just a good day."

"Maybe for one of us."

"Something wrong?"

"Struggling. I came by to see if you can join me for a drink."

"Sure," Dick says, the day getting better by the minute.

———

Pro Sports Grill is crowded, but at the far end of the room, Graham waits at one of the few bar tables. Dick stops in his tracks when he sees him. His friend is not alone. Seated on his right is Joanne. At first, Dick almost doesn't recognize her. Her dark hair, normally pulled tight, cascades around her shoulders, and she has swapped out her trademark business skirt and jacket for a light blue sweater and jeans.

Graham flags him over.

"Hey, buddy. Look who decided to join us." He toasts Joanne with his half-empty mug.

"Hi, Richard. I hope you don't mind that I crashed your party," Joanne says.

Dick's mouth's gone dry, but he manages to say, "Not at all. It's nice to see you—" He stupidly gestures at her with his hand. "You know, not . . ."

"Pressed and tucked?"

Sheepishly, he shrugs, feeling like the class nerd at a school dance who's stumbled into the prom queen. He slides onto the stool beside her and reminds himself that she is his boss and that breasts are nothing more than mammary glands that provide nourishment for infants, and that her red-painted lips and fingernails, while designed to stimulate, are not designed to stimulate him.

Dick orders a scotch, and Joanne orders a beer. While they wait for their drinks, Graham carries the conversation, telling jokes and stories about the lab that almost make it sound like an exciting place to work. If Dick didn't know better, which he does—Joanne one Y chromosome short of Graham's type—he'd say Graham was flirting.

Only after they are on their second round does Dick realize the stories Graham's telling all involve him, and that Graham is flirting, but not for himself. He is working very hard to be a surrogate flirt on behalf of his inept friend who has not managed to utter a word since the stupid words he uttered when he first sat down.

"So, Richard, you were the one who figured out Cameron's Cocktail?" Joanne asks, sounding impressed.

"He was," Graham says, slapping Dick on the shoulder. "But, modest boy that he is, he never took credit."

The story is partly true. Cameron's Cocktail was named after its creator Jake Cameron. When it was given its name, it had been a drug to save lives. When Dick intervened, after Cameron's death, it had become a death potion. Dick was given the responsibility of figuring out why. Credit was never taken or given because the horrible oversight that led to multiple deaths was a blight on Pentco that nobody wanted remembered.

"So Joanne," Dick says, anxious to shift the attention away from himself, certain Graham's exhausted all the highlights of his very mundane life, "what got you started at Pentco?"

She wipes the condensation on her glass with her finger, creating a clear line, and shrugs. "It's just where my path took me. I started out in marketing, but there was nowhere for me to go there, so when the management position opened in the lab, I applied. I didn't think they'd hire a non-chemist, but they liked the idea of having a 'big-picture thinker'"—she uses her hands to make quotes in the air—"at the helm. So here I am."

She takes a sip of her beer and smiles. Crow's-feet define her eyes, and Dick wonders how old she is. She looks younger than Caroline, who is his age, thirty-nine, but he's never been a good judge of age or of women.

"Where'd you go to school?" he asks.

"Columbia."

"Impressive," Graham says.

"Class of 2010," she says, which makes Dick's estimate about right.

"Okay, enough small talk," Graham says. "I'm starting to feel like a third wheel."

Dick looks at Joanne with what he hopes is an expression of apology, letting her know he had nothing to do with this, but when his eyes catch hers, she's not looking at him like she's put out. Instead, she is smiling, her head tilted as if contemplating him, looking at him in much the same way Janelle did, as if trying to decide if he's okay looking or not.

"Let's get to it," Graham says, rubbing his hands together. "The reason we are gathered here today to join this man and this woman and this man in holy drinking is so they can help poor Graham out of the quagmire of ethical uncertainty he's found himself mired in."

Joanne giggles while Dick toasts him and frowns. He understands far too well how the ethics of a project can cut you down as quickly as the science.

Graham explains that the New England Research Institutes just released a study showing obesity to be more a personality trait than a physical one. If this is true, then is it ethical for Graham to continue what he's doing, knowing the genetic solution he's exploring could end up altering personality traits to cure obesity?

"There are definitely going to be some who take issue with that sort of meddling," Joanne says.

"Exactly," Graham says. "Could you imagine if I took my drug and ended up skinny but dull?" He flicks his head at Dick, and Dick laughs.

The server stops at the table, and though Dick's already tipsy, he's enjoying himself so much he orders another.

The conversation continues, Graham taking the side of defending DNA alteration; Joanne outraged at the idea of messing with people's personalities; and Dick straddling the middle as he wonders if there might be a way to isolate the overeating trait without altering other traits.

The conversation is impassioned and riveting, and Dick can't remember the last time he's enjoyed himself so much.

An hour later, Graham, mockingly upset, stands. "Heathens, both of you! Robbers of science and lovers of blubber! I cannot tolerate another second of this blasphemy in defense of mental sanity and morality." He storms off, leaving Joanne and Dick laughing.

The bill arrives, and Dick reaches for it, but Joanne puts her hand on his stopping him. He tries not to react to the jolt of electricity down his spine.

"Pentco's got this," she says.

"No," he says with surprising confidence. "My treat."

She doesn't argue, shocking him for the second time in a day with how well his assertiveness worked with a woman.

27

Steve is on his third cup of coffee and his second dose of Advil. He didn't sleep last night, his burden too heavy, Denise swimming in and out of his thoughts. She called last night, but he didn't answer, his thoughts too muddled and still too unsure of what to do.

"Memphs was picked up last night."

Steve looks up to see Anthony Briggs, the young agent who covered for him while he was in California.

"I thought you'd want to know," Briggs says.

He stands in a deliberate pose of cool, his hands loose at his sides and his weight shifted to his left leg. Steve remembers when he first started at the agency and the effort it took to act over the bad moments of the job. The kid's shoulders are too high, and he can't quite decide how to position his mouth.

"Picked up?" Steve says, leaning back and taking a slow breath through his nose. He doesn't act anymore. He doesn't have to. Twenty years on the job has made him genuinely tough.

"He kidnapped a sixteen-year-old, then raped and killed her in a trailer he'd rented. And get this, the police show up on a tip from a neighbor, and Memphs answers the door with the legs of the girl sticking out in plain sight behind him." Briggs guffaws and shakes his head.

Steve doesn't see the humor.

His burden delivered, Briggs leaves.

Steve unearths Memphs's casefile from his stack and drops it into the "To be Filed" bin. Beneath it is the Parsons file. He pulls it in front of him and leafs through it, pausing on the note Parsons sent Denise from prison:

Dear Denise,

Congratulasions. I understand you had a BOY! Isn't that lucky? For you and for ME. I can not wait until I am out of this place so I can MEET him. Thanks to you I have so much time to think and PLAN. Take care of HIM for me and enjoy the time you have. It goes so fast.

Otis

Steve stares at the ugly scrawl and thinks about how Denise must have felt when, at eighteen and a new mom, she got the letter, and then when Parsons was released and her beautiful son was eleven.

His phone buzzes, interrupting his thoughts and letting him know he has a message.

He swivels toward the window before looking at it.

Missed u last night. B safe today. I
want you in one piece. Xoxo. D.

He runs his thumb over the glowing words as a lump forms hard in his throat.

He texts back:

Missed u too. Needed to close
the Parsons case. Now you can be
done with me.

Her reply is instant.

Done w u? I just got started :) !

He swivels back to his desk and places the Parsons file on top of the Memphs file, and for the first time in a day, his heart unclenches, and for the first time in a long time, he remembers how it feels to be alive.

28

A thin, black-clad hostess leads Dick and Kiley to a corner booth. Dick did careful research to find this place. They are known for their extensive offering of low-carb items, and he is pleased when he opens the menu to see heart symbols peppering the page, making it easy to know what items are safe for South Beach dieters.

"How's school?" he asks.

Kiley doesn't answer, her eyes on the menu.

When she sets it down, he tries again. "How are things? Are you still dancing?"

"I haven't danced for a year."

"Oh," Dick says, thinking he might have known that but not sure.

He can't think of what else to say. Fortunately, the server arrives to take their order.

He nods to Kiley.

"I'll have the fettuccine alfredo, and an extra order of garlic toast."

Dick's certain this wasn't one of the heart-marked entrees but keeps the thought to himself then, afraid of offending his daughter, changes his own order.

"I'll have the same. But no extra bread."

He was going to order the antipasto salad with light vin-aigrette. His diet's been going well, and already he's lost five pounds. He will consider this his cheat meal for the week.

The server leaves, and again, there's silence.

"Have you been enjoying the Heelys?" he asks, the roller sneakers he bought her for her birthday feeling like a safe sub-ject since she was the one who asked for them.

Shrug.

A basket of rolls arrives, and as Kiley grabs one and but-ters it. Dick sips his Miller Lite and looks at her, overwhelmed by his feelings as he often is around his kids. Though a million sonnets, songs, and stories have been written about a parent's devotion to their children, he never truly understood it until the first time he held Kiley in his arms. He can still remember how small she was, the smell of her newborn skin, the flutter of her tiny heartbeat, the heat of her wee body.

It's hard to believe how much she's grown, filling out and getting curves, which make her look a lot like Caroline. They share the same dark curly hair and broad shoulders, though Kiley has narrower hips, and her face is defined by a deep cleft chin.

His breath catches in the back of his throat like he's almost choking on something, and his eyes narrow on the dimple Ki-ley's had since she was born but which he's never fully considered before.

"You okay?" Kiley asks, her lip curling.

His skin sizzles, and he shifts in his seat.

"Two fettuccini alfredos, one with extra garlic toast," the server announces and sets their dinners in front of them.

Kiley digs in, while Dick's dinner sits untouched, his eyes returning again and again to Kiley's chin that moves up and down as she chews. How could he never have noticed? Cleft chins are like brown eyes or the ability to roll your tongue; you can only get them if one of your parents has the trait. Dick's chin is long and square. Caroline's is small and pointy. There are no dimples on either.

When finally Kiley finishes her last bite, he says, "We need to go."

"Go where?"

"Home . . . I need to take you home," he stammers.

"But I want dessert."

In the thirteen years Dick's been a father, he can't recall ever telling his children no.

"No."

Kiley blinks. "You said dinner. Dinner includes dessert."

She doesn't use the word *Dad*, and he tries to think of the last time she said it and realizes it's been so long he can't remember.

"Kiley, we're leaving."

She crosses her arms.

"Fine," he says, standing. "Stay." He throws three twenties on the table. "Buy whatever dessert you want, then call your mother to pick you up."

He starts for the door, then reconsiders. When he turns back, Kiley is grabbing for the money. He pulls the straw from her Shirley Temple and continues on his way.

29

Dick is sitting in his cubicle at Pentco, staring at the screen-saver of bouncing balls on his computer. The lab is deserted and silent except for the buzzing fluorescent lights and soft whirring computers. He's been here since he left Kiley at the restaurant, his rage at critical mass.

The straw is in a baggie on his desk, and every other minute he looks at it, stunned and disgusted with himself that it took this long before he figured it out, thirteen years of his life given to a lie. He rubs his eyes hard, then rests them on his knuckles, his fists pushing against the sockets. He met Caroline when he was in Boston getting his PhD. She worked at the bagel shop where he bought his breakfast each morning. She was attractive with large breasts, and Dick's always had a weakness for well-developed glands. One morning, she asked him out. It stunned him, but he said yes. They went to a movie and after had sex. Then she asked him to go out the following week, and he agreed. It had continued that way for about a month when she dropped the bombshell that she was pregnant. It never occurred to Dick it might not be his.

He rubs his eyes again as if trying to erase the memory.

Until tonight, he believed his mistake had been having sex with Caroline, now he knows it was believing her when she told him the baby was his, then doing the noble thing and marrying her.

What destroys him is how much he loves Kiley regardless of all that. He would still lay down his life for her. Meanwhile, he now knows the feeling isn't mutual. She no longer considers him her "Dad," and he wonders how long she's known. Certainly not as an infant or toddler. In those early years, they'd been close. Caroline didn't have much patience, and Kiley was difficult, so Dick was the one who rocked her to sleep and soothed away her tears. He taught her to count, to read, and how to ride a bike. He was the one who helped her with her homework, filled out her school forms, took her to the doctor and dentist.

Elementary school graduation, he thinks, the sudden memory like a slap. She refused to take a picture with him.

Two years!

Spots swim in his brain, and sickness roils his gut. For two years, Kiley has known he wasn't her dad and kept it from him.

Why?

But as soon as he asks the question, he knows the answer. *Money.* Caroline didn't want to lose the child support she was going to get for Kiley when they got divorced.

His brain on fire and desperate for a distraction, he pulls a yellow notepad in front of him, feeling like he needs to do something or else go mad.

He starts to write. Doing what he's been avoiding for more than a week, the numbers burning a hole in his brain. *Knowledge is power.* And he feels so powerless. He will get it out of his system and be done with it. Figuring it out doesn't mean he needs to do anything about it. It simply proves it can be done. His pen flies across the page as he exorcises the thoughts from his head.

Statement of problem: Released repeat pedophiles pose an imminent risk to society, and the law is powerless to do anything about it until it's too late.

Implications: Countless innocent children are being senselessly victimized.

His body buzzes, and he's slightly concerned by his excitement:

Hypothetical solutions: Theoretically, potential threats could be analyzed, their behaviors predicted, and their crimes prevented by preemptive neutralization or elimination if dangerous, portentous symptoms are exhibited (i.e. predatory or depraved behavior).

He taps the pen on the pad, thinking for a moment before continuing.

Possible contributing factors to irremediable predatory disposition:
- *Previous offense(s)*
- *Boy victim(s)*
- *Victim unknown to perp*
- *Never married*
- *Male*
- *Level of violence*
- *Age of perp*
- *Age of victim(s)*

He's surprised how clear the criteria are in his mind. He thinks about the countless articles he read on the pathologies and continues to write:

- *Paranoia*
- *Low motivation for treatment*
- *Age of onset of offending*
- *Negative relationship with mother*
- *Diverse sex crimes*
- *Release date*

Throwing down the pen down like he just completed a timed exam, he blows out a breath and leans back in his chair.

Still pumped, he takes a sip of his cold coffee, wakes his computer, and opens the statistical program he uses for lab analysis. He programs in the contributing factors and sets the Mendoza Line. The Mendoza Line is not a technical term, but it's the name he uses to describe the breakpoint of a study. The phrase was coined after Minnie Mendoza, a Minnesota Twins player from the seventies who never hit over .200. A batter "under the Mendoza Line" isn't considered a threat. If you don't make the line, you don't belong in the big leagues.

All that's left is to input the data. The more cases he analyzes, the more accurate the results. Based on historical data, the program will analyze which factors contribute most to future outcomes, ultimately providing an algorithm that can predict the statistical probability for recidivism of an individual. In other words, when he's done, Dick will know with a fair amount of certainty which recently released pedophiles are most likely to strike again.

The data is at his fingertips. Thirty years ago, the founder of Pentco made an arrangement with the director of the BOP, Bureau of Prisons, that allowed Pentco access to the prisoner database so the company would have a wealth of potential human guinea pigs. There's nothing illegal about it. Participants gladly sign waivers over the potential health risks of drug trials to receive upgraded housing, better food, or just a break in the monotony of prison life. They never lack for volunteers.

It's a slow process. First he needs to first narrow the search to sex offenders who committed crimes against minors, then he needs to analyze each of those files for the contributing factors. Each file takes twenty minutes to parse, and when he finally shuts down the computer near midnight, he's only gotten through a dozen of the hundred randomly chosen subjects of his data set.

He returns on Saturday and works all day, only taking a two-hour break in the afternoon to coach his team. There's no one in the office, and the work is tedious, but Dick doesn't mind. Methodical researching and analytical thinking are his gifts.

On Sunday, he doesn't take a break at all, and a little after one in the morning, he finishes. Eyes blurry, and brain buzzing from caffeine, he stares at the buzzing blue "calculate" button in the lower right corner of his screen.

Click and get your prize.

Except, he's now more certain than ever, it's a prize he doesn't want. His self-preservation angel has returned and sits squarely on his shoulder. Knowledge may be power, but in this case, it would be nothing but an enormous burden he wouldn't have any idea what to do with. He is no hero. What he did with Otis, he did because he had no choice. Otis was threatening his family. Beyond them, none of this is his responsibility, and the only thing knowing will do is make it feel like somehow it is and make it so he never sleeps again. And he really needs to sleep.

With a yawn, he closes the program and drags the file he named "Pepper" for "Program of Predictability of Recidivism" into the "Stuff" folder on his desktop, where he intends for it to remain.

30

Seven hours later, Dick is back at Pentco. On his way to his cubicle, he stops by the lab.

Graham nods in greeting from his lab bench. "What's up?"

"I was hoping you could run a DNA test for me." Dick sets two Ziploc baggies on the table. In one is the black straw from Kiley's drink, in the other a Miller Lite bottle.

"What am I testing for?"

"Paternity."

Graham arches his eyebrows then, with a sympathetic frown, nods.

Dick continues to his desk and stares at the screensaver of bouncing balls that spares him from the "Stuff" folder and the blue "calculate" button that, despite his earlier vow, has not left his mind.

"You okay?"

He startles and turns to see Joanne.

"Hey," he says, blinking to get his bearings.

"You didn't stop by to update me," she says.

He's surprised how nice it is to see her. She's back to her corporate self, "pressed and tucked" as she said—a tailored skirt and jacket and her dark hair pulled tight. But he sees past it now to the laughing woman from the bar with the radiant smile and quick wit.

He glances at his watch to see it's 8:30. He was supposed to meet with her at 8:15.

"Sorry. I guess I got distracted. I'll be right there."

When she's gone, he gathers his Freeway notes and hurries to her office.

Her jacket is off, and she is leaning against her desk, her ankles crossed in front of her as she reads a file, and he thinks the pose is intentional and that it's possible she is viewing him differently as well.

He explains the progress he's made and how he's now confident in his theory that the recently developed binding agents being used in some chemotherapy treatments are a viable solution to resolve the issues he had with his failed version of Freeway. He'll know more after the conference, but the research is promising.

"Sounds like you're on to something," she says when he finishes.

He nods, and she tilts her head. "Richard?"

"Huh?"

"I'd think you'd be more excited."

"I am," he says, trying to imbue the enthusiasm she's looking for.

She frowns. "Is something going on?"

He shakes his head, though he's never been very good at lying.

"Girl troubles?" she asks playfully.

He laughs, but then thinks of Kiley and Caroline. *Yes, girl troubles.*

"No," he says. "At the moment, there are no girls in my life to be in trouble with." He only realizes how flirty it sounded after the words are out of his mouth.

She grins, then shocks him with, "Good to hear."

Not knowing what to do with that, he looks away.

"So, what is it then?"

He shifts his weight, then shifts again. "You know when you were a kid, and you used to have those dreams where you were a hero, where you ran into a burning house to save your family or invented a cure for cancer or came up with a solution to help the homeless?"

"Yes to all of the above except curing cancer. I sucked at science even as a kid."

He smiles, imagining her as one of those smart girls who killed it in the humanities—history, English, social studies.

"Well, do you ever wonder where all that went?"

She chuckles. "I used to really want to be like Jane Goodall. But I wanted to live with pandas, not chimpanzees."

"You know pandas eat bamboo like fourteen hours a day and sleep the rest of the time?"

"I was eight."

"Fair enough. Anyway, for whatever reason, that's what I've been thinking about, wondering when I stopped dreaming of being like Sir Fleming or Jane Goodall and just started trudging along."

"Sir Fleming?"

"The microbiologist who discovered penicillin."

"Oh."

"I guess I've just been wondering when I lost sight of that, of trying to do something . . . I don't know . . . something more . . . more than myself?"

"But you are?" Joanne says. "With Freeway."

Dick shakes his head, frustrated with his inability to explain the feelings he's been struggling with since Otis's death. He thinks of his dad. His father served in the army, then worked his whole life at a fish hatchery doing maintenance. He never did anything grand, but there wasn't a moment he didn't stand up for what he believed in or do what was right.

"Most of us are just doing the best we can," Joanne says. "You know, trying to get by."

"But what if you *knew* you could do something that could change things?"

"Like save the pandas?" she says with a grin.

He thinks of Jesse. He thinks of Otis. He thinks of the boys on his team.

"Exactly. What if you knew you could stop something bad from happening?"

"Richard, what's this about?"

Realizing he probably sounds insane and that the whole thing is insane, he says, "Nothing."

"You can't say all that then say 'nothing.'"

He smiles at her mock annoyance, enjoying the banter and thinking how long it's been since he's had that with a woman.

"It was just a thought I had, wondering why most of us never become the heroes we believed we were going to be when we were kids."

"Wouldn't it be amazing if we did?" She pushes off the desk and puts her fists on her hips. "Joanne Humphries, superhero of pandas."

"I can totally see it. All you need is a cape and some bamboo."

"Well, until we figure out how to be superheroes, how about we just keep working on saving the world from hay fever?"

31

"How long has she known?" Dick says as Caroline scowls from the doorway.

"What are you talking about?"

"How long has Kiley known I'm not her father?"

Caroline's ruddy face loses its pink, the truth plain in her beady brown eyes. Dick's never been a violent man, but for the first time, he understands how a man might hit a woman. He thrusts the printout Graham gave him toward her and, when she doesn't take it, drops it at her feet.

"She's still my daughter," he says, "and if you do anything to interfere with that, so help me, I'll petition for full custody of Jim and sue you for damages for the past thirteen years."

"She doesn't want anything to do with you," Caroline spits.

"Yeah, well, you might want to convince her otherwise, unless you want to lose everything you lied so hard to get."

He whirls, feeling like the blood in his veins is blistering his skin.

———

Dick tosses and turns for two hours, then gets up and tries to read the novel he started a month ago. Losing interest, he tries to sleep again, and finally gets up and packs his bag for Las Vegas. His flight leaves this evening, and he's heading to the airport straight from work.

As he eats his breakfast of grapefruit and shredded wheat, he reads the paper. As always, he starts with the national news, moves to the local section, and saves the best—sports—for last.

He never makes it to the photo of the Angels' pitcher concussing the Giants' catcher as he slides into home to score the winning run. On the front page of Section B is a quarter-page article topped by the photo of a crying woman being held by an older one. In the middle of the column is a smaller photo of a little boy with brown curly hair and freckles. The headline reads, "Missing Irvine Boy Found, Two-Time-Convicted Child Molester Arrested."

> Eight-year-old Jerry O'Neill's body was found dismembered in a suitcase that had been abandoned in a dump in Santa Ana. Fibers found on the bag led detectives to arrest Leonard Fedorov, a child molester who had been released nine months prior . . .

The shredded wheat sits soggy in the bowl.

———

The office is empty except for the janitor running a vacuum over the carpet on the other side of the room. Dick jiggles his mouse to wake his computer, opens the "Stuff" folder, clicks on "Pepper," and without hesitation, clicks the blue button.

The results are nearly instant. If a subject meets the

minimum threshold, there is a 93 percent probability of a positive result within five years of their release. In other words, all the other losers like Otis who are let in the world will, nine times out of ten, repeat their crimes within five years of their release.

He accesses the prison database, finds Leonard Fedorov, scrolls through his file for the contributing factors, and punches them into the program as he goes: two previous convictions, boy victims, never married . . .

Twenty minutes later he is finished. If the analysis returns a cumulative score over sixty-three, it's positive.

Click.

Subject 1: Leonard Albert Fedorov – 67

The number sears into the occipital lobe of Dick's brain. From the moment Leonard Fedorov was released, there was a 93 percent probability he would strike again. Dick throws the mouse at the monitor, and the screen cracks, the data mutating into a starburst rainbow at the point of impact, the green sixty-seven still glowing.

He thinks of the curly-haired boy in the paper—Jerry O'Neill—his apartment only a few miles from Dick's own.

32

The Pentco planning department rented Dick a cherry-red Chrysler Sebring convertible. Dick exchanges it for a white Nissan Sentra.

Things are clear now. He's not certain where this path will lead, but this is the path he's chosen, or perhaps the path chose him. Either way, there is no turning back. Jerry O'Neill is the last burden he will carry. He's never held much belief in karma or God having a hand in destiny yet has lived long enough to know sometimes there's no explaining things. All he knows is he feels a personal responsibility, even if it's simply because he's the only one who understands the numbers and the cold, hard truth they represent.

Dick had a coach once who said, "Fear has two meanings: Forget everything and run. Or face everything and rise." And he knows now, the time has come to rise. Jerry is Jesse. Jerry is Jim. Jerry is him. And shame will not shadow his life again.

When he is away from the airport, he pulls onto a secluded road and exchanges the plates on the car with the temporary ones he brought from home. Then he climbs back in the car to review the profile he printed at Pentco before he left. The subject's name is Kevin Shea, and he is the most recently released two-time pedophile in Clark County, Nevada.

He was an easy choice. There were a dozen others who were recently released, but when Dick read Shea's file, he had a hunch Shea would fly past the Mendoza Line. And he did, scoring a whopping sixty-nine, six points past the minimum.

Only forty-two, he's already been convicted twice on multiple counts of kidnapping, rape, and sexual assault. His psychological profile reveals a damaged soul who suffered a badly abusive childhood that would almost make you feel sorry for him if he hadn't turned out to be such a monster himself. His juvenile records are sealed, but the fact that he has a juvenile record and that his first conviction dates back to when he was eighteen doesn't bode well for when his sickness began.

A full moon watches as Dick pulls into Royal Palms Trailer Park. He drives slowly past the pale blue mailbox with the number 60324 and studies the rusted trailer it belongs to. The home is dark, and an old, one-time-red Chevy truck is parked out front.

Dick pulls back onto the highway and parks at the 7-Eleven on the corner. Though he's tired, he does not sleep. He keeps his eyes on the drive that leads to the trailer park. At six thirty the next morning, the truck emerges, and Dick follows. Half an hour later, they arrive at the Sunny Hills Packinghouse, a meat factory the size of a city block.

Dick sets his phone timer to buzz in seven hours and drives to the conference. He spends a few hours at the show and a few resting at his hotel.

His phone wakes him, and he returns to the packinghouse and parks in the lot with the other cars in a spot with a view of the entrance. Half an hour later, employees begin to trickle out. Some reach into their pockets for cigarettes, and Dick feels a sympathetic craving. It's been two weeks since he last smoked, and of all the things he's given up, it's what he misses most.

He scans the faces, searching for the one that matches the photo he has of Shea, an average-looking man with mud brown hair and thick, straight eyebrows. The windows of his car are down, and snippets of conversation float on the breeze. He listens absently as he continues to scan.

"Shea, fantasy money's due tomorrow."

Dick's head snaps sideways to see a heavyset man talking to a leaner one sitting on one of the loading docks. The thinner man's shoulders are hunched, and his trucker's hat is pulled low over his eyes. With a nod, Shea drops to the ground, crushes out his cigarette, and walks to his truck.

Dick waits until the truck pulls onto the highway before following. He thinks Shea is going home, but a few miles from the trailer park, the truck turns into a self-storage facility. Dick drives past, then circles back and parks in a visitor spot.

He puts on the "What Happens in Vegas Stays in Vegas" hat he bought at the airport and, head down, walks the grounds. Shea's truck is in front of building C, unit 104, and Shea is nowhere in sight.

It's another hour before Shea's truck pulls out of the storage park. Dick yawns as he watches, the adrenaline rush that's sustained him since he read the Jerry O'Neill article thirty-five hours earlier worn off and replaced by deep exhaustion. He could follow Shea, but his gut tells him what he's looking for is behind the orange door of unit 104C.

33

At nine the next morning, Dick is back at the U-Store complex wearing his hat, along with oversized sweats, blue sneakers, and non-prescription glasses he bought last night at Walmart. A girl around twenty wearing a fluorescent green tank top sequined with the word "Sexy" sits at the desk reading a magazine.

"I'd like to rent a unit," Dick says.

She hands him a form and returns to her reading.

"Are there any units available in block C?"

She lets out a sigh, noisily closes her magazine, takes her feet from the counter, and glances through the ledger.

"210C."

"How about on the bottom level?"

She rolls her eyes like Dick is the most annoying customer in the world. "108?"

"That will be fine."

He fills out the form.

"License and credit card," she says when he's done.

"I'd like to pay cash."

Another eyeroll. "Fine. License."

He hands her the license he created using a superstore

membership card and a decal he printed at the local copy shop that he mocked up from an image of a New Hampshire driver's license of a man vaguely resembling him.

The girl barely glances at it. She makes a copy and returns it, and he gives her first and last month's rent.

He parks the Sentra in front of Shea's unit, pulls on a pair of latex gloves, and using bolt cutters he also bought last night, removes the lock from the door. He practiced in his hotel room and is glad he did. It turns out being a criminal is not so different from planning out an experiment. Consider everything before you start. Run it and rerun it in your head with every conceivable hitch. And have a contingency plan for everything. A good plan is 99 percent preparation and 1 percent execution. The first lock he tried to cut took over five minutes. This morning, he clips the shackle in under one.

He returns the bolt cutters and broken lock to his trunk, then, with a quick glance around, walks back to the unit and opens it. The noise is deafening, and his heart goes haywire and causes him to dive beneath the half-raised door and slam it down behind him.

He fumbles with his phone to turn on the flashlight. The beam comes to life and shines on the gray concrete floor. He takes a gulp of air and regrets it, a vile stench causing bile to rise like a fist in his throat. Pinching his nose against it, he squeezes his eyes tight to keep it down as every instinct in his body screams at him to flee. Whatever this is, he wants no part of it. His eyes sting with tears, and his muscles twitch. *Urine, feces, something metallic.*

Sipping air sparingly through his teeth, he waits for the sickness to pass, then slowly lifts the beam. In the left corner, a bare mattress is wedged between the wall and a white chest freezer. The mattress is old, the faded pinstripes barely visible beneath the stains of brown, rust, and yellow. The freezer hums, a slight chill escaping its seal.

———

Dick is in the Sentra, his head between his knees as he breathes into a Krispy Kreme donut sack, the technique not working, his breath wheezing and his extremities numb. He counts, loses track, starts again. He reaches thirty before the carbon dioxide begins to seep into his bloodstream and his breathing begins to settle. When he's out of danger of passing out, he leans his head back against the headrest and stares at the gray felt of the car's ceiling, afraid to close his eyes for fear of seeing what he saw again.

Dick has seen dead bodies before. In school, he dissected a cadaver. And as part of his post-graduate study, he worked with a chemist who specialized in treatments for terminally ill cardio-pulmonary cases, and he witnessed the autopsies of several of the patients after they passed. Death does not bother him, but the story the two young corpses in that freezer told of their last days has turned his stomach to acid and his lungs to lead.

With a deep steeling breath, he straightens, then pulls out the prepaid cellphone he also bought last night and calls 9-1-1. "I'd like to report a crime."

"What sort of crime?"

He hesitates. The list is extensive, but he decides the litany is unnecessary. "Serial murder."

"Are you in danger?"

"No. The murders already happened."

"Excuse me?"

"Two kids were murdered, and I'm calling to report it."

"Kids?"

"Yes."

"Already dead?"

"Yes."

"Hold on," the operator says, her voice turned tight. "I'm connecting you to one of our detectives."

An eternity that's probably less than a minute passes, then an authoritative voice comes on the line. "This is Detective Harris. With whom am I speaking?"

"I'd rather not say."

"Okay. Then what should I call you."

"Smith."

"Fine, Mr. Smith. How can I help you?"

"I have information regarding a murder. Actually, two murders."

"Two murders?" His voice pitches high, disbelieving.

"Yes."

"You witnessed these murders?"

"No, but I found the bodies."

"You *found* them?"

Dick hesitates. "Yes."

"How did you happen to find them?"

"I'd rather not say."

"Why?"

"I don't want to be involved."

"Sounds like you're already involved."

"I'm not. I just want to do the right thing and report a crime."

"If you're not involved, why can't you tell me who you are?"

"Do you want the information or not?"

"I do, but I want to verify the source."

"There are two young boys lying dead in a freezer. See for yourself." Dick's voice loses its cool, and he feels his chest tightening again. He recites the address and is about to hang up when Detective Harris asks, "Do you know the suspect?"

"Yes," Dick says, then quickly corrects it to, "No. I don't actually know him, but I know who he is."

"How?"

"I just do. He's a child molester who was paroled from Nevada State Prison three months ago. His name is Kevin Shea."

The detective's in the middle of his next question when Dick ends the call. Grabbing the Krispy Kreme bag, he places it back over his nose and mouth and sucks air deep into his lungs.

———

After numbly wandering the conference floor for several hours, Dick returns to the packinghouse, arriving a few minutes before Shea's shift ends. Shea's truck is still in the parking lot, and Dick wonders if he's already been arrested.

Same as yesterday, at four o'clock a stream of employees leaves the building, and Dick is shocked when he sees Shea among them. Leisurely he smokes a cigarette, then gets in his truck and drives from the lot.

Dick follows as he takes the same route as yesterday.

Dick parks again in a visitor's spot of the storage facility, wondering if the police are staking out Shea's unit so they can apprehend him at the scene of the crime.

A few minutes pass, and the Chevy reappears. Driving fast, it peels from the U-Store drive onto the road.

Dick swivels his head back toward the storage units expecting to see the police in hot pursuit, but the drive is empty.

He looks at Shea's truck as it continues to race away, then jerks his car from its parking spot and slams on the accelerator—20 mph, 30, 40, 50 . . .

He slams on the brakes and skids to a stop on the shoulder. *What the hell am I doing?*

His eyes fix on Shea's taillights fading in the distance.

Damn it! The small car's tires kick up gravel as he tears back onto the road.

34

For two hours, Dick trails the Chevy on Highway 15, his thoughts vacillating between confusion and incredulity. *Where were the police?* Every other minute, he considers calling them again and, each time, thinks better of it.

The needle on his gas gauge hovers at the quarter mark, and he wonders how much gas Shea has. He passes a sign that says, "Cedar City 40 miles," which means Dick has approximately thirty minutes to formulate a plan.

———

It's almost dark when Dick follows Shea off the freeway into a gas station.

He watches from the shadows as Shea shells out several bills to the attendant, then returns to his truck to fill it up. As Shea waits, he leans against the fender and smokes. He stretches his arms over his head to work out the kinks in his muscles. His red T-shirt has a waving American flag emblazoned across its front, with bold letters over the top that read, "Made in the U.S.A."

When the pump clicks off, he crushes out the cigarette, then climbs back in his truck and drives to the diner across the street. Dick fills up the Sentra, then parks a few spots away.

Through the window, he watches Shea sitting at the counter. The back of his shirt says, "Land of the Free."

Dick calls the Las Vegas Police. "Detective Harris, please."

The call goes to voicemail.

He punches zero to reconnect to the switchboard. He explains that it's an emergency, and the operator says she'll page the detective. Dick recites the number for the prepaid cellphone and hangs up.

Inside the diner, Shea drinks coffee and studies the menu. A server with bleached hair and therapeutic shoes takes his order, and Dick thinks of Dee as he wonders how long the server's been working at the diner and if, at one time, she had been pretty.

On the first ring, Dick snatches up the phone. "Detective Harris?"

"Mr. Smith? Where are you?"

"The question is where the hell are you? Did you find the boys?"

"Yes. Who are you?"

"It doesn't matter."

"Yes, it does. How'd you know about those boys being in that freezer?"

"It's irrelevant."

"It's not."

"What matters is the guy who put them there is sitting in a diner in Utah eating a patty melt."

"Utah?"

"Yeah. Big surprise, when he realized his secret had been discovered, he decided not to stick around."

"You followed him?"

"What was I supposed to do?"

"How are you involved in this?"

"I'm just a guy that had a bad hunch about another guy and who's trying to do the right thing."

"That's quite a hunch and a hell of a commitment, following a convicted felon to Utah."

"That wasn't my plan. Where were you?"

"Warrants take time. We got to the storage unit a little before six."

Dick looks at his watch. It's almost eight. "Who were those boys?" he asks, his head throbbing with the image of the two frozen faces as he stares at Shea's back.

Harris ignores him. "Where are you?"

Dick drops his forehead to the steering wheel. He's so tired. "Who were they?" he asks again.

"It won't help," Harris says.

"Probably not. But I'd like to know."

Harris's gruff voice softens. "We're not sure. Our best guess is they're a couple kids from Winchester. The first was reported missing six weeks ago, the second, two weeks later."

"Can you tell me their names?"

"Will you tell me yours?"

"No."

"Germaine Johnson and Willy Pierce."

"Route 15 Diner, ten miles south of Cedar City," Dick says and hangs up.

Shea says something to the server, and she laughs. He must be a funny guy.

————

A few minutes later, Dick watches two patrol cars pull into the parking lot. Two officers walk into the diner and, within seconds, Shea is splayed on the counter, his face pressed to the gray Formica as they cuff his hands behind him.

35

"Agent Patterson?"

"Yeah?"

"This is Detective Thad Harris out of Nevada. I understand you're in charge of crimes against S.O.s."

"That's right."

"Then I thought I should pass this along. A con by the name of Kevin Shea was collared yesterday for kidnapping and murdering two boys."

"I only handle crimes against sex offenders."

"I know. Thing is, we wouldn't have caught him except for an anonymous tip we got about the bodies."

"Okay?"

"The warrant got bogged down at the courthouse, and by the time we got to the scene, Shea had figured out someone was on to him and had bolted. We caught up with him but only because the anonymous tipster followed him and called to tell us where he was."

Steve's quiet. A stalker. It's rare, but it happens. Citizens who feel it's their responsibility to keep an eye on ex-felons. "Send me the report."

"Will do."

Steve hangs up and blows out a breath. Is it his imagination or are the number of bad guys and the evil they're capable of growing exponentially?

His phone buzzes, letting him know he's been messaged. He smiles and taps to retrieve his prize. An image of pink painted toes appears, below it, the message:

I changed the color, do u like?

His fat thumbs struggle with the keys as he taps his reply:

Love it. Wish I could see it in person.

Her timing is amazing. She's amazing.

An email pops up in his inbox—the report from the Nevada detective—a single page outlining the two calls the detective received along with the address and phone number of the storage unit where the two boys were found.

Steve doesn't expect much as he dials.

"U-Store and a whole lot more," a bored voice recites on the other end of the line.

Steve explains who he is, and the clerk becomes more animated. "It was like totally crazy. There were all these police and reporters . . ." She chatters on, and Steve lets her, knowing this is possibly the most exciting thing that's ever happened to her.

When she finishes, he asks, "Did you know Kevin Shea?"

"I don't really get to know the people who rent here. I see them come and go, but there ain't no reason to talk to them."

"But you saw Mr. Shea coming and going?"

"Every day. He'd come about the same time, usually around five."

"And how long would he stay?"

"Don't know. I'm off at six, and he was usually still here."

"Did you notice anyone else hanging around about that time?"

"Nope. This place is pretty quiet. Most people just store their junk, and it sits here."

"So yesterday, you didn't notice anything before the police arrived?"

"Not really. I rented a unit, but that's about it."

The slightest buzz of nerves. It could be nothing, but small nothings often turn into somethings. "You rented a unit? Do you have the renter's name?"

"Hold on." Barry Manilow's "Copacabana" fills the earpiece.

She returns. "Abraham Stoker from New Hampshire." She rattles off a driver's license number and address.

When Steve hangs up, he leans back in his chair and looks at the note. *Abraham Stoker.* Something about the name is familiar. He punches it into the FBI database. Nothing. He retypes it in Google—61,700 hits. Bram Stoker wrote the book *Dracula.* He also wrote the book *Famous Impostors.*

Cute joke. Steve doesn't laugh.

A concerned citizen tracks a bad guy to the scene of a crime, reports it, follows him when the cops' response is too slow, then calls the cops again, and the perp gets busted.

Pursuing this would take effort and resources Steve doesn't have. And even if they caught the guy, no jury is going to convict him. He would be hailed a hero, possibly even be thrown a parade. Steve archives the email and moves on to his newest, most pressing case.

The Riley family moved to Concord, Ohio, three months ago. Mr. Riley is the night manager at a twenty-four-hour drugstore. Mrs. Riley is a homemaker. Their two boys are six and nine. Mr. Riley is also a convicted rapist. Two days ago, in the middle of the afternoon, the Rileys' house burned down. No one but Mr. Riley was home at the time. He was asleep, but the smoke alarm woke him, and he got out. Their cat died.

The local police declared the fire an accident, but Mr. Riley and the Rileys' pastor believe it was arson. The pastor called the State Department, and that led him to Steve.

According to the pastor, from the moment the Rileys moved to town, they have been harassed. A rock was thrown through a window. Mr. Riley's car was tagged with spray paint. The family received several threatening letters warning them to leave. The Rileys had already moved several times and were determined to make this new home work. The church had become a haven, and Mr. Riley's new job was good. So they ignored the threats.

Steve pulls up Mr. Riley's criminal record. When he was twenty-two, he pled guilty to first-degree rape. The victim was a nineteen-year-old college student. He served ten years of a fifteen-year sentence and was released twelve years ago. No priors, and nothing since.

Steve dials Mr. Riley's number. "Mr. Riley?"

"Who wants to know?"

"My name is Steve Patterson. I'm an agent with the FBI."

"I'm on the straight."

"Relax. I'm not calling to hassle you. I'm calling because I understand a crime may have been committed against you and your family."

"If you consider trying to burn a man alive a crime."

"You're sure it wasn't an accident?"

"I smelled the gas, and my wife don't let me smoke in the house. Wasn't no accident. They tried to light me up, and now we've lost everything."

"I'm sorry."

Grunt.

Steve's never been good at condolences, too little able be fixed with words.

He's considering what to say next when Mr. Riley continues, "You know what a fire's like? It's like a giant eraser. Takes everything you have, everything you worked for, all your memories, and erases them like they ain't never existed."

"Were you insured?"

"Not for fire due to negligence, which is what they're calling it. Damn pigs, probably the ones who threw the match."

"The police?"

"Even if they weren't the ones who did it, don't mean they ain't responsible. I told them about those boys, but they didn't care. Told me maybe it was best if we moved on."

"You're talking about the Olsen brothers?" Steve says, referring to the file.

"That's right."

"Mr. Riley, I'm going to look into this."

"Won't help. They'll just tell you what they told me, that I oughta have been more careful. Damn fire captain didn't even go inside. Declared the fire an accident from the sidewalk."

"The pastor said you're staying with him for the time being?"

"Just until Sunday. He's got six of his own. The church will be taking up a collection at the service, then we'll be moving on."

"Well, if this turns out to be arson, you'll have an insurance claim."

Silence for a beat before Mr. Riley says, "What happened wasn't right. I know what I did was wrong, and every day I need to live with that. But in this life, I did my time. That ain't to say I'm forgiven and that I don't still deserve a penance. But my wife and kids, they didn't do nothing. Not sure why, but God gave me a second chance. He gave me my family, and they're good and decent. I messed up, worse than I'll ever be able to make up for, but for twelve years, I've been doing right, and that should count for something."

Steve finds himself nodding. It's exactly right. Doing right needs to count for something. Otherwise, what's the point of even trying? One foot in front of the other, Danny would say each time Steve asked how he was holding up. "I'm not moving real fast, but I'm still standing and managing to put one foot in front of the other, and I suppose eventually it's going to take me somewhere."

"I'll be in touch," Steve says.

The line disconnects, and Steve sets the phone down at the exact moment it buzzes. He picks it up again and looks at the screen.

> How about next weekend? They
> really are much prettier in person.

His insides do somersaults.

Not sure why, but God gave me a second chance, Mr. Riley's words replay in his head.

He books a flight to California with a day layover in Dayton, Ohio, an hour from the Rileys' burned down home.

36

Dick wakes to his phone ringing. He glances at the clock on the bedside table: 10:03.

The room is bright. He forgot to draw the curtains. Out his hotel room window, blue sky blazes.

"Hi, Joanne," he says, trying not to sound like he just woke up.

"How's it going?" she asks.

"Good," he lies, his head pounding like he has a hangover though he hasn't even had a beer in days.

"Good?" she says. "That's it?" She sounds irritated.

He grabs the water bottle on the table beside him and guzzles down the last few sips.

"Did you find a binding agent that might work?"

"Maybe. Not really sure. The seminar on chemo agents is this afternoon. I'll know more after that." He thinks the seminar is this afternoon. He's completely lost track of things.

"Will you call me when it's over and let me know?"

"I can just talk to you when I get back," Dick says, only realizing how ungrateful it sounds after he says it. "I'm leaving for the airport after the seminar," he adds.

"Then I'll meet you for a drink when you land," she says.

"That won't be until nine."

"Richard, is something wrong?"

Yes. "No. Sorry. I'm just preoccupied. There's been a lot to take in."

"And I want to hear all about it. Call me when you land."

37

It's a little past nine when Dick walks from the plane into Orange County Airport. He hesitates, then dials. "I'm back," he says, trying to sound bright.

Joanne's voice is sleepy like he might have woken her. "How was your flight?"

He imagines her on a sofa curled up with a blanket.

"Good. I'll tell you the details in the morning. It's late. I just called because you asked me to."

"I'm glad you did. Are you tired?"

"Actually, no. I slept on the plane."

"Perfect. You're awake, and I'm bored. Let's meet for a drink, and you can fill me in on the conference until we're ready for bed."

He doesn't answer, his mind stuck on the innuendo and whether there was one.

"Are you still there?" she asks.

"Uh, yeah. Sure. Sounds good."

He hangs up and stares at the glowing panel of his phone. *Was she flirting?* No. She's just excited about Freeway.

He glances at his reflection in the glass of the terminal as he walks, and the distorted image confirms it. At best he's average, not offensive but a good measure short of good-looking. And Joanne's a looker. He sighs in disappointed relief.

———

Joanne sits at a small table in the corner, the bar empty except for the two of them and the bartender polishing glasses. Joanne wears a lavender tank that leaves her arms bare and reveals a bit of lace from her blush bra beneath.

"I ordered you a scotch," she says. "That's what you drink, right?"

Dick feels like a beer. "Perfect."

"So tell me everything," she says excitedly.

For an hour, Dick fills her in on the conference and the promising prospects for Freeway, exaggerating how much he learned during the limited time he actually spent at the conference.

Two scotches later, the topic exhausted, he says, "So, have I sufficiently bored you so you can sleep?"

"Not yet. You'll have to try harder." She smirks and looks at him through mascara-coated lashes with an expression that definitely does not seem all business.

"Let's get out of here," he says, shocking himself and her, her eyes pulsing wide and causing him to backtrack. "Sorry. I shouldn't have said that. I don't know why I did."

She sets her hand on his, stopping him. "Walk me to my car."

Dick throws too much money on the table and, eyes avoiding hers, leads her from the bar. When they're in front of her Lexus, she places her hand on his right cheek and pecks him on the left. "Richard, thank you for meeting me tonight. I had a wonderful time."

He wants to reach out for more, but she's already turned away.

38

Concord, Ohio, is a quintessential middle-American town—more churches than restaurants, more pickups than cars. Steve drives through the dinky town of Concord into endless fields of sprawling wheat and corn spotted with large barns and small houses set back from the road. Ten minutes later, he turns the agent car he borrowed from the field office in Daytona onto a rutted dirt driveway that leads to a house sagging with neglect and age.

"Are you Rudy or Tommy Olsen?" Steve asks the boy-man standing in the doorway—160 pounds of farm stock with sinewy muscles tan from the biceps down that hang from well-worn overalls. Overgrown sandy hair surrounds a simple face.

"I'm Tommy."

"Is your brother here?"

"Out back."

He follows Tommy around the house, the side yard filled with rusted cans, overgrown weeds, and the smell of a broken sewer. Behind the house, standing beside a tractor is Tommy's twin, except Rudy is a couple inches taller, thirty pounds heavier, and his face is not as simple or kind.

Rudy extends his hand, his grip a vise and the skin thickly callused.

"I'm here to talk to you boys about the Riley fire," Steve says, and the quick glance between them—shame in Tommy's and warning in Rudy's—tells Steve all he needs to know about their guilt. Yesterday, the state fire marshal visited the site and confirmed the fire was arson. The house had been doused in kerosene and lit. The Rileys have a claim, and these boys are likely responsible.

Before Steve can continue, the back screen door opens, and a young woman shuffles forward carrying a tray of tea. Her straw hair hangs in her face, and her eyes never leave the ground. Without a word, she thrusts the offering toward Steve.

He takes a glass and so do each of the boys.

"Thank you," he says, and she recoils like a frightened bird before shuffling away.

"That's Elaine," says Rudy.

"She's our sister," adds Tommy.

And suddenly, life makes sense. Rape victims each deal with the crime differently, but in general, the methods of coping fall into three general categories. Victims get angry and rise up hell-bent on being a survivor and proving it. Or they figure out a way to work through it internally, making some sort of peace with what happened and moving on. Or the most traumatized curl into themselves and become terrified of the world.

Elaine Olsen is the latter.

Steve sets his glass on the tractor's hood and returns his focus to the boys. "You need to confess," he says.

"To what?" Rudy says, pulling his shoulders back.

"To burning down a man's home with him in it and killing his cat."

Rudy's jaw tightens, and his eyes tick side to side, figuring out his response.

"Fortunately, nobody was hurt," Steve goes on.

"Maybe we should get a lawyer?" Tommy looks from his brother to Steve then back again.

"Tommy, shut up," Rudy says.

Tommy shoves his hands in the pockets of his overalls and toes the ground with his boot.

"Are your parents around?" Steve asks, taking in the dilapidated barn and rusted tractor. The brothers are in their twenties, but they're still boys and they are in way over their heads.

Tommy shakes his head as Rudy spits, "What's that got to do with it?"

"I'm just trying to figure out if you boys are on your own?"

Rudy swallows, his bluster faltering before returning full force. "Get the hell off our property!"

"Not without you and your brother," Steve says calmly.

"You're arresting us?" Tommy gulps.

"Actually, you're turning yourselves in," Steve says.

"To hell we are!" Rudy says.

"I'm trying to help you. Turn yourselves in, and I'll talk to the DA about a deal. Make me arrest you and drag a team out here to investigate, and you're on your own."

Tommy's shoulders have crept up his neck. Meanwhile, Rudy's shoulders have dropped with the weight of his clenched fists, and his jaw is thrust forward aggressively.

"The easy way or the hard way," Steve says. "Either way, you're coming with me."

Rudy is still beside the tractor, and Steve is certain he is considering the wrench lying inches from his hand. The screen door slams open again, and Steve turns to see Elaine looking at them from the porch.

Rudy seizes the opportunity and snatches up the wrench. He swings it wildly at Steve as he charges, and Steve sidesteps, whirls, then shoulder tackles him from behind, sending both of them crashing to the ground. Getting his arms in position, he thrusts his legs beneath him and lifts Rudy with him as he stands. Rudy cries out as the full nelson wrenches his arms and neck.

Tommy bobs and weaves, trying to join the fight, but the boy's no fighter and is entirely uncertain how to hit Steve without hitting his brother.

"Stop squirming," Steve says, struggling to hold Rudy as the boy inflicts immense pain on himself.

On the porch, Elaine hasn't moved, her eyes following as Steve sidesteps with Rudy toward the side of the house. He swears at himself for not bringing zip cuffs and for not ramming Rudy with his left shoulder instead of his right, the damaged joint screaming in pain.

"Tommy, you coming?" Steve wheezes. "Or do I have to come back and tussle with you as well?"

Tommy has given up trying to attack and stares stupefied as Steve drag-carries his brother along. Steve applies pressure to the back of Rudy's neck, and Rudy yelps. "Tell Tommy to come along," Steve hisses. "This will go better for both of you if you voluntarily turn yourselves in."

"This is voluntary?" Rudy grunts.

"If you both get in the car and don't give me any more trouble, that's what we'll call it."

"Screw you."

Steve bears down again, causing another yelp. "Listen, Rudy, if you want to spend the next ten years rotting in prison, that's fine, but just remember, you're bringing Tommy with you. I'm throwing you a lifeline. Turn it down, and both of you are going to pay the price."

Rudy's struggle lessens, and he looks up from his hung head toward Tommy. "Tommy had nothing to do with it."

"If that's how you want to spin it, that's fine, but you both still need to get in the car."

"Tommy walks," Rudy negotiates.

"It's not up to me."

Rudy's eyes slide to Elaine. "He has to walk. One of us has to."

"Get in the car, tell Tommy to do the same, and I'll turn the radio up loud."

"How the hell's that going to help?"

"It's a long drive, and my hearing isn't what it used to be. You can get your stories straight."

Rudy's head bends forward, relieving some of the tension, and Steve knows this is the moment of truth, the instant he will either acquiesce or explode. Steve braces for it, then breathes when his sandy head nods.

Tommy sighs in relief and almost trots toward them.

True to his word, Steve turns the radio up and tries not to listen to the brothers' conversation as he drives. But when they pass the Riley ruins, Tommy leans forward and says, "We didn't know he was home," remorse clear in his voice.

"Tommy, shut up!" Rudy snaps.

"But it's true, Rudy. We thought he was gone."

"Geez, Tommy, I told you, you wasn't there. Okay? You don't know anything about what happened."

"He's not the judge," Tommy says.

"No, but he's a cop."

"I'm just saying, we wouldn't have done it if we'd have known he was there."

Steve can't help but like the younger boy.

Rudy mutters, "The bastard wouldn't leave."

"He has to live somewhere," Steve says.

"Not in our town."

"He did his time."

"There ain't enough time to be done for a man who did what he did, going and destroying something just so he can get off."

Steve nods along with the first part. He agrees rape's about the lowest crime there is, but Rudy's wrong about the motive. "It's not about sex."

"Bull. Guy can't get a decent woman, so he takes what he can't have."

"It's about anger and control," Steve says.

He's been at this a long time, and he knows this isn't just a theory in psychological textbooks. Rape is raw and cruel, and there's nothing loving or mate-driven about it.

"That don't make sense," Tommy says. "Why would you want to have sex with a girl you're angry with?"

Steve almost smiles, then thinks of Mr. Riley and the awful thing he did when he was twenty-two and the joy turns sour. The girl he raped had humiliated him earlier that day by mocking him when he asked her out. He took a nasty trip on LSD, tracked her down, and did the unthinkable. His testimony made it clear he was out of his mind at the time, so much so he couldn't recall most of what happened.

Steve pulls up to the Lake County Sheriff's Office. He opens the back door, and Tommy pops out. Before Rudy can do the same, Steve slides into the back seat beside him.

"Tell the truth," he says. "It will go better for you."

"Tommy had nothing to do with it," Rudy says, shaking his head obstinately.

"Rudy, Tommy's not going to weather this well. They'll break him, or he'll break himself. I'll put in a good word but don't try and lie your way out of this. You already have one damaged sibling; you don't need another."

The boy's eyes well, belying his bluster. "But Elaine—"

"Elaine needs help, more help than you or Tommy can give her. I'll talk to social services—"

His face hardens. "We take care of our own."

"Rudy—"

"You said you wouldn't tell what you heard. Is your word good?"

"Rudy—"

"Is your word good?"

Steve nods.

"Then let me out."

With a sigh, Steve steps from the car then leads the boys into the station. Tommy isn't much older than Danny was when he was locked up, and he won't fare any better. Elaine was raped. The Rileys' house was burned. Tommy and Rudy Olsen will go to prison. All of it a waste.

On his way to the airport, Steve calls social services and requests they make a house call to Elaine Olsen. He also calls Internal Affairs. The Concord police captain and fire captain have some explaining to do.

39

Dee smooths the satin of her dress and runs her hands over her waist, her stomach still flat. Serving has kept her fit. As she rubs lotion on her legs, she thinks about a country song she heard a few days ago, something about doing it better in the next thirty years. She can't recall the rest of the lyrics, but the chorus has stuck with her.

Dick didn't need to buy the dress for her, but she's glad he did. And his smile as he paid for it said he got more pleasure from that than anything else she did for him that day.

She puts her head upside down and shakes out her hair, her insides lit up. She hasn't felt this way . . . hasn't allowed herself to feel this way . . . since she was seventeen. But now, Otis is gone, and with his death, the dark cloud that has shrouded her life has lifted. And not only has the sun appeared, but like an unexpected rainbow after a storm, so has Steve Patterson.

After Joe died, she never thought she could love anyone like that again. She was certain of it. Since they were children, Joe had been her destiny and she his. How could that ever be replaced? Yet, the night Steve showed up to ask about Otis's death, she got the shock of her life—strong, steady, good. It was like pulling on a pair of worn leather shoes that fit just right, familiar and certain, as if made specially for her—valiant like Joe, gentle like her father, a survivor like her.

She thought it was only for a night—comfort in a storm. But then it wasn't. He came back, and they spent another night in each other's arms, and another morning talking and laughing.

Jesse likes him, and Steve is good with him. The second time Steve was here, they played catch with a football in the street, and after, manned the grill to make burgers for lunch. Watching them, she realized how hungry Jesse was for a man in his life. He has his uncle, but Dick's rarely around, and Steve and Dick are so different. Already Steve and Jesse joke and rib each other the way guys do. They even tussled once over the television clicker, Steve playing keep away as Jesse leaped around, over, and on top of him, both of them laughing, which made her insanely happy.

When Steve left to go back to D.C., she told herself it wasn't real. He was a mirage concocted by her euphoric, overwrought brain because Otis was gone, an amalgam of those she already loved melded into a phantasmic hologram that would disappear when he was gone. But when he got home, he called, and she knew he was no illusion, Steve as real as the fear she felt at the thought of loving him. The last time she felt this way ended so tragically it nearly destroyed her.

She takes a sip of wine to calm the butterflies flittering inside her. It's been two weeks since they last saw each other, and though they've talked almost every night, she wonders if it will be as magical.

A car pulls into the driveway, and she hurries from the house.

The car is too small for him, or he's too big for the car. Awkwardly he unfolds himself to get out, and her nerves are erased, the sight of him causing her heart to skitter around wildly and her grin to spread so wide her dimples hurt.

In his arms is a bouquet of red roses. Then he lifts his head, and there they are—his eyes, his soul, chocolate brown, sincere, and honest. And when she feels the light pressure on her spine, she knows Joe is watching, encouraging her forward with a smile not entirely different from Steve's.

"No," he says, holding up his hand.

Her heart stops.

"Please," he says, his voice a rasp. "I just want to look at you."

It beats again, and she smiles impossibly wider.

His gaze starts at her shoulders, travels down her body, then stops on her pink toes. She watches as a grin spreads across his face, then his head comes up and his gaze settles on hers. "Hi," he says.

"Hi." And she runs into his arms.

40

Dick parks behind the Enterprise Rent-A-Car that occupies his usual spot. The guy Dee's seeing is visiting. She has not stopped buzzing since the relationship started, and he knows he should be happy about it since it was what he professed he wanted, but his true feeling is distinctly the opposite, like an interloper has encroached on his turf. Since Jesse was a baby, Dick has been the only man in their lives, and it's turned out he relished the role more than he knew.

The door opens, and Dee steps out and hugs him. He scans over her head for the intruder, who it turns out is easy to spot. Walking from the kitchen is a large dark-haired man in khakis, a navy blue golf shirt, and a red-flowered apron that reads, "World's Greatest Mom."

Dee glances back at him, then looks again at Dick, and the giant smile that spreads across her face almost convinces Dick to like the man.

"Dickie, this is Steve."

Steve extends his hand, and Dick gives an extra-firm handshake.

"Dick, it's nice to finally meet you. Dee and Jesse have told me a lot about you."

Dick offers what he hopes is a smile. "Yeah, well, I know almost nothing about you."

Dee shoots him a be-nice look, and he realizes his smile must not be convincing.

"I was just getting the barbeque going," Steve says. "Why don't you join me, and you can ask anything you like?"

Despite his effort to be a tough sell, Dick finds himself liking the guy as he follows him out back. He's got an ex-military, good-guy vibe—low-key and unassuming, yet also like he could whip off the apron, turn it into a cape, and take down an assassin.

Steve sets to work lighting the grill while Dick pops open a beer. The desert heat is just short of bearable, and Dick bristles when he realizes the misters that have been broken for months and that he's been meaning to fix are on and that Steve must have been the one to fix them.

"Where's Jesse?" Dick asks, feeling like he could use an ally.

"Camping with a friend."

Dee emerges with the burger patties, sets down the tray, then wraps her arms around Steve's waist as if it's the most natural thing in the world. Steve rests his hand on her shoulder. He towers over her, and it's impossible to look at them and not to think of Joe and how he and Dee used to stand just like that.

"Shoot away," Steve says. "What do you want to know?"

What are your intentions? Is that what Dick's supposed to say?

Dee saves him. "Steve, tell Dickie about the tickets." She looks up adoringly, and Steve pecks her on the lips, and Dick's blood turns hot despite the damn misters.

"I understand you're a baseball fan," Steve says as he untangles himself from Dee's hold to put the burgers on the grill. "A friend of mine, a guy I served with a lifetime ago, went on to become an announcer. Guy's name is Mike Mitchell—"

"The Angel's announcer Mike Mitchell?" Dick says.

"Yeah, that's him. Anyway, I called him and told him I had a girl I was trying to impress"—he winks at Dee—"who has an eleven-year-old son, and he hooked me up with four tickets and said we could sit with him in the announcer's box for a bit while he calls the game."

Despite himself, Dick's insides buzz. Mike Mitchell's the real deal, a true authority on the game who really knows the players and loves statistics.

"Your sister's not much of a fan," Steve goes on, "so she suggested we make a guys' day of it—you, your son, me, and Jesse."

Dick isn't sure if Steve's trying to show off, but it's working. Jim's going to be blown away.

"The game is the Saturday after next. They're playing the Mariners, so it should be a good game."

For the next hour, over burgers and beers, he and Steve talk sports, the wonderful bonding agent of most male relationships. Dick's more knowledgeable about the history and statistics, while Steve's more passionate about the players and teams.

"So, Dick, I understand you're a chemist?" Steve says when the conversation's been exhausted.

"I develop anti-allergens," Dick says with a shrug, knowing his job is boring to most people.

"Tell him about Freeway," Dee says. "Dickie's working on a new drug that's amazing."

Dick blushes at his sister's pride. It's been a long time since he's felt that.

"*If* it works, it will be amazing," Dick says. "The good news is, as of this week, it's looking more promising."

"You figured something out from the conference?" Dee asks.

"Maybe."

Dee turns to Steve. "His boss, who is awesome, sent Dickie to a conference in Las Vegas a week ago to help find a binder for the drug he developed, which is the only thing he needs to figure out to make it work."

That's not exactly true. There's still a lot of science to figure out and testing to do, but he doesn't correct her.

"Did you place my lucky bet?" Dee asks.

"Twenty on red after three blacks have hit on the wheel," Dick says.

Dee's hands are in front of her prayer fashion. "Did I win?"

Dick reaches into his wallet, fishes out two twenties, and lays them on the white plastic table.

"I won! I always win!" She pulls the money toward her and kisses it then turns to Steve and pecks him on the lips, catching Steve off guard. "You okay, babe?" Dee asks.

Steve offers half a smile, then returns his attention to Dick. "When did you get back from Vegas?"

"When?"

Steve nods.

"Last Friday."

"So you were there during the week?"

Dick hesitates before answering, unsure if he's imagining it or if Steve's tone has changed.

"Yep. The conference was Wednesday through Friday," he says as he stands. "Excuse me. The beer seems to have gone right through me."

He hurries to the bathroom, his pulse beating out of rhythm. There is no connection between Shea and Otis, and what he did in Las Vegas wasn't even illegal. He knew about a crime and reported it. Anonymously. Harris had no idea who he was talking to. Yet that distinctly felt like Steve was questioning him.

He splashes water on his face, takes his time drying his

hands, then returns to the patio and, from the doorway, says, "Dee, I know it's early, but I need to get going."

"You just got here."

"I've got some things I want to get started on." He forces himself to look at Steve. "Steve, it was nice meeting you."

Steve stands and, his face a mask, shakes Dick's hand, squeezing a little too hard as Dick wills himself not to flinch.

41

Steve sits at his desk, the phone to his ear. The world below glints gold with the rising morning sun. It figures, the single time he turns his back on the law, it comes back to haunt him.

Dr. Richard Raynes, brother of the woman he loves, has anointed himself supreme righter of wrongs. He scoffs. Dick is either going to end up in prison or get himself killed.

A bus wheezes to a stop below, and he watches as people disembark then as others climb on board.

The on-hold music that's supposed to be soothing is giving him a headache. The sad truth is he likes Dick. He's exactly as Denise described—sweet, shy, awkward, and trying hard to do right by her and Jesse.

The Enterprise Rent-A-Car administrator comes back on the line. "Four hundred and seventeen miles," she says, and Steve sighs out heavily and thanks her.

Dick drove over four hundred miles during his three days in Las Vegas when he was supposed to be at a conference.

He takes the elevator to the basement and waits for a clerk to retrieve the Parsons file. He removes the DNA analysis on the sweat from the sliding door and delivers it along with a longneck beer bottle he took from Denise's. The chain of evidence won't hold up in court, but the Parsons case isn't going to court. This is for personal confirmation.

Steve scans the Las Vegas papers from the time Dick was there for other crimes that could possibly be attributed to him and is relieved not to find any. Next, he looks at the papers for Irvine, California, where Dick lives. There's a horrible story about a little boy who was molested then cut up and discarded in a suitcase at a dump, and another about a twelve-year-old girl who was raped inside her home, but there are no crimes against past felons that he can find.

He'd like to believe Dick is done, the Las Vegas incident an anomaly, and that he's gotten it out of his system. But Steve's gut tells him otherwise. Dick doesn't strike him as an impulsive person. As a matter of fact, he seems the opposite, a man measured and deliberate, which means he made the calculated choice to pursue Shea, and Steve doesn't imagine it was a one-time deal.

The question is why. Otis he understands. It was personal. But Dick had no connection to Shea.

Over the years, Steve has encountered his share of zealots, those who feel so strongly about a cause they're willing to risk everything for those beliefs. Dick doesn't seem that passionate. If anything, he comes off apathetic, a bit melancholy, and almost bored. He cares about his work and the project he's working on. He likes baseball and coaches his son's team. And that's about it. Vigilante crusader just doesn't fit.

――――

"Steve."

He swivels from the window to see his boss, Mitch Gelson, standing in front of his desk. Steve is seated, but they're still almost eye-to-eye. Five-feet-flat, the man attempts to make up for his lack of stature with shoe inserts, fastidious grooming, and an abrasive personality.

"Mitch."

Neither extends their hand. It isn't often Steve sees Gelson. While technically Gelson is Steve's boss—a formality Gelson relishes and Steve ignores—the man has nothing to do with what Steve does.

Gelson drops a sheet of paper on Steve's desk and, in a baritone voice that belies its weedy source, says, "Make this go away. And remember, we're the good guys."

"I'll take a look at it," Steve says, setting the paper aside without a glance.

"It needs to be looked at now," Gelson says, remaining in front of Steve's desk.

With a sigh, Steve slides the sheet in front of him, thinking he was right when he was in charge and rejected Gelson each time he came up for promotion.

"I want an update by the end of the day," Gelson says and, with a military heel turn, marches away.

Steve's about to set the paper back in his inbox when he sees the name at the top. The case was a while ago, but Steve remembers it. Diego Ramirez was convicted of raping a six-year-old, the rape so brutal the girl needed a hysterectomy. According to the report, Ramirez was released two weeks ago.

He dials the number listed, and a clipped voice picks up. "Captain Goh here."

"Hello, Captain. This is Agent Patterson with the FBI. I'm calling in regard to Diego Ramirez."

Silence.

"Captain?"

"I'm here."

"You've been named in a lawsuit filed by Mr. Ramirez against the Santa Ana Police Department for harassment."

The line buzzes empty between them.

"Captain Goh?"

"I don't know what you want me to say."

"Are you harassing him?"

"We're keeping an eye on him."

"It says here that you've been following him and that your officers have been hassling him."

"I don't know of any misconduct by my officers."

"Captain, Mr. Ramirez has rights. Without probable cause, he needs be allowed to go about his business and should be treated the same as any other citizen."

"He's not any other citizen," Goh hisses. "Ramirez is a child-raping bastard who's going to hurt more children if we don't do our job."

"Our job is to uphold the law."

"Our job is to protect society."

"We do that by following the law."

"Yeah, well in this case, the law is wrong."

Steve takes a steeling breath.

"I was the first officer to arrive at the scene of that little girl's rape," Goh says. "I thought she was dead there was so much blood, this little blond girl lying on this red-soaked floor."

The words heavy, Steve says, "I'm sorry."

"I'm not," Goh says. "Because now I'm in charge, and the bastard's back, and this time, I can do something about it."

"No," Steve says. "You can't."

"A lawsuit's not going to stop me."

"Maybe not. But I am."

"The feds?"

"It's my job."

"What's your job?"

"To make sure released offenders' rights are protected and that they have a chance to return to society." Though he's said the words a thousand times with conviction, they come out hollow.

"That's bull, and you know it. Ramirez is not going to return to society in any way that's good."

"That's not for us to decide. He did his time. He gets his chance."

"At what price? The price of another Ally? Another ten Allys?"

"I hope none."

"Well, your hope isn't good enough."

"Captain, you need to back off."

"Are we done?"

"You might not like it, but Diego Ramirez has rights, and you need to abide by them. If you don't, it will be you, not him, defending yourself in court."

"And what about the next little girl who ends up his victim?"

"You won't be doing her much good if you lose your job."

A beat of silence and Goh hangs up. Steve blows out a breath, his head pounding like there's a sledgehammer between his ears, moments like these impossible to reconcile with the reason he chose to do this.

42

It's the antiseptic quality of the photos that make them particularly gruesome. Alison Cleason's six-year-old blue eyes are un-maimed, while her unsmiling mouth is swollen and raw. Somebody had brushed her hair. It's wispy thin, light blond, and curls at her shoulders.

He sets the photos aside, reads the file in its entirety, then makes a call. While what he said to Goh was true, it doesn't mean Goh's concern isn't warranted. Steve has a bad hunch about why Ramirez went to the lengths he did to file a complaint about Goh harassing him, and it's not what Goh thinks. Ramirez's been in prison fifteen years, and over that amount of time, priorities can change.

Aside from Alison Cleason, there were believed to be three other victims. All refused to testify, too traumatized by the threats Ramirez made while they were in his captivity. Alison Cleason was the youngest and the only one brave enough to defy him, and it was her testimony that put him away.

Steve calls Alison Cleason and leaves a message.

He hangs up at the exact moment his phone buzzes, and he looks at the screen to see another text from Denise:

???

He needs to call her. She's left two voicemails, and this is her third text. The problem is as soon as he calls her, she's going to ask him what's going on, and he doesn't want to continue to lie. Her brother's gone rogue, and until Steve's certain he's not going to continue to go rogue, he feels like he's walking a tight-rope between his loyalties.

He decides to take the coward's way out:

> Sorry. Swamped. New case.
> I'll call tonight.

He almost hits send, then thinks better of it and adds:

> Can't stop dreaming of u.

He's about to set the phone down when it rings.

"Hello, Mr. Patterson," a young woman says, her voice smooth and confident. "This is Ally Cleason. I'm returning your call."

"Miss Cleason—"

"Please, call me Ally."

"Okay. Ally. I'm calling regarding Diego Ramirez—"

"Because he's been released."

"Yes."

"And you're concerned for my safety."

"Yes," Steve says, her plain-spokenness surprising. "Miss Cleason . . . I mean, Ally, I've been at this a long time, and in my experience, men like Diego Ramirez tend to harbor grudges that, in prison, can often fester and grow."

"Are you trying to scare me?"

"I'm trying to tell you that I think, now that he's out, you need to be careful. I believe he is dangerous, specifically to you."

"Mr. Patterson," Ally says, "as long as you say you've been at this, I've likely been thinking about Diego Ramirez longer. Since I was six. For fifteen years, I've watched, tracked, and worried about him and the day he would be released."

Steve takes a long, slow breath and closes his eyes, imagining the little girl in the photos grown up into this self-possessed, confident young woman. She has what his mom calls moxie. In the army, you learned to recognize it, the soldiers with true mettle in their bones.

"And do you want to know the conclusion I've come to?" she says.

He waits, eyes still closed.

"I've decided he's taken enough from me. And that, regardless of where he is or what he is doing, I am not going to live my life based on that."

Steve's jaw clenches with her words. The problem with the best soldiers is they're usually the ones who end up in early graves.

"I understand, but I think, at least a while, you should consider taking extra precautions."

"What do you suggest? A dog? A bodyguard?"

Her sarcasm is warranted. Steve's read Ramirez's file. He is a brilliant, cunning psychopath—vindictive and ruthless. A dog, a bodyguard—neither would make a difference.

"Maybe just think about laying low."

"Hide?" she says. "Live my life in fear, waiting for him to find me?"

"Ally, the threat is real—"

"For how long? A month, a year, the rest of my life? You think I should give this man, who has already taken so much—my innocence, my ability to have children—you think I should now also give him my present and my future?"

Steve closes his eyes, his pulse pounding.

"Mr. Patterson, while I appreciate your concern, I've considered this moment for a long time, and I'm not going to run, and I'm not going to hide. I'm no longer a six-year-old little girl who got separated from her mother, and if Diego Ramirez comes after me, he'll have more to contend with than he did back then."

While Steve applauds her bravado, he's seen too much and knows how often monsters like Ramirez win.

43

Dick is concerned as well as impressed that somehow the cogs of justice came together to allow Steve to make the connection between Otis's death in California and Shea's arrest in Utah. He sits at his desk, staring at the bouncing balls, his eyes seeing nothing as his mind mulls over his visit to Independence and his introduction to Agent Steve Patterson.

A million morons get away with ill-conceived, poorly executed crimes every day, and yet Dick somehow managed to implicate himself in both offenses. Dick's not sure what bothers him more, that he was outsmarted or that Steve knows the truth. While he feels justified in what he's done, there's a distinct sense of shame along with a low burning compulsion to defend it.

Explaining Otis is easy. He was protecting Dee and Jesse. But what about Shea? How do you explain stalking a total stranger and then following him to Utah?

In retrospect, Dick realizes how reckless and stupid that was and how easily things could have gone sideways. Yet, even with sober hindsight, each time he thinks of those boys in that freezer, the alternative is unthinkable—Shea still out in the world with the next Willy or Germaine at his mercy.

Fortunately, at the moment, he doesn't need to worry about it. Thanks to what he learned at the conference, he now has the green light to move full steam ahead on Freeway, and between that and the Little League playoffs, for the first time in a long time, his life is so full he doesn't have time for anything else.

"Big game tomorrow?"

He looks up to see Graham. "Yep. If we win, we stay in it."

The playoffs are double elimination, and so far, his Cubs have won one and lost one. If they make it through this next game, they secure third place and move on to the finals. Jim called three times today to discuss the lineup.

Graham attempts a smile, but his lips don't quite curl.

"Something up?" Dick asks.

Graham shakes his head but says, "What if I don't figure it out?"

Dick's first instinct is to appease him with, *What are you talking about? Of course you'll figure it out.* How many people said similar things to him right before his own professional life imploded?

Instead, he levels his eyes on his friend's and tells him the truth. "It will be bad. Worse than you imagine. You'll get depressed. Your life will fall apart. You'll struggle like hell to make peace with it and tell yourself you're over it and that you don't care and want nothing more to do with it. But no matter how many times you tell yourself that or how much time passes, it will continue to eat at you, churning in your brain and gnawing at your insides, until finally you go back to it, knowing the second time will be the end, and there will be no recovering if you fail again."

A thin smile crosses Graham's face. "That's what I thought. Good luck tonight."

44

They are driving home from the Angels game, Dick smiling from the passenger seat of Steve's rental car as Jim retells the story of the Cubs' season-ending loss. Though they didn't come out on top, Jim hit a double and snagged a fly ball, so it was an amazing final game.

True to his word, Steve got VIP treatment at the ballpark, and they spent over half the game in the announcer's booth with Mike Mitchell. Jim even got to say, "Play ball!"

It was an amazing experience, and Jim and Jesse really connected. Since the divorce, the cousins haven't gotten together, and even before that, Caroline despised going to Independence and Dee wasn't a fan of Caroline, so the kids rarely saw each other. Jesse and Jim are only a year apart, and neither has a brother, and Dick wonders if maybe this could be the start of something deeper between them. After the third inning, Jim asked if Jesse could spend the night at the house for a sleepover, and Dick agreed.

They get to Caroline's, and the boys climb out.

"Later," Jim says.

"Peace out," Jesse says with a peace symbol.

Steve huff-laughs, and Dick smiles.

The car door closes, and Steve says, "How about a drink?"

The last thing Dick wants is to have a drink with FBI Agent Steve Patterson. The entire night, despite appearances, tension pulsed between them. The day after they met at Dee's, Steve sent a text confirming that the strange vibe Dick felt wasn't imagined.

> I believe we have a mutual
> acquaintance, Detective Harris.

Dick chose not to respond, and yesterday Steve followed up with another message:

> I will see you tomorrow at five
> and would like to confirm you are
> no longer pinch hitting in the big
> leagues. Two hits and no errors you
> should stop while you're ahead.

Dick thought long and hard about how to answer and finally texted back:

> I am looking forward to the
> game. See you tomorrow.

"There was this place somewhere around here where Mike took me once. It has a kazillion beers on tap," Steve says.

"Henry-N-Harry's," Dick says, the bar legendary.

"Yeah. That's the place."

Dick directs him to the old saloon, and they take two stools at the mostly empty bar. A sign above the mirror says, "141 beers on tap," and Dick studies it for a moment, wondering what made them stop at 141. Why not go for 150? Or stop at a clean 100?

"What's your poison?" Steve asks.

With 141 selections to choose from, it seems like a loaded question. Normally, he orders Miller. Lately, he's been drinking Miller Lite. He sees one called "Hoppy Ending" and, hoping it's an omen, chooses it. Steve smiles, then orders an Arrogant Bastard, and Dick smirks back.

"So, Dick," Steve says after their beers are delivered. "I have a problem."

Dick knows what Steve's problem is but doesn't help him out. Turning his beer in his hands, he says nothing.

"The problem I have is I know about Otis, and I know about Shea."

"I don't know what you're talking about," Dick says.

Steve's eyes lock on Dick's. "Let's not do that, okay? Just say nothing, and I'll fill in the rote lies for myself. I'm not looking for a confession. I'm just going to tell you the situation in the hopes that you and I can come to an understanding."

Dick takes a sip of his beer, Hoppy Ending surprisingly smooth.

"The thing is, I'm in love with your sister, and your sister loves you."

Dick startles. While he knew Steve and Dee were seeing each other, he had no idea it was already that serious.

"Otis I get. You were protecting your sister and Jesse. But what I'm worried about is that you're now on some sort of crusade."

Crusade? The word sounds warriorlike and not at all like what this is, which is more like a concerned bystander noticing an accident about to happen and doing what he can to stop it.

"All I want," Steve goes on, "is your assurance that this is where it ends, and that from here on out, you'll go back to doing your job and leaving the cops to do theirs."

"Unfortunately they can't," Dick blurts, the words out of his mouth before he can stop them.

Steve lifts a brow.

Dick's given so much thought to this it's like there's a pressure cooker inside his head.

"The law, as it stands," he says, "makes it so the cops can't do anything about men like Otis or Shea." His heart tightens as it does each time he thinks about Willy and Germaine. "Our system is founded on the principle of presumed innocence, and it allows forgiveness for past mistakes. It's what makes America great but also what leaves it vulnerable. The police can't track down a threat and eliminate it. They can only react to a crime after it's been committed."

It's very small, but Dick watches as Steve's left eye twitches, the smallest tell that he might not entirely disagree.

But when he responds, it's to say, "And you think rogue justice is the answer? No trial. Guilty by presumption?"

"More like suspicion by assumption," Dick says. "A rational monitoring of an abhorrent segment of society that's already proven to be a danger."

"Abhorrent?" Steve says, his voice pitching high and losing some of its cool. "You do realize not every sex offender is *abhorrent*? Some are good people who just made a mistake or did something stupid. And some are extremely remorseful?"

"Agreed. Which is why you don't presume them guilty as you said. But you also don't ignore the statistics and the known pathologies or fail to recognize that there are men who are predators, raptors without conscience who, once released, will inevitably prey again." He feels his own emotions rising and works to tamp them down. "And therefore, you watch them, and if they exhibit predatory behavior, you stop them."

"By killing them?"

"Shea was arrested."

Steve squints hard. "So your argument is that any average Tom, *Dick*, or Harry should be able to take it upon themselves to follow any released felon they think might commit a crime and deal with them as they see fit?"

"Not exactly," Dick says, then stops himself from going deeper into the analysis he created. "But since the law is powerless to stop high-probability threats from manifesting into heinous, violent crimes, then yes, it makes sense for there to be monitoring and possible action outside the law."

Steve shakes his head. "Could you imagine the anarchy that would lead to? It would be open hunting season on ex-felons."

"Only if the rogue justice, as you call it, was widespread and if its enforcement wasn't moral, judicial, and careful. Which, in the instances of Otis and Kevin Shea, it was. Otis was going to hurt Jesse. Kevin Shea had two dead boys in a freezer."

"And now, because of that, you've anointed yourself rebel enforcer of justice and moral righter of wrong? That's ludicrous!"

Dick looks hard at his beer as he tries to figure out a way to explain it.

"My whole life," he says, "as far back as I can remember, I've watched as bad things have happened around me, feeling like I had no control. Then, out of nowhere, Otis became my burden. No one else could do anything about it, so there was no choice but to do something myself. And yes, that changed things, made me realize I have more power than I believed."

He stops, frustrated with his inability to express himself more clearly.

Finally, he says, "Tell me, do you believe in God?"

Steve tilts his head. "I don't know. I don't think about it much, but I suppose I hope He exists."

Dick nods. "Before all this, I couldn't convince myself

of some higher, all-powerful force looking down on us and controlling the minutiae of the world, or that anything so magnificent would give a crap about me and my petty existence." He looks up at the massive chalkboard with the 141 different beers, then back at his nearly empty Hoppy Ending. "But now, I know I was wrong."

"So you're doing this because you've found God?"

Dick shakes his head. "The opposite. I realize now, I was right. God is not some supreme Buddha sitting on a heavenly perch passing judgment and hurling lightning bolts of mercy or penance at his flock. He's not that at all. He is the mundane and the ordinary, the everyday and the unremarkable. He is everything. But mostly, He is you and me and every other trapped soul walking this earth trying to do right. Some might call it morality. I call it the collective human spirit of good that stands up against that which is not, whether through kindness, good deeds, or noble actions that stretch beyond our individual selves. It is the all-powerful, irrepressible shared conscience within us that dictates that we be accountable for our actions and hold others accountable for theirs. Maybe what I'm doing is a crusade, as you called it, or maybe it's even a calling. Call it what you like, but now I believe."

45

This is not going well. Steve really thought he would confront Dick, tell him he knew about Parsons and Shea, and that would be the end of it. But that's not what is happening. Instead, Dick has been sitting beside him calmly sipping his beer as he defends his actions and affably argues that continuing his outrageous vigilante quest is the morally right thing to do.

"So, thanks to your newfound faith," Steve says, "you're not going to stop? And what, you think I should just turn a blind eye?"

"Isn't that what you've done so far?"

Steve winces. His whole career, he's never come close to crossing the line of his sworn duty, and now, it's being thrown back in his face by the very person he did it for.

"Look, Steve, I get that you have a job to do," Dick goes on. "And I appreciate that, but you know as well as I do that what you do is often at odds with what's right."

Steve hates that the words cause Ally to fill his mind. Diego Ramirez is only one city away, and he has not left his mind since his conversation with Captain Goh.

"And you think," he says, "that somehow, because of what happened with Otis, you're the person to determine that?"

"No," Dick says. "Actually, you are."

"Me?"

Dick nods. "It's just sort of worked out that way. Somehow . . . quite impressively, by the way . . . you figured out what happened with Otis and Kevin Shea, and you decided not to pursue it. I assume because you found what happened to be warranted."

"No! I didn't pursue it because of your sister!" Steve feels his blood pressure rising and hates that Dick is getting the better of him.

Dick infuriatingly shakes his head. "You said it yourself, you let it go because you understood what I did was necessary to protect Jesse and Dee."

"Because they're your family. We all do things we might not normally do for people we love."

Dick's eyes flash, revealing deeper, underlying fire. "Really?" he says. "And those boys in Las Vegas, they didn't deserve justice because they weren't my family?"

Steve didn't see the photos of the Las Vegas scene, but judging by Dick's response, he imagines it was bad.

"Tell me, Steve," Dick goes on, "how many little boys needed to end up in that freezer before you would have considered my intervention justified?"

"And tell me, Dick," Steve counters, "what would you have done if the cops didn't show up at that diner? Continued to follow him? Tried to stop him yourself?"

Dick looks away, and Steve watches as he swallows, the fear from those moments clear on his face, and Steve can't help but feel respect. True courage isn't never being afraid, it's charging into the flames despite it.

"I don't know," Dick says, head shaking.

Steve imagines Dick has never been in a fight in his life, and that, if he was in one, he'd most certainly lose.

"Dick, you're walking on a tightrope, and if you keep going, you're going to slip, and when you do, there won't be a net."

Dick nods as he stands. "Thanks for the beer. I'll take an Uber."

Steve watches him go, thinking how much he and Ally would get along, and in the next minute, thinking how they'll likely never meet because attitudes like theirs are going to get at least one of them, most likely both of them, killed.

It's close to midnight, but knowing he can't sleep, he drives to Diego Ramirez's home a half hour away. He parks at the curb across from a hipster work-live complex with art galleries on the lower level and sleek condos above. In a cruel twist of fate, Ramirez's fame as a psychopath combined with a gift for painting made him a world-renowned artist while he was in prison.

The sign on the gallery door reads, "By appointment only." Steve looks at the large vivid canvases through the glass—vibrant, bold splashes of light and color—and wonders how such a twisted mind could create such beauty. Despite his impassioned argument to Dick to the contrary, Steve knows there are those who are *abhorrent*. And while some may argue we are all born good and it's circumstances that turn people evil. Steve disagrees. Men like Memphs and Ramirez came into this world with something essential missing from their DNA, the humanity gene left out of the mix.

In the window above, a silhouette crosses behind the shades. *Ramirez.* He thinks of Ally. Then before he can stop it, another thought passes dark over his mind, belying every fervent point he made only an hour before, his hands tightening on the steering wheel as he imagines knocking on the door, and when Ramirez answers . . .

46

Group three is acting sluggish. All four mice have burrowed into the wood shavings, their bodies flittering with rapid heartbeats as the other groups scurry around. Dick takes out one of the rodents, extracts a small drop of blood, and examines it under his microscope. The problem is the same as before; the binding agent is not metabolizing and is therefore building up in the system. Dick documents the results, which are exactly what he expected from groups one and three.

The other two groups are exhibiting very positive results. The anti-allergen appears to be working with no notable side effects. Group four is especially encouraging. The mice are not only responding well to the treatment, but there's indication that the animals' immune systems might be contributing. If this is true, eventually the mice will be able to be weaned from the medicine, and the allergies will be held at bay by the host unaided.

He returns to his cubicle. Now that the study is up and running, there's not much to do but wait. He pulls up his baseball team's stats from the last game and tabulates the final batting averages. He smiles at Jim's on-base percentage.

He texts him:

.426 OBP! Great job.

Jim's response is almost instant:

Cool!

He looks at the starburst crack on the screen of his monitor, his focus narrowed on the epicenter. Despite the bluster he showed two days ago while talking to Steve, he's not eager to return to the pursuit, his nights haunted by what happened in Las Vegas.

He jiggles the mouse to wake his computer and, for a long time, looks at the small red chili in the upper right corner of his screen, which is the icon he created for "Pepper."

Blowing out a breath, he opens a program called Family Watchdog and types in the address for Pentco. He restricts the search to a twenty-five-mile radius and, in seconds, gets the results. Within twenty-five miles of where he is sitting, there are seventy-two registered sex offenders who committed crimes against children.

Seventy-two. How many of those will rank above the Mendoza Line? He really doesn't want to find out, knowledge a great burden he doesn't want to bear.

His phone pings, and he looks at it to see another message from Jim:

My OBP is the same as Trout's!

Seventy-two released felons who have hurt children live within minutes of his son . . . his daughter . . . the boys on his team.

He texts Jim:

Amazing!

Then he sets down his phone, copies the first name from the Family Watchdog list, and pastes it into the name search field in the prison database. He reads through the record for the contributing factors and moves on to the next name on the list.

When he leaves for the day, he's completed six of the seventy-two files. He saves his work to a thumb drive along with "Pepper," then scrubs the files and search history from his desktop. He has no idea if Steve is watching, but he's not going to take the chance.

47

It took ten days to get through the list, the files so repulsively fascinating Dick found himself lost in the reading. It was like getting an up-close, intimate look at the dark sordid underbelly of society. Over the years, Dick's read plenty of stories about abuse by priests and other figures of authority such as teachers and coaches, but the occupations and personality types of the pedophiles living a stone's throw away were hardly confined to the predictable. They included anybody and everybody. There was a gardener, a dentist, a butcher, two psychiatrists, even a surgeon who abused his victims while they were under anesthesia. Every case had its own underlying story. Many of the perpetrators were victims themselves, while others came from seemingly perfect backgrounds and circumstances.

His mouse hovers over the calculate button, his excitement concerning. He knows he shouldn't be enjoying this but is unable to help himself. It was a difficult task parsing the files, and now that he's finished, he is undeniably eager to see the results.

Click.

Like a crystal ball, the screen refreshes, and he scrolls through the results to see four of the seventy-two names highlighted green. Within the next five years, four of the seventy-two reg-istered sex offenders of children within twenty-five miles of where he is sitting have a 93 percent probability of reoffending.

He leans back and blows out a breath, relieved. The result is better than he feared. He had thought it would be at least twice that.

The scores range from sixty-four, one point above the break point, to sixty-eight. Number five on the list catches his eye. The score is sixty-two. The next highest is fifty-five. Dick looks back at the file of the sixty-two, a man by the name of Diego Ramirez. His victims were girls, and he only has one conviction, which is what kept him below the Mendoza Line.

He thinks about this. He doesn't like to fudge. Precise an-alytics dictated the score where a significant statistical change in probability occurs, which in this case was sixty-three. The number isn't arbitrary, and Diego Ramirez is below it.

Just the same, he reviews the file, and a small note in the psychological profile causes him to reconsider, "Mr. Ramirez has deep resentment toward his victims, which manifests itself in a need for their total acquiescence. If they do not submit, it's likely he will seek revenge."

Dick thinks about Otis and the note he sent Dee when he was convicted. It's not one of the contributing factors, too difficult to measure, but he decides to add it as an "extra criteria." If resentment toward the victims is evident, the subject receives a bonus point.

He erases the other profiles, keeping only Ramirez and the other four. Seventy-two possibilities winnowed down to five. He feels a perverse sense of accomplishment, the thrill of knowing he's done something very few could do.

It's after seven, and he's tired. He saves his work, scrubs his computer, and tucks the thumb drive in his pocket. He'll decide what to do with his newfound knowledge another day. For now, he's earned a beer.

48

Dick walks into his apartment around seven, buzzed from two beers and the Angels' victory over the Astros. He checks his phone, hoping for a distraction, but now that Little League is over, his weekends have returned to long days of going for morning runs, then attending to the mundane errands of life like laundry and shopping.

He glances at the switch plate beside the door, and with a sigh of resignation, flips the switch plate open to retrieve the thumb drive from its hiding place. He plugs it into his laptop and looks at the five Pepper files neatly listed in order from highest to lowest score—PPR1 through PPR5. He considers this, wondering if he should reverse it, start with Diego Ramirez to get his feet wet, then move on to the more dangerous numbers.

No. He's not sure how far he'll get, so better to deal with greatest threats first. He opens PPR1's file, a man by the name of Irving Grayson Ingberg III. Ingberg only has a single conviction, but he received six extra points because, prior to his conviction, three other accusers had leveled charges against him. Two of the cases were resolved without going to court. The third was dropped by the DA for insufficient evidence. Finally, six years ago, one of the cases stuck, and Ingberg was sentenced to five years in prison.

Twenty-two months ago, he was paroled after serving forty-eight of his sixty months. Dick reads through the file, which is remarkably sparse. The case was pled out, so there was no trial, and during his four years of incarceration, Ingberg was a model inmate. There's not even so much as a doctor's note. His mugshot shows a silver-haired man with piercing blue eyes, who even in a drab prison uniform, looks dignified. Under aliases is listed a single name: Grayson Ingall. There's also a photo of his accuser, a thin-faced boy by the name of Devin Heinz. He was ten, the same age as Jim, when Ingberg molested him.

Dick shuts down the laptop, returns the thumb drive to its hiding place, and leaves the apartment.

He drives to the address listed in the file, surprised when he finds himself in an affluent area of Orange of sprawling grand estates. He winds through hills until he comes to an iron gate surrounded by a tall brick wall.

No parking is allowed on the street, so Dick can only drive by. As he passes, he catches the glimpse of a large white house surrounded by red rose bushes.

Irving Grayson Ingberg III is going to be a challenge.

Not ready to go home, he grabs a yogurt at a strip mall near the freeway and considers the four remaining options. PPR2 lives in Huntington Beach, PPR3 in Cypress, PPR4 in Lake Forest, and the last, Diego Ramirez, is in Santa Ana, one town away.

———

The Diego Gallery is located in a gentrified part of the city with newly constructed live-work complexes clustered around the Orange County Center for Contemporary Art. Like pieces of contemporary art themselves, the edgy galleries blaze bright and bold from the impoverished seediness around them.

It's art walk night, and the streets are bustling. Dick needs to park several blocks away. As he walks back to the gallery, he is struck by the dichotomy of the neighborhood. The right side he would describe as California barrio, the smell of tamales and carnitas mingling with salsa music and Spanish voices that float from windows and yards of houses with barred doors and pitted drives. And he would guess the monthly income of most of the households is probably less than the price of a single canvas being sold in the glitzy, hipster galleries across the street.

He reaches Diego Ramirez's gallery and joins a dozen others in the showroom as they mill around, admiring the art. The paintings are large, each canvas at least six feet tall by four feet wide. Broad strokes of vivid colors leap and swirl this way and that, and Dick isn't sure what to make of it.

A well-put-together silver-haired gentleman beckons a forty-something woman with indigo hair. The blue-haired woman ignores him, and instead walks to a millennial-aged man in faded jeans and a paisley shirt standing in front of the largest painting in the showroom.

"Stunning, isn't she?" the woman says with a nod toward the painting.

Dick edges closer.

"Is he here?" the man asks, eyes intent on the painting, which is all yellows and blues except for an unexpected splash of red toward the bottom.

"I'm afraid our genius is a bit reticent this evening."

Dick scoffs at the pretentiousness and glances up the stairs toward the residence of the "genius" who destroyed a six-year-old girl and who knows how many others.

"Does this piece have a name?" the man asks.

"She does. Diego calls her *Alison*."

Dick falls back a step and into the person behind him. "Excuse me," he says, the words strangled as his eyes spin over the painting—blond, blue, red—*Alison*—the little girl he raped who bravely testified against him.

He looks at the painting beside it—brown, hazel, red. Next to that—gold, green, red. He reaches for the wall to steady himself.

"How much?" the man asks, rapture in his voice, clearly even more enamored now that he knows her name.

"Unfortunately, this one's not for sale," the blue-haired lady says, "but perhaps I can interest you in one of the others?"

"No," the man says. "I want this one."

Dick swallows as he sizes the man up, knowing he's someone used to getting his way.

"I'm sorry. Diego has a personal connection to this piece and won't part with her. He's had many offers."

Dick interrupts. "Excuse me. Where did you say Mr. Ramirez is tonight?"

She looks Dick up and down and is about to ignore him when the man helps, "Yes, where is Diego? I'd like to speak to him directly."

The blue-haired woman's eyes dance, and she leans in and whispers conspiratorially, "He has a new muse. And from what I understand, she's playing hard to get."

49

"She's dead."

"Captain Goh?" Steve says, switching the phone to his other ear and giving the conversation his full attention.

"Are you happy?" Goh says. "Your justice was served, and now Ally Cleason is dead, and Diego Ramirez is gone."

Steve squeezes his eyes shut as the words pierce in his brain.

"He stalked her, waited to get her alone, then slit her throat and left her in the parking garage beside her car to bleed out."

Evil trumps good. Steve knows it. He knew it when he called Ally to warn her. He knew it when he was sitting in his car outside Ramirez's studio.

"But don't worry, he made sure he said goodbye. On his way out, he smiled at the security camera and gave us the bird."

He sounds drunk.

Steve pinches the bridge of his nose. "He's gone?"

"Of course, he's gone," Goh slurs. "The only ones we even have a chance in hell of catching are the stupid ones, and Ramirez isn't that."

"There was no choice," Steve says, the words hollow even to him. "We had to wait until he was guilty of a crime."

"Is he guilty enough for you now?"

"It's still not up to me." The words are laced with acid.

"It was. It was up to *you* and *me*. *We* knew who Ramirez was, and that girl's death is on us. Not the system, not our forefathers and their deluded vision of justice. *Us*. We're to blame."

"We serve the system," Steve says, hand clenching the phone so tight it trembles. "It's not our job to make the rules, only to enforce them. If we don't, the lines become blurred."

"Tell that to Ally. Oh, right, you can't."

———

Steve drives to Chincoteague, buys supplies, and sets sail. The passion that drives him is confused, and he needs to get some perspective.

When he is far enough from the harbor he can no longer see the shore, he drops anchor and drifts. The sun roasts his skin, his stomach rumbles, and the wind blisters his lips, but he pays it no mind, grateful to feel something other than the throbbing in his brain.

For the system to work, it has to be protected. Civilians and cops cannot take justice into their own hands. Yes, some guilty get off, and some innocents get hurt, but society as a whole is better for it, the system not perfect but the best shot we have for not ending up at the mercy of those in power. It's what safeguards us from becoming a mutinous, violent society ruled by paranoia, prejudice, assumption, and fear. And who is he or Captain Goh or Dr. Richard Raynes to question that?

The arguments make sense, so why does it feel like such a load of idealistic crap?

His job is to protect and serve. The military and his career in law enforcement have drilled that into his head. And when he was in war, he preached it with sincerity to his men, men he led into battle knowing some wouldn't make it back. The greater good. You needed to believe in it. The understanding that the sacrifices you were making were for something worth saving, the betterment of the country and her future. It was imperative to have confidence that wiser men and higher causes existed and that the orders you were following, staking your life and the lives of others on, served a greater purpose, and to accept, without question, that commands and rules were to be followed regardless of the perceived consequences or price.

Ally Cleason was the price.

This is where the argument falls apart. The price too high . . . too arbitrary . . . too ignored, disregarded, and unappreciated. Dick said it's the thing that makes America great but also what leaves it vulnerable. Could he be right?

Since their conversation, he's kept tabs on Dick and his possible future targets, a list of thirty-some recently released pedophiles in his area. Diego Ramirez was on the list. And when Steve realized it, as much as he wants to deny it, he knows part of him wished Dick would do what Goh could not.

Perhaps he's stayed in the job too long. Maybe it's time to step down and let someone new take over, someone less hardened to those they've sworn to defend.

His life is changing, or maybe it's him.

50

Dick stands in front of Joanne's desk with a shy, proud smile on his face.

"You did it," she says, her cheeks stretched wide with her own beaming grin.

He shrugs like it's no big deal, though both of them know exactly what a big deal it is. Dick has successfully created the first continuous-release oral anti-allergen as effective as its nasal steroid counterpart. The drug still needs to be tested in a clinical trial then sent to the FDA for approval, but Dick is confident it will sail through both, which means Freeway could be on shelves within a couple years.

"Amazing," Joanne says, smoothing her hand over the report.

She looks especially pretty this morning. Her hair is down so it drapes over her shoulders, and her lipstick is a softer shade, more coral than red.

"I'll submit it to the board this afternoon for trial funding." She looks up at him. "I can't believe you figured it out so fast."

Dick knows it was slower than she realizes. For ten years, he's considered and researched what went wrong and how he would fix it if he ever got the chance. It's confounding how quickly

things have turned around, a domino effect set off by, of all
things, Otis's return. Like a rail lever pulled at the last second
that veered a train from a cataclysmic crash, he was forced into
action, which set off a chain of events, which diverted his life and
set him on a course entirely different from the one he was on.

"Maybe we should celebrate?" he says. "How about I take
you to dinner?"

Her smile freezes.

"Or not," he says, eyes and confidence dropping.

She walks past him, closes the door, then returns to lean
against the desk.

"Here's the thing," she says slowly, measuring her words.
"I've thought a lot about this . . . you and I . . . you know . . .
and the idea of us going out."

He nods. For two months, they've been almost flirting.

"And?" he manages.

"And I don't know. I was considering it. But then . . . I got
this weird feeling."

Dick cocks his head.

"You're going to laugh," she says, looking at him through
her brow.

"Try me," he says, unsure if he's flattered that she was considering dating him or insulted by her ultimate rejection of the idea.

"I can't put my finger on it," she says, "but I recognize it.
Like I said, you're going to laugh, but there's something about
you that, for lack of a better word . . ." She smirks with embarrassment. "Is dangerous."

Dick does laugh. He's been called a lot of things in his life,
dangerous not among them.

Joanne chuckles as well. "Fine. Laugh." She grabs a piece of
paper from her desk, crumples it, and throws it at him.

He bats it away and continues to smile.

"The thing is I have a history of choosing guys who keep secrets from me and lie, and I don't want to do that again."

The humor stops, and Dick drops his eyes and says nothing.

"Exactly," she says. "I just don't trust it."

51

It's been four days since Dick reported his results to Joanne. The board meeting started an hour ago, and he's waiting anxiously to hear what they had to say. Turning side to side in his chair, he looks at the bouncing neon balls and thinks about what Freeway's success will mean for allergy sufferers and for him.

Pentco's policy is that half a percent of the proceeds of any product developed using a scientist's discovery goes to the scientist. Singulair, the current number one asthma and allergy medicine, did $735 million in sales last year. If Freeway does that, Dick will earn $3.7 million. Per year.

"Morning," Joanne says, startling him from his thoughts.

Dick swivels around to see her leaning against the frame of his cubicle, and his blood warms, embarrassed and turned on, their conversation in her office a few days ago undoubtedly having increased the "dangerous" vibe between them.

"I just got out of the meeting," she says. "And they said no."

His heart stops, and his throat goes dry.

"Kidding," she says quickly.

"Oh." He blinks several times, the joke not funny.

She smiles apologetically. "They were very impressed."

He nods, still recovering from the stun.

"The vote to fund the trial was unanimous with just one small change." She pinches her finger and thumb in front of her.

"A change?"

He considered the protocol very carefully, ran it and reran it dozens of times in his head, thinking about it from every aspect.

"While they love that you took the initiative to explore ideas beyond the scope of the project, they prefer you focus your energy on the task at hand and narrow your pursuit to the second compound."

He tilts his head as the words play, rewind, then play again. "But that makes no sense. Compound four is the breakthrough. Did they not understand? It boosts the user's immunity—"

"They're very excited about compound two," she interrupts. "And you have their full support."

"But we're talking about a possible cure."

"Yes, but at the moment, they want you to focus on two."

Some of the joviality has slipped from her voice, and Dick's pulse ticks up several notches as he realizes what she's saying.

"Oh," he says, eyes leveling on hers.

She nods and smiles, pleased he's caught on.

"Because four is a cure," he says, confirming it. "Which means eventually patients wouldn't need their medicine."

She touches her finger to her nose, and her grin grows, the crimson lips spreading to her cheeks.

He looks away from them to the floor before lifting his face back to hers and saying plainly, "No."

The grin drops. "Richard—"

"No," he repeats. "Four is a cure. We have a cure. You can't keep that from people."

Her expression tightens with her frustration. "Richard, this is *good* news. Freeway's been resurrected, and it's going to be one of the most significant new medicines of the decade." She uses her hands to emphasize the point, the red talons flicking and flying. "It will be Pentco's new crown jewel, and think about it, the results are the same. People will no longer suffer from allergies."

He can't believe this is happening. Only moments before, he had been contemplating how great his life was going be and what the windfall of money would mean for his kids, and in a matter of sentences, all that hope and happiness has been deflated.

Fortunately, he hadn't gotten too used to the idea. With a resigned sigh, he says, "Please thank the board for their consideration, but let them know that, while I appreciate their support, I only want to proceed if we pursue both compounds."

Her eyes widen with shock before she recovers and they narrow like lasers. Venom practically spitting from her lips, she says, "Richard, this is not up to you. The board made a decision, and I'm telling you, as your boss, to drop protocol four and proceed with protocol two."

When he doesn't respond, she says, "Do you understand?"

Filled with the same flat feeling he had when Freeway failed the first time, he says, "Yes. Perfectly."

"So, you'll start on compound two?"

"I'll move on this afternoon."

She nods her approval, then, cooling her tone, paints on a smile and says, "Richard, this is a *good* thing. We should be celebrating. What do you say you and I go out for a drink?"

"No thanks," he says and swivels away to start what's next.

52

Dick's letter of resignation takes five minutes to write, but destroying every trace of Freeway takes most of the afternoon. He smiles as he pours the vials down the drain and washes away the evidence.

The advantage to being low man on the totem pole is that Dick didn't have an assistant or anyone looking over his shoulder. He's the only one who understands how and why the drug works, and its molecular code is unique as a fingerprint. The chemistry that makes the drug work only exists in two places, Dick's head and his laptop at home.

When he's certain there's not a trace of Freeway left to be found, he packs up a file box with his personal belongings and places the letter of resignation on his keyboard.

When he gets to his apartment, he backs up the Freeway files from his laptop twice onto two separate thumb drives, then scrubs the hard drive clean. The computer questions and warns him several times before following the command. The first thumb drive he puts behind the switch plate beside the door, the second he drops in his pocket.

He drives to the Goodwill store and leaves the laptop in the electronics donation box. The data's erased, but he doesn't want to take the chance it can somehow be recovered.

At the office supply store down the street, he buys a new laptop and mails the second thumb drive to Dee. The note that accompanies it reads:

Dear Dee:
    Please put this with Papa's things.
                            Thanks,
                            Dick

Dick's grandfather had installed a safe under the cinder-block bench in the cellar. Along with an assortment of militia artillery and ammunition are a few military bonds and the birth certificates and documentation of the Raynes family for several generations.

The past and the future in a safe beneath the desert.

53

Steve is several hours early but was terrified of being late. For a week, he's had paranoid thoughts of not being at the airport when they got off the plane. He's dreamed of flat tires, hurricanes, and terrorist attacks. Denise and Jesse have never left California, and neither has ever flown.

At the gift store, he buys a newspaper, a box of candy, and two Washington D.C. tourist T-shirts, size adult small and children's large.

He scans the paper as he waits. The world is still at war, crime's still occurring on every front, and the Knicks are still having a bad season. Steve waits at the arrival gate, his FBI badge allowing him the pre-9/11 pastime privilege. Through the glass, he watches the three-dimensional dance of the airplanes taxiing, landing, and circling above. Danny used to love standing at the window with his hands spread wide and his nose pressed to the glass, his breath making a foggy circle on the pane. The thought makes him smile, and the realization that thinking of Danny has made him happy instead of destroying him surprises him and makes him smile again.

He pulls out his phone, and his ex-wife answers on the first ring.

"Steve? Everything okay?" Her concern fills his heart.

"I'm good. It's why I'm calling. I wanted to let you know I'm okay."

He can hear her sweet smile. "Oh, babe, I'm glad."

"I still have my moments, but I think I might finally be coming out of the tunnel."

"You've met someone?" she says, showing how well she knows him.

"Yeah," he says, feeling guilty, though she's the one who moved on first.

"Oh."

"Sorry."

"No. It's good. Just hard."

They both fall silent. He imagines her sitting in their back-yard, a book on her lap, her new dog, a terrier mix, at her feet.

"I'm glad you're doing better," she says.

"Thanks. I love you."

"I love you too."

————

Denise and Jesse are almost the last passengers to deplane, and Steve's nearly having a heart attack by the time they finally appear. He embraces them both so hard when they finally get to him he crushes the candy and knocks the wind out of Denise.

"Sorry," he says sheepishly as he releases her.

Jesse has moved to the windows and is watching the planes.

"How was the flight?" Steve asks.

"Terrifying. Thank goodness Jesse was with me. People are not meant to fly. We are meant to have our feet on the ground."

Steve hugs her again, this time more gently. "Thanks for coming."

She stands on her tiptoes and kisses him lightly on the lips, her arms around his neck. "What are a few gray hairs and years off my life when the payoff is you?"

Jesse's back. "I made a list of the places I want to go while we're here. We can talk about it while you drive. There are sixteen must-sees, twelve hope-to-sees, and twenty-two would-like-to-sees."

"Sounds like we have our work cut out for us," Steve says, grabbing Denise's carry-on.

And as they walk through the airport, Denise on his arm and Jesse talking a mile a minute, he wonders if the people around him are jealous.

54

Dick googles Irving Grayson Ingberg III and doesn't get any hits, but when he types in his alias, Grayson Ingall, the search reveals 691 results. Ingall comes from old money and invested his fortune in several businesses, the most well-known a modeling and talent enterprise called Ingall Talent Agency. He is known for his philanthropy and generous support of the arts.

What's interesting is there is no mention of his criminal life. Somehow, Grayson Ingall has managed to keep the crimes of Grayson Ingberg III from being associated with him. One article in *Riviera Magazine*, a glossy publication on the who's who of Orange County, is titled, "Where is Grayson Ingall?" The article, published a few months after his sentencing, explained that Ingall was taking a sabbatical from his company to be treated for an undisclosed illness. Dick could practically hear Ingall's publicist whispering the story to the reporter.

There are lots of photos of Ingall and his highbrow life, and Dick thinks again how difficult it's going to be to infiltrate his world. He searches next for his accusers. The first boy, thirteen when he accused Ingall of raping him, is now thirty-three and impossible to trace. His name is Steven Roche, and there's no way of knowing which of the fourteen million results are the Steven Roche Dick is trying to find. He moves on to Kirk Krasner, whose accusation was made three years after Steven's, and gets nothing. The third accuser, Cayman Riegler, was the complainant whose case was dropped by the DA for insufficient evidence. There are three results, all for a chiseled, honeycomb-haired model who lives in New York. The first is for a Tommy Hilfiger runway show that happened last spring.

The second is for a model management company. According to Cayman's profile on the site, he is twenty-seven and has been working as a model/actor since he was twelve. His credits span from print ads to commercials to fashion shows.

The third entry, published three years ago, is for a blog called *GuiltFreeSurvivor*. Dick clicks the link:

Blog entry 127

Cayman: The hardest part was that I trusted him and that my parents adored him. It was such an honor that this esteemed guy had taken an interest in me and my career. He'd done so much for my family, always making sure I was short-listed for casting calls, using his influence to ensure I had steady work. My family struggled financially and he knew it so I thought he was doing it to be kind.

The first time he invited me to his house I was so excited. I remember rubbing it in my sister and brothers faces bragging that I got to stay at a mansion with a pool.

It started off exactly how I imagined. We had an amazing dinner that his cook prepared then went for a swim in the pool. When we were done I followed him to his bedroom where he told me I could change. I started for the bathroom but he told me to undress in the bedroom. I didn't know why but didn't think it was a big deal. I took off my swim trunks, and he took off his. That's when I got a bad feeling. I should have put my clothes back on. I should have left the room. Instead I just stood there. My family counted on the money I made.

He told me to touch his penis. He said it would mean a lot to him. So I did. Then he told me to rub him. I did that also. It was like I wasn't even there anymore. I know it sounds stupid. But I was just a kid. He told me to do things and I did them.

When it was over he told me to get dressed then he took me for a walk outside so he could show me his garden. He explained that I was now one of his special boys and that each special boy was represented by a rose bush.

This is really awful but when I saw how many rosebushes there were I felt better.

He told me he loved his roses and took care of them just like he would take care of me but that in order to do that I couldn't tell anyone our secret.

The next day I went home and when my parents asked how it was I said great. I bragged about the pool and the great dinner we had.

That week I got the biggest commercial of my career.

A week later I was invited back to his home. The day I was supposed to go I got sick.

The next time he invited me I went. The first thing we did was plant a small rose seedling beside his back porch. He said it was special because it was the first bush planted beside the house which meant it was closer to him.

That night he raped me. I remember begging him not to though at the time I wasn't even entirely sure what I was begging for.

Within days I started having nightmares and wetting my bed. My parents grew concerned and asked me what was wrong but I didn't tell. Shame more than fear stopped me.

Several more times I went back. It didn't seem to matter anymore. I was ruined and numb and all that was left was to please him so my career would continue and I could continue to help my family. But life had another plan. I shared a room with my brothers and I started having night terrors. It didn't take long for my parents to figure out what was triggering them. My parents went to the police and I lived through the ordeal of telling my story a dozen times to a dozen different strangers only to have the monster set free because he had lots of money and a team of fancy lawyers.

My parents guilt was as hard to bear as my own unhappiness.

For the first few years I tried to bury what happened put it behind me and go on with my life. But I never really got past it. In high school I started abusing alcohol and drugs. I purposely got into fights, drove drunk, put my family through hell. My senior year I tried to kill myself. I lived and my parents got me into rehab. It was there that I first confronted my demons and that I discovered Prozac a wonder drug that numbs the edges enough for me to stagger forward without wanting to destroy everything around me.

This is no story of triumph. I know this site is

called GuiltFreeSurvivor but I don't feel like a survivor.
I am simply alive. I remain because I don't want to
hurt my family any more than I already have. When
my parents leave this world so will I. There's nothing
here for me. I can't carry on a meaningful relationship
without running away at the first inkling of intimacy.
I cannot even say the word sex. The concept is forever
tainted in my mind. Sex for me is dirty, ugly, humil-
iating, and shameful. I hate sex. This makes me very
alone, out of touch in an aspect of life everyone else
takes casually and enjoys immensely.

I do not want him to continue to have this power
over me yet I seem powerless to stop it. He still follows
me. I see him in every authority figure in my life—
teachers, rabbis, bosses. He forever lives in the corner
of my mind like the thorny roses he loves. His story is
mine and I fear one day my story may be his.

———

Dick runs until he can't catch a breath, then stops and bends
over his knees wheezing, the first blind rage gone and the cool
night air helping clear his head of the fury. He glimpsed the rose
bushes surrounding Ingall's house. Dozens, perhaps hundreds.
He spits on the sidewalk and wonders how many were planted
in the fifteen years since Cayman was twelve.

55

"Morning, Joanne," Dick says brightly as he answers the phone.

He looks at his watch. It's 8:07. She must have gone to his cubicle first thing to check on him and just found the resignation letter.

"Richard, this is ridiculous. Come back and bring the formulas, and we'll forget all this nonsense."

"Forget that you want to cause people unnecessary suffering to line your pockets?"

"Forget that you are in violation of your contract and that, by taking those formulas, you are committing grand larceny."

"Arrest me."

"Don't think we won't."

He scoffs, the idea amusing, and he realizes he is relishing this, long pent-up resentment toward Pentco and their indifferent dismissal of him ten years earlier bubbling to the surface.

"You'll never work in this industry again," she says.

"That's okay. I've lost my taste for it."

Her voice turns almost saccharine as she changes tact and says, "Richard, this is silly. What about all the people Freeway could help?"

"I'd rather they were cured."

The sweetness returns to sour. "So that's it, all or nothing? We bend to your will, or you walk?"

"I already walked."

"Richard, come back and let's talk about this. We'll start with compound two and revisit four down the road."

"Don't patronize me."

"I'm not—"

"You are," he says. "You want the formulas?"

"Of course I want the formulas. They're ours. They belong to Pentco."

"Set up a meeting with the board," he says. "I have a proposition."

"Why don't you and I meet instead and see if we can figure this out?"

He scoffs again. "Trying to save your hide? No, thanks. The board makes the decisions; that's who I want to meet with. As a matter of fact, as far as I'm concerned, you don't even need to be there."

"You son of a—"

He ends the call before she finishes.

———

Dick sets the bag from the electronics store on the counter and smiles when he pulls out his phone to sees the voicemail symbol glowing. It took less than two hours for Joanne to call back. Her voice is deliberately slow, and he can hear the effort it takes for her not to scream, which makes him grin wider. The meeting with the board is set for a week from today.

He considers the delay and realizes they're buying time to see if they can end-run him, get one of the other chemists to unlock the key. He's not concerned. There aren't many things he's certain of, but his unique knowledge of oral anti-allergens is one of them. If there were another chemist who could do it, it would have already been done.

Dick opens his laptop and punches "Diego Gallery, Santa Ana" into his browser. Because of Diego Ramirez's twisted art, he has moved to the top of Dick's list.

Breaking News: Famed artist, Diego Ramirez of Santa Ana wanted for questioning in the brutal murder of his past accuser Alison Cleason.

Dick's pulse races as he reads the article, which includes a photo of a pretty young woman who looks very much like the little girl in Diego's file from fifteen years earlier. The murder occurred Saturday night, the same night Dick visited the gallery. Alison Cleason was walking back to her car from the UCI library after attending a study group when she was allegedly brutally killed by Diego Ramirez, who was waiting for her in the parking garage. She was found by another student. Alison was twenty-one.

Dick thinks of the *Alison* painting, his stomach roiling, and he wonders if the blue-haired lady will now be allowed to sell it, and then wonders if the man who wanted it so badly, on discovering its real cost, will want it more or less.

The fury Dick felt earlier after reading Cayman's post returns, but he doesn't have the strength to run again, so instead, he sits quiet, trembling with rage and regret for not having done something sooner. If he could line them up—Otis, Shea, Ingall, Ramirez—he'd have no problem running a machine gun across their bodies. It wouldn't give him joy, but it would give him peace. Alison, Cayman, Germaine, Willy, Jerry, Ed—all of them worth so much more than the parasites that destroyed them.

He whispers a prayer for Alison's soul, then opens Pepper to consider who's left. Ingall is stalled until he can figure out a way to infiltrate his life. Which leaves three prospects. PPR2 and PPR3 have equal scores of sixty-five. Dick chooses Ray Hamilton because he's in Huntington Beach as opposed to Kristian Knott, who lives in Cypress, which is farther away and inland, which means hotter.

He rereads Hamilton's file—three convictions, but the first was plead down to a misdemeanor for fondling a fifteen-year-old boy when Hamilton was nineteen. His crimes aren't violent, but all the other criteria fit. Packing up his laptop, he grabs the electronics bag, and heads out the door.

———

Huntington Beach was reborn from a sleepy beach town of surfers and oil wells into a tourist haven of Starbucks and chain stores a decade ago. It's easy to find Hamilton's complex. It sits on the Coast Highway across from a large expanse of beach.

Dick parks his Volvo near Hamilton's assigned spot, which is occupied by an old silver Nissan pickup, circa 1970 something. It's almost noon, and Dick is hungry, so he opens the Wendy's bag beside him and pulls out his taco salad.

The first forkful doesn't make it to his mouth.

Hamilton walks toward his truck mostly unchanged from his most recent photo—chin-length gold-blond hair, bronze skin, and a jaunty gate that belies his age of forty-two. He climbs into his truck and pulls onto the Coast Highway.

Dick follows, and they end up in an industrial part of town. Hamilton turns into a driveway between an auto salvage yard and corrugated barrel buildings with rollup doors. Dick drives past, then doubles back and pulls into the driveway. The first barrel houses a furniture refinishing company, the next is a custom-art framing business, and the third has a small sign above the open door that reads, "Hamilton Signature Boards."

Dick parks beneath a eucalyptus tree beside the furniture refinisher and watches from a distance as Hamilton works on a surfboard. He wears a backward baseball cap and a respirator mask. Eighties rock and roll plays from a boom box, and Hamilton bobs as he uses what looks like a large sanding block to smooth a board that lies on two sawhorses inside the bunker.

Dick returns to his lunch, content to watch Hamilton work. He admires Hamilton's meticulousness and skill. Every few minutes, Hamilton takes a gauge from the table beside him to measure a particular dimension, then documents it into a computer. It reminds Dick of working in the lab.

Hamilton's been at it almost two hours when an old red Volkswagen bus, the kind with highlights in the roof, pulls up beside the shop. A curly-headed, golden-haired kid in his mid-teens hops out, and the van drives away. Hamilton comes out of the shop with two bright orange surfboards under his arms. He throws them in the bed of his truck as the kid pulls down the rollup door.

Dick follows them to a parking lot near the Huntington Beach pier and watches as they grab the boards and trot into the water.

Dick walks to the pier and, as he watches the pair swim out on their boards, wonders if surfing is the Holy Grail. Hamilton is three years older than Dick but looks a decade younger—his body lean and muscled, his gold skin kissed by the sun and unwrinkled.

Like his expertise in the shop, Hamilton is impressive in the water. Powerful and efficient, he gauges each swell, lines himself up before taking a few powerful strokes to join its momentum, then pops to his feet and cuts back and forth effortlessly as if it's no more difficult than breathing.

An hour later, the waves starting to die down, Hamilton gives a shaka symbol to the surfers around him, catches the next wave and rides it toward the shore. When it dissolves to white-water, he squats, grabs the rails of his board, and flips upside down to ride the rest of the way on his head.

The beachcombers stare and point, and he emerges to a small ovation. Taking it in stride, he offers a humble smile, tucks his board under his arm, and walks farther onto the beach.

A few minutes later, the kid joins him. The two knock knuckles, and the kid hands Hamilton his board. He takes off on foot as Hamilton walks toward his truck. Dick considers following Hamilton but decides instead to follow the kid.

It's much more difficult following someone on foot, and Dick finds himself needing to double back half a dozen times. Finally, a mile from the beach, the kid turns into a neighborhood of tract homes and, two blocks after that, walks into a tidy blue home with white shutters. Dick makes a note of the address and returns to his apartment.

56

Dick doesn't have a job. It's hard to get used to. For twenty-three years, since he was sixteen, he's worked. Of course, not having a job makes his side proclivities easier to pursue. Which he's not so sure is a good thing. He wishes he was still coaching. Obsessing over bad men and the bad things they might do twenty-four hours a day is a depressing way to fill the time.

After his run, he returns to Huntington Beach. The blue house is dark, and the Camry that had been in the driveway is gone. Dick pulls a magazine and a small stack of junk mail and bills from the mailbox. Everything is addressed to Nancy Skolnick, except *Surfer Magazine*, which is addressed to Jason Skolnick.

From his car, Dick calls the local high school. If they're on the same schedule as Irvine, this is the final week before summer break. Using the pretense of verifying references for an internship at Pentco, Dick discovers Jason is a senior, which makes him seventeen or eighteen.

Dick frowns. With Hamilton's record, he probably shouldn't be hanging out with teenage boys, but Jason doesn't seem like a victim. He considers moving on to Kristian Knott in Cypress.

Hamilton seems on the up-and-up, and unlike the others, Dick likes him.

Dick taps his thumbs on the steering wheel. There was a time Dick liked Otis as well.

It's probably a waste of time, but since all he has these days is time, and since being near the ocean is nicer than driving to Cypress, he decides to stick it out another day.

He drives past Hamilton's shop. Hamilton's truck is parked outside, and white dust floats from the open door. Dick continues to the condo and walks around the complex until he finds Hamilton's patio. It's easy to spot with all the wetsuits and towels draped over the wall. He pretends to be examining the stucco as he looks inside the window right of the patio doors to see a bedroom which is a horrible mess—cans, food wrappers, and clothes strewn on every surface.

With a quick glance around to make sure no one's watching, he sticks one of the two webcams he bought at the electronics store in the upper corner of the window in the shadow of the balcony above. He glances at the window on the left, which probably leads to the living room, and decides against placing the second unit. There is no shade, and the round black webcam would be too obvious.

When he gets to his car, he pulls the camera up on his phone, his heart pounding as if he did something truly daring. The image is dark, and it takes a minute before he's able to discern what he's seeing. Part of the windowsill blocks the lens, and he realizes he should have been more careful when he placed it. But even with only a partial view, he's able to make out the bed, the door, and part of the floor.

He drives to the lot beside the pier, buys a coffee and Danish, and sits on the same bench he sat on last night to watch the surfers. The soothing rhythm of the waves, salty air, and warmth of the sun lull him into a languid, dreamy state, and he finds himself wondering if it might be possible for him to learn. He's only thirty-nine. Maybe it's not too late.

He glances at his phone and notices the lighting has changed, the image brighter, and he realizes a light beyond the bedroom's been turned on. A second later, a shadow enters . . . Hamilton. Followed by a slightly taller shadow with curly hair . . . Jason.

Dick watches as clothes are unceremoniously discarded, and Dick's thankful the image is small and vague and soundless. He turns away when the two begin to roughhouse and kiss, no longer proud of his accomplishment and feeling more like a peeping Tom watching something he shouldn't be. When a long time has passed, he glances back at the screen to see them sitting on the bed, Hamilton leaning against the headboard and Jason on the edge smoking what looks like a joint.

Dick returns to looking at the water. Yes, Jason is underage, but none of what just happened was criminal. Again, Dick considers giving up on Hamilton.

In no rush, he watches the sun set on the water and silently counts down as it disappears on the horizon . . . *six, five, four, three, two, one . . .*

The horizon still aglow, he packs up his trash and is carrying it to the bin when Hamilton passes. He is alone and looks like he's heading toward the diner at the end of the pier. A young couple waves to him, several fishermen nod, and a group of kids carrying skateboards run up.

"Hey, Ray," the tallest of the four says.

Dick moves closer and leans against the rail. He only catches snippets of the conversation, the breeze carrying every other word away. The kids leave, and Hamilton continues on and disappears into the diner.

Dick looks at the glass door then at the boys goofing off

on their skateboards. He thinks of Hamilton's file and his past victims. Both were pre-teen boys that he had befriended before taking advantage of them.

It's a beautiful night, and he has nothing better to do, so he decides to wait. He treats himself to a scoop of rocky road ice cream and watches the people around him—families walking with dogs and strollers, surfers bronzed and salty from the ocean, sunburned tourists, young couples holding hands—everyone out and about and enjoying the evening.

As Dick watches, he tries to remember feeling the way these people look, carefree and unburdened. Like a tingling on his tongue, he can almost taste it, but it's faint and very faraway, and he knows it was before his mother got sick.

Hamilton walks from the restaurant, and the boys swarm him again, only three now, the fourth one gone.

This time Dick positions himself so the wind is in his favor.

"So?" the spokesman of the group says. "Did you think about it?"

Hamilton laughs, a great hearty rumble that is surprising. "Matt, you're too ugly for me to teach," he says without an ounce of malice.

"Ah, come on," Matt says.

"How about me?" pipes the lanky one beside Matt.

"Too skinny," Hamilton says and starts to walk away.

"What about Frankie?" Matt says to his back.

Hamilton turns to look at the last boy, who hasn't said a word. "Frankie, you want to learn to surf?" Hamilton asks.

The boy looks like he just swallowed his tongue. He's smaller than the other boys by half a head and has a bookish charm that's both endearing and pitiable at once.

"Man, that's not fair," Matt says.

"That sucks," the skinny one says

"What do you say, Frankie?" Hamilton asks.

The boy glances at the two boys, then at Hamilton. "Sure?" he says, more question than answer.

"No way," Matt says.

"Saturday," Hamilton says. "Be here at noon."

57

Steve is holding Denise's hand as they walk through the Vietnam Memorial. Jesse is trying to find the name of a great uncle among the 58,178 names inscribed on the wall. The names are listed chronologically, and Denise has no idea when her mother's brother died during the fourteen-year war, so the search is close to impossible, but Jesse is trying anyway.

"Come on, Mom. You don't even know if it was early in the war or close to the end?"

"I told you, Jess, no. My mom died when I was a baby. Uncle Dickie might know. Here's my phone, call him."

"How is your brother?" Steve asks, hoping the question sounds innocent.

"Good, I think. Dickie doesn't say much, but he seems okay. He said you went out for a beer after the game. You didn't tell me that."

"I must have forgot."

"So, what did you talk about?"

"You."

"That must have taken all of two minutes. What else did you talk about?"

"I don't know. I don't remember."

Steve's conversation with Dick has replayed in his head so many times he could recite every word verbatim. Since he learned of Ally's death, it's been the third track on an endless playback reel of the conversations he had with Captain Goh, Ally, and Dick.

"Come on," Denise prods, nudging his shoulder. "My brother hardly talks, and now you're stonewalling me as well. You two just sat and stared?"

"Let's see." He pretends to try and recall. "We talked about crime and how justice doesn't always prevail. Your brother has very strong opinions."

"He does?"

"You don't think so?"

"I don't know, Dickie's always been pretty removed from things that don't involve his work . . . or baseball." She smiles.

She has the nicest smile. It embodies her whole face—her cheeks, her eyes, and her lips.

"You should have seen him with Caroline, his ex. He'd just let things go, roll off his back, no matter what she said or did."

Steve watches her jaw tense and gets the feeling she's holding back her own very strong opinions about her ex-sister-in-law.

"Yeah, well, he definitely has opinions about justice," Steve says.

"You mean Otis?"

They're entering dangerous territory, both attempting nonchalance as their entwined fingers strain not to clench. His own opinions have become muddled in a distinctly unsettling way. Ally's been dead almost a week, and there's been no sign of Ramirez. More to reassure himself than convince her, he says, "Yes, like Otis. He doesn't see anything wrong with someone murdering him. I'd say that's pretty opinionated."

"Killing him," she corrects, her hand releasing his to sweep an invisible hair from her face.

Steve wraps his arm around her shoulder and kisses the top of her head, deciding to drop it. It's a beautiful day, and he's the happiest he's been in a long time. He doesn't want to ruin it. She curls into him and slides her hand into the back pocket of his jeans, a habit that seems second nature to her and that drives him wild with how familiar and intimate it is.

"Though I suppose, when I think about it, Dickie's always been a bit black and white about things," she says after a minute. "Even as a kid."

She smile-huffs as if caught in a memory.

"You know how much he loves baseball?"

"He does know his MLB," Steve says.

Dick and Mike had an amazing exchange in the announcer's box trading facts and statistics, past and present.

"Well, when Dickie was thirteen, he was on a team that made the playoffs, and there was this kid who wasn't very good, and he and Dickie were kind of friends, odd men out sort of thing."

"You know this story from when you were three?"

"My dad told it to me. My dad didn't say a whole lot, but every once in a while, he'd tell a story with every detail, and when he did, it was like time stood still."

Her love for her dad radiates, and Steve imagines how close they must have been. He's seen photos of the man—in a military uniform, in a suit when he got married, in a workman's uniform at the hatchery. A small man with a straight spine and an earnest face.

"The rules said every player needed to play at least two innings and bat twice," Denise goes on. "So the coach calls Dickie's friend and tells him not to show up for the first playoff game."

Steve rolls his eyes. It's amazing how many grown men act incredibly childish when it comes to their kids' sports.

"So," Denise goes on, "Dickie being Dickie decided to talk to the coach and tell him it's not right not to include his friend." She stops and faces Steve. "Could you imagine the courage that took?"

"And let me guess," Steve says, "the coach told Dickie to get lost."

"Yep. Coach told him to mind his own business."

"So that was the end of it?"

"Nope. That's the thing. Dickie couldn't let it go. He went straight from talking to the coach to calling the league president."

Steve shakes his head. "The president do anything?"

"Nope."

"So the kid didn't play in the playoffs?"

"Actually, he did. Dickie quit the team, and they didn't have enough players, so his friend got to play, and Dickie never played again."

"He didn't have to quit," Steve says, irritated by the story and angry at the idiot coach, the stupid league president, and at Dick for not realizing how the idiot coach and stupid league president would respond.

"That's just it," Denise says. "He did. Dickie couldn't play for that coach anymore. It wasn't even an option."

Denise sighs out and looks dreamily at Jesse, who is still running his fingers over the names. "I could tell my dad was proud," she says, "but all I could think when he told me the story was, *For what?* Dickie did all that, and it turned out to be for nothing."

No, Steve thinks, *it was for everything.*

58

It's Saturday morning, and Dick's back in Huntington Beach sitting on a bench beside the pier, eating a burger from Duke's Surf Shack. As he eats, he peruses the news, looking to see if there's been any update on the search for Diego Ramirez. Today, the two-week-old story doesn't get a mention.

The day is stunning, spring in its finale. The sky is cloudless blue and the wind sweet and light.

Hamilton arrives first, two boards under his arms. Frankie shows up a few minutes later. They walk to the smooth sand near the water, and Hamilton lays the boards between them. Dick watches as Hamilton gestures to the water, and he realizes he is explaining the currents and describing the different kinds of waves. Dick wishes he were closer so he could hear the lesson. The more Hamilton talks, the more Frankie seems to relax, at one point even working up the courage to ask a question.

Hamilton lies on one of the boards and demonstrates how to paddle and pop to your feet. Frankie lies down, and Hamilton makes a few adjustments, the two now laughing like old friends. Frankie tries popping up like Hamilton did, and Hamilton playfully shoves him off and takes his place. Frankie tries to shove him off the way Hamilton did to him, but it's like the guy has glue on his feet. His body moves this way and that, but he never loses his balance.

Dick finds himself smiling as he watches and getting excited when, finally, they tie the leashes to their ankles and walk toward the water. Frankie steps tentatively into the frigid Pacific, while Hamilton seems immune.

When they're thigh deep, Hamilton holds Frankie's board so he can climb on, then he lies on his own board, and together they paddle out. The waves are small, but each time one hits, Frankie tumbles. Patiently, Hamilton waits for him to scrabble back on, and they set off again. Finally, a dozen spills later, they've made it past the break and are straddling their boards with a dozen other surfers. Though they're too far for Dick to see their expressions, he imagines Frankie smiling wide.

A set rolls in from the horizon, and Hamilton slides off his board and shoves it out of the way so he can get behind Frankie.

"Paddle!" he yells, the command loud enough for Dick to hear on the beach.

Dick holds his breath as Frankie flails his skinny arms and as Hamilton motors him from behind. The wave catches up. Hamilton disappears. Frankie topples off.

When Hamilton pops up, he has hold of Frankie's board. Frankie scrabbles back on, and they paddle back out. They wait for another set and do it again.

Frankie's definitely no natural. He looks like a slippery eel trying to paddle on a stick of soap. But what he lacks in innate ability, he makes up for in determination. Though he looks exhausted, with barely enough strength to pull himself back onto the board, time and again he returns to the other surfers.

Finally, Hamilton says something that ends it, and Dick watches, disappointed, as they paddle back toward shore. He feels terrible for Frankie. He was trying so hard, and surfing is tougher than it looks.

Halfway to the beach, Hamilton says, "Stop."

Dick looks past them to see a wave breaking a hundred yards away. Like before, Hamilton ditches his own board and gets behind Frankie.

"Paddle!" he roars.

The whitewater races toward them, and Frankie swims with everything he has. Dick can barely see Hamilton but knows he's there by how fast Frankie is moving, his board being propelled by Hamilton's amazing strength.

Go! Dick encourages. *Go. Go. Go.*

And it happens. The whitewater takes hold, and Frankie is no longer paddling but instead is holding on for dear life, his face a mix of terror and exhilaration, and it's all Dick can do not to cheer.

He makes it to within twenty feet of the beach before tumbling off, then pops from the water, a huge grin on his face. He looks back at Hamilton, who is still treading water a hundred yards away, and raises his fist in triumph. Hamilton gives a shaka wave back, then climbs on his own board and rides to shore to join him.

Hamilton high-fives Frankie, then grabs both boards and heads for his truck.

Frankie bounds after him. "Wait. Mr. Ray?"

Dick smiles at the kid's polite use of "mister" in front of Hamilton's name.

Hamilton turns, and Frankie says, "I want to go out again. Will you take me out again?"

Hamilton smiles warmly, much nicer to Frankie than he was to Matt or the skinny kid. "Frankie, you did great, and that was fun, but I can't just give lessons away for free."

"How much do they cost?" Frankie blurts, his joy buzzing so bright Dick feels it all the way to his spine.

"Fifty an hour."

"Oh," Frankie says, his energy deflating. "Okay. Well, thanks again for today."

Hamilton starts to turn but then lets out a sigh and turns back. "Tell you what, maybe we can work something out."

Frankie brightens. "What? I'll do anything."

The words send a shiver down Dick's spine.

Hamilton thinks, then his eyes widen with an idea. "Housework," he says.

"Housework?"

"Yeah. My house is a mess, and I was going to hire someone, but if you want, we can make a trade instead."

Frankie swallows. "I guess I can do that."

Hamilton sticks out his hand, and Frankie shakes on it. "Meet me here tomorrow. You'll clean my house, then we'll surf."

The shiver grows. Frankie's around twelve, and Hamilton must know, with his record, having a twelve-year-old boy alone in his house isn't a good idea.

"Does it have to be tomorrow?" Frankie stammers. "It's Sunday, and my family goes to church. Can we do it another day?"

"Fine," Hamilton says, seeming to lose patience. "Wednesday, four o'clock."

"That would be great," Frankie says excitedly, eager to please. "Thank you, Mr. Ray." He bounds away, and Hamilton continues toward his truck, a smile on his lips Dick can't quite read.

Dick watches Hamilton go. Today is Saturday, which means he has four days to figure out if teaching Frankie to surf is all Hamilton has in mind. He really wants to believe it is and for this to turn out exactly as it seems, surf lessons in exchange for a bit of housework.

He turns in the direction Frankie is walking to see him disappear into an arcade. Dick follows and catches up just as Frankie is exalting Matt and three other boys about his lesson, making his success far grander than it was.

Dick interrupts. "Hey, guys."

They all look at him.

"I'm a reporter with *Orange Coast Magazine*, and I'm doing a story on local surfers. I overheard you talking. Who are you talking about?"

Matt jumps in. "Ray Hamilton. Guy's sick on a board."

"And he gives lessons to you kids?"

Matt frowns. "Just *some* kids." He jerks his head at Frankie. "Wieners like this."

"You're the only one he's taught?" Dick asks.

"Nah," Matt says before Frankie can answer. "He also taught Zack."

Dick pulls out his phone. "Can I get your name?" he says to Frankie. "For the story."

"Frank Kramer."

"And Zack's name?"

"Zack Kuchinskis."

"Do one of you boys happen to have his number?"

59

Dick's meeting with the Pentco board is this morning. The fact that the meeting is still on is a good sign. It means the other chemists failed.

Before Dick leaves his apartment, he tries calling Zack Kuchinskis, the boy Hamilton gave surf lessons to before Frankie. There's no answer on his home phone, and he's uncomfortable leaving a message.

It's strange how much Dick is rooting for Hamilton. As he drives to Pentco, he finds himself daydreaming of Zack telling him Hamilton's a great guy and that he taught him to surf and that was it, end of story. Ninety-three percent probability is not a hundred percent, and he wants Hamilton to be the exception.

He yawns. Frankie won't leave his mind, and it makes sleep impossible. Yesterday, he spent the day with Jim. They went to an Angels game, and it took his mind off it for a few hours, but when he dropped Jim off, his worry was ten times worse. Frankie and Jim have similar builds and the same color hair, and last night, the two kept getting mixed up in his nightmares.

The conference room overlooks the suburban sprawl of Orange County and is furnished with a thick glass table surrounded by sixteen sleek leather chairs. Eight Pentco executives and Joanne are on one side. Dick takes a seat on the other.

Joanne sits rigid, her eyes focused on the middle of the glass, hate radiating. Her lips are crimson, and her hair pulled so tight her skin is stretched.

The only board member Dick recognizes is the older man with sharp blue eyes sitting opposite him, Pentco's CEO, Jon Katz.

"So, Doctor," Katz says in the silky, unwavering voice that's earned him a reputation as a gentleman and a shark, "you finally deliver the oral anti-allergen we hired you to deliver a decade after it was supposed to be completed, and the gratitude we get for our patience is you hijacking our product?" His piercing gaze lasers into Dick's brain. "You understand taking corporate property is a felony?"

And withholding a drug that could potentially cure millions from a lifelong affliction is morally reprehensible. Dick holds his tongue.

After a breath, he says, "I thought we were here to discuss a solution that suits us both?" He's surprised and pleased to hear his own voice is nearly as smooth as Katz's.

Katz's thin lips curl at the corners, perhaps surprised as well. Despite Katz's ruthless reputation, Dick has always respected the man. He's a giant in pharmaceuticals, and his steadfast leadership of Pentco over the past two decades has catapulted Pentco to the front of the pack in a crowded field of competitors and has resulted in vaccines, medications, and cures for billions.

"Doctor, like the great country we live in, I, too, do not negotiate with terrorists."

Dick cocks his head, nods, and replies, "Okay, my misunderstanding." He stands.

He played this exact scenario through in his head, along

with a dozen others, and he is proud of his forethought, especially when he sees the small twitch in Katz's right cheek. Dick turns and starts for the door. The theatrics seem a bit ridiculous, but if it's a show Katz wants, Dick's willing to play along.

He's halfway to the door when Katz says, "What is it you want?"

Dick gives a silent cheer, then straightens his face before turning. He returns to his seat, clasps his hands on the table in front of him, and eyes solely on Katz, says, "I want out. Pentco wants Freeway but only the medicine that suppresses allergies, that's fine. I don't like it. I think it's greedy and wrong, but I accept it's not my decision to make. Compound two will help millions. I want you to produce Freeway, and I want it to be successful."

Katz's icy glare holds Dick's a full second before he nods for Dick to continue.

"But in exchange, I want you to release me from my contract with Pentco, specifically the clause that prohibits me from pursuing competitive study with another company. And I want ownership of compound four. And in exchange for the royalties I would have received for Freeway, I want a one-time payment of two million dollars."

"That's ludicrous!" the man to Katz's right exclaims, a ferret in a slick suit who Dick believes is Katz's lawyer. Beside him, Joanne glares. Two others shake their heads, and the man on Katz's left leans in aggressively.

Katz holds up his hand. "Why would we do that?"

"Because otherwise you get nothing."

"But neither do you. You won't get a dime, and your precious project will never see the light of day."

Dick doesn't have to act, the anguish he feels as real as his plea. "Mr. Katz, we both want the same thing. You want Freeway to be produced and to succeed, and so do I. We both know the numbers. This is a windfall. It's foreseeable that this drug will replace Singulair and catapult Pentco to number one in anti-allergens. Two million isn't even one year's royalties."

"It's not the money that concerns me," Katz says.

"You don't want compound four."

"But I certainly don't want someone else to have it."

"Four might not even be viable," Dick says. "It has at least two years of development left, and it's not a sure thing. We both know showing promise is a long way from a solution. Even if I do figure it out, by the time I do, Pentco will have cornered the market with Freeway."

For a long moment, Katz studies him. No one else moves. The air conditioning clicks on. A bird flies past the window.

Finally, Katz folds his long fingers together on the table, and his voice barely above a hiss, he says, "Freeway is Pentco's, and so is compound four. You have twenty-four hours to hand over the formulas, or we will pursue legal action."

The man on the right nods, and Joanne squints maliciously. Dick pays them no mind. His nose pinched against his emotions, he lifts his eyes to Katz's. "Mr. Katz, I'm sure you are a good businessman and an excellent poker player, but you've just made a mistake."

Katz silver brows arch.

"You cannot win against a man with nothing to lose."

Dick feels their eyes following as he leaves Pentco for the very last time.

60

From outside the Subway where Dick had lunch, he tries Zack's number again. This time a young man answers, and Dick's heart jumps. He hadn't realized how much he was hoping Zack would be home.

"Zack Kuchinskis?"

"Yeah."

"I'm a reporter with *Orange Coast Magazine*," Dick says, "and I'm doing a story on local hotshot surfers."

"I'm not one." The kid laughs at his own joke. There's a croak in Zack's voice, which makes Dick think he's thirteen or fourteen.

"A couple of kids at the pier told me about a guy named Ray Hamilton. They said he was a good guy who sometimes gives local kids surf lessons for free, and they mentioned your name."

Silence.

"Zack?"

"Yeah?"

"Is it true? Did Ray teach you to surf?"

"They weren't free," Zack says. "I traded."

"Traded what?"

"What difference does it make? They weren't free. Okay? Ray's a jerk. I'm sure there are better guys to write about."

Dick's throat tightens. "You don't like Ray?"

"No. The guy's a loser."

"Did he do something to you?"

"No." The response is quick.

"Zack, there's another boy who's supposed to trade Ray for lessons this week."

"Good for him."

The phone goes dead before Dick can ask anything else.

The guy's a loser, what does that mean? That was not the conversation Dick was hoping for. Wednesday is two days away, and he still isn't sure about Hamilton.

———

The day's a bust. This morning, Dick's hopes for Freeway ended with a thud, and this afternoon, his conversation with Zack only made matters worse. He rubs his neck as he stumbles up the stairs to his apartment, intent on drowning his misery in beer and baseball.

He goes to put his key in the lock to find the door ajar. He steps back as a lump forms in his throat. Not once, ever, has Dick forgotten to close and lock his door.

He looks around. The complex is mostly quiet. Someone a few doors down is watching television with their window open, and a gardener trims a hedge near the street. He looks again at the door then, after another long moment, pushes it open.

His vision goes red with anger. It's just like they show in the movies when someone's place gets tossed, except Dick has less stuff, so there's less of a mess. The card table and chairs are flipped over. The drawers in the kitchen are emptied on the floor. The cushion and pillows of his couch have been slit open and the stuffing removed. He walks to the bedroom and bathroom, then back to the living room, glances at the switch plate beside the door, and almost musters a smile.

Grabbing Lucille from the coat closet, he leaves, unsure where he's going but knowing he can't stay in the apartment.

He's a block away when he spots the tail, mostly because they're making themselves known. A shiny black Suburban with dark windows rides his bumper. They stay with him as he drives aimlessly, the entire thing so cliché he would laugh if he wasn't scared out of his mind.

For a nanosecond, he considers trying to outrun them, and then does laugh—him, everyday schmo, gunning his twenty-year-old Volvo station wagon in an attempt to shake professional hired guns in their souped-up commando SUV.

So instead, for an hour, Dick meanders through the streets of Irvine considering what to do, his tail attached.

When he spots a diner, he pulls into the parking lot and parks beside a marquee advertising breakfast twenty-four hours a day. Before stepping from the car, he pockets the second webcam.

It's not yet four in the afternoon, but Dick is exhausted, and as he shuffles toward the entrance, he thinks what he'd really like is to fly off to a secluded beach somewhere, far from Hamilton and Ingall and Frankie and red rose bushes and ominous-black vehicles with apartment-ransacking men in them, and take a long, dreamless nap.

He's reaching for the door when he reconsiders.

Returning to the Volvo, he opens all the locks along with the trunk, grabs Lucille, and with a nod and shrug to the two men watching, returns to the diner.

While eating a bowl of minestrone soup, Dick watches the man who was in the driver's seat of the Suburban go through his car. The man is the size of an NFL linebacker, and the Volvo lilts with the man's weight as he rummages around inside.

Dick looks away from the destruction, irrationally having feelings for the car. They've been together a long time, and it pains him to have her torn apart.

"Would you like anything else?" the server asks.

"Refill his coffee, and I'll have a cup as well."

Dick looks up to see a man of average build with stick-straight, military-short brown hair. He wears a suit, and Dick names him 001 in his head—James Bond wannabe.

The man sits down.

Lucille is against the window, and Dick's cellphone is on the table.

The man glances at Lucille, then lifts Dick's phone, powers it down, and sets it back where it was.

"Dr. Raynes, I've been asked to retrieve something from you that belongs to my client."

"Your client and I discussed that this morning," Dick says, "and unfortunately, we were not able to come to terms." His voice wavers, and the man's mouth twitches with a smile.

"It doesn't belong to you."

"Well, it certainly doesn't belong to him," Dick says. "You can't own the intelligence of another man. You can only treat them right and hope they share it with you. This morning, I made a fair offer, and Mr. Katz turned it down. If he doesn't like it, he can sue me."

001 appraises Dick. "Mr. Katz would rather not involve the law."

"Of course he wouldn't. He's not an idiot, and neither am I. We both know how damaging this story would be to Pentco and to him if it got out. I can see the Anderson Cooper inter-view now, wondering why his company would want to withhold a drug that could cure millions."

001's eyes are steady on Dick's. "Are you threatening us?"

"Are you threatening me?" Dick shoots back as he glances at the linebacker, who is now leaning against the Suburban.

"I'm here to convince you to return the formulas."

"And if I don't?"

"It's in your best interest to cooperate." The man's eyes glint.

"Otherwise, you'll hurt me?"

"Let's hope it doesn't come to that."

"And if I go public with the story?"

"I'm not going to let you do that."

"You'll stop me?"

"Yes, I will stop you."

"Mr. Katz would go that far?"

"Doctor, let me make this clear. Mr. Katz is not going to negotiate. He is not going to allow you to sell his drug to a competitor. The only thing Mr. Katz is willing to do is let you walk away if you return the formulas. Do you understand?"

"Perfectly," Dick says.

Dick looks again at the window and waits for the man's eyes to follow. When, finally, they do, he turns back to see the man's face gone dark.

"Where's that going?" he says with a nod toward the webcam on the windowsill, its small round body concealed behind Lucille and its lens pointed at 001.

"A friend."

It's actually being sent to Dick's cellphone.

The man doesn't flinch, but his right dimple tightens. "Goodnight, Doctor."

001 walks from the diner, and he and the linebacker climb into the Suburban and drive away. Dick's hands shake as he emails the video to Greg Larson at the hatchery. The carefully composed message reads:

Hi Greg, I ran into a bit of trouble at work. Please hang onto this video in case something happens. If it does, send it to Agent Steve Patterson at the FBI. He's one of the good guys. Best if you don't tell Dee. Thanks. Dick

He laughs at the irony of Steve Patterson being his avenging angel in the event of his death. The server refills his coffee, and he sips it slowly, his nerves jacked up high. For all the bluster he showed 001, he is scared out of his mind.

An hour later, he climbs back in the Volvo. "Sorry, old girl," he says, surveying the damage.

The door panels have been pried off and the seats slashed, but she's still drivable.

His phone buzzes, and he sees an email notification. He opens his inbox to see the response from Greg Larson:

Trouble seems to follow you, or do you seek out trouble? Do you need me to send help your way?

Dick glances in his rearview mirror. Nothing but night.

Thanks, but for now things are fine. Just a precaution. Thanks.

Katz is a scientist and a businessman, his mind rational like Dick's. He beat his chest, hoping Dick would flinch, but instead, Dick raised the ante. Fairly certain Katz isn't going to kill him—at least tonight—he returns to his apartment, and with Lucille at his side, lies down to rest.

———

Ringing wakes him, and remembering his peril, he bolts upright as his eyes scan wildly. It's still dark, and he squints at the clock on his nightstand to see it's five forty-seven.

"Hello," he says, heart racing.

"You win, Doctor." Katz's says, his icy smooth voice unmistakable. "Give us the files, and we'll agree to your terms."

Dick looks at his ransacked apartment and considers the night before. "The price has gone up. I, too, don't like to be terrorized."

Silence for a long moment. "What do you want?" Katz says finally, the silky smoothness slipping.

"Three million."

"Fine," Katz says, almost sounding relieved. "Drop off the files, and my attorney will draw up the papers."

"No," Dick says.

"Doctor, my patience is wearing thin."

"You hold all the cards, and I don't like the way you play. Draw up the papers, wire the money to the account I specify, and when I'm satisfied you've met your end of the bargain, I'll give you the files."

"What assurance do I have that you won't just take off?"

"Because, Mr. Katz, I know who you are, and I don't underestimate you."

"You shouldn't."

61

Denise and Jesse have only been gone two days, but the hollowness of Steve's life returned the moment the plane lifted off the tarmac. The decision that followed took only one minute more.

"Gelson," Steve says, walking into Mitch Gelson's office, "I've decided to put in for a transfer."

Gelson looks up from his desk and leans back. He folds his hand on his lap, and a rat's smile spreads across his face. This is probably the best news Gelson's gotten since his promotion. Though Steve stepped down as assistant director three years ago, his previous rank and reputation garner far more respect than Gelson will ever get, which is a constant thorn in his side.

"You know," Gelson says, the smug look still in place, "your position is not transferable."

"I understand that. I've decided to return to being a field agent."

"Field agent?" Gelson scoffs. "Assistant director to special investigator to field agent. You do realize you're going the wrong direction?"

Steve ignores the jab. "I'd like to be involved in finding my replacement."

"That won't be necessary."

"I know it's not necessary," Steve says, straining for patience. "But I created the position, and I know what it takes, so I'd like to find my successor."

The rat's smile twitches. "It won't be necessary because, once you're gone, I see no reason to continue it. The position was only created as a sympathy bone thrown to you because of your son."

"A bone?" Steve hisses, hating the emotion that's crept into his voice. "You know how many cases I handle and the amount of work there is. Who the hell's going to take care of it?"

"It will get taken care of the way it did before."

"It didn't get taken care of before. That's why the position was necessary."

"Steve, this is your own personal crusade, no one else's."

"It's the crusade of the law . . . of the constitution."

Gelson shrugs. "I guess that's the way it goes. When you leave, so do the rights of the bottom-feeders you've made it your mission to save."

"And damn the Fifth Amendment?" Steve says.

"Damn your holier-than-thou attitude toward saving the scourge," Gelson spits.

Steve's hands ball as blood rises to his face, and his first thought is to reach across the desk and smack the smarmy grin from Gelson's face with his fist. In his younger days, he would have. But older and wiser, instead, he wheels away, angry for allowing the worm to get to him.

He returns to his desk, which is littered with dozens of new cases unattended to because of the time he spent with Denise and Jesse. Before setting to work, he searches the Orange County papers and blotter to check on Dick. It's been nearly a month since their beer, and though there's been no sign that he's up to his old tricks, Steve is certain it's only a matter of time.

His search turns up nothing. The weather in Irvine is sunny and beautiful. Ramirez is still missing. Two more recently released sex offenders have settled in Orange County.

Feeling cantankerous, he decides to send Dick a text:

> I just spent a lovely week with
> Denise and Jesse. You are lucky
> they live so close and that you
> have the freedom to see them
> whenever you please.

He smiles as he presses send, then returns to his work.

At eight, he calls it quits, grabs a bite at his favorite Italian restaurant, and returns to his apartment.

Three large boxes block the door. He checks the Pottery Barn labels, certain there must be a mistake. The addresses are correct, so he pulls out one of the packing slips. Next to "Gift Sender's Name" is: "Denise Raynes."

Steve carries the boxes into his living room and, like a kid at Christmas, tears into them, embarrassed by his eagerness. The first contains new bedding, a soft duvet in blue with matching pillowcases and a set of crisp white sheets. There's even a dust ruffle, which Steve needs to look at the photo to know what that is. The second box contains towels and a bathmat. And the last is filled with a rust chenille throw and four pillows for his couch.

The gift message reads, "I love you too much to see you living in such sorrow."

Steve, still sitting on the floor, leans back against the couch and hugs one of the pillows to his chest. He buries his nose in its softness and breathes in its warmth. He can't remember the last time he cried. It wasn't when Danny died. He often wonders about that. The unforgettable saline taste touches his lips, and he's certain it hasn't been since he was a boy.

62

Dick deletes Steve's text then goes for his run. *Freedom.* The word Steve intentionally used pulses with his steps, and he thinks of the great irony that, somehow, he has ended up on the wrong side of the law when one of the things he has always been criticized for is his intransigence when it comes to bending rules or doing what's right.

He gets back to the apartment, showers, then faces the mess. His couch and bed are unsalvageable, so he calls a hauling company for a pickup. The rest he is able to put back in order in under an hour, the sum of his belongings so little that he's almost embarrassed by what 001 and the linebacker must have thought as they ransacked the place.

Dick sets the last chair in place and leaves the apartment to head back to Huntington Beach. It's Tuesday, his last day to figure out if Frankie is in danger. His plan is to scope out the nearest middle school in the hope of spotting Frankie or one of his friends. It's a long shot, but other than trying to find Frankie and warn him, he is entirely out of ideas.

He's almost to the car when his phone rings. It's Katz's secretary calling to let him know the papers are ready and that they need to be signed today. He hangs up, stunned how quickly they managed it, then realizes Katz planned for this. His lawyers probably started drafting the agreement the moment Dick left the meeting yesterday morning in case the formulas weren't found. All they needed to do this morning was change the value from two million to three million.

He stands for a moment looking at the phone, a tightening in his chest that takes a second to recognize as the long-ago feeling of pride. He did it. Freeway has been saved, and compound four is his.

He calls Greg Larson.

"Score one for the little guy," Greg says when Dick tells him the story.

"Don't break out the champagne just yet. I need a lawyer to make sure the deal's on the up-and-up."

"Jeb Cobb in Fresno," Greg says without hesitation. "Most honest, ball-busting lawyer you'll find."

The name alone makes Dick like the man.

As he climbs into his car, he thinks of Frankie but pushes the thought away. He will deal with Hamilton tomorrow. Today, he has a lawyer to see.

————

Jeb Cobb is a thick, squat man with no hair on his head, a copper walrus mustache, and a bone-crushing handshake. His office is pine-paneled with an enormous, mounted large-mouth bass on one wall and a pair of bull horns on the other.

"Ready to have some fun," he says, the words slightly muffled by the mustache.

Dick feels a rush to his bloodstream. The words might have been different, but to Dick they sounded like, "Giddy up. Let's ride."

Jeb frowns as he reads the agreement, scratches notes in the margins and draws lines through entire paragraphs. Ten minutes later, he picks up the phone on his desk and dials the number at the top of the letterhead.

His voice never gets loud, yet his argument thunders as he talks to Katz's attorney, and Dick knows Greg Larson was right to recommend him. Jeb goes through the contract line by line, and though he can't hear the attorney on the other end, Dick can tell he's getting frustrated by how much more he talks than Jeb.

Finally, Jeb says, "Fine. If that's how you feel. We understand." He hangs up, lifts his head, and smiles.

"What happened?"

"They disagreed with everything I said."

"So what does that mean?"

"It means we need to wait for them to finish having their tantrum." He glances at the clock on the wall. It's almost five. "Drink?" he asks.

"Sure," Dick says, the place and the man making him want to sip whisky, polish his gun, and shine his spurs.

Jeb pulls a bottle and a couple glasses from his desk.

As they drink, they talk about Fresno and Independence and Greg Larson and their families. They're halfway through their second bourbon when the secretary pokes her head in to say Mr. Nelson, Katz's attorney, is on the line.

"Here we go," Jeb says, straightening in his chair.

Dick's pulse ticks up a notch.

Jeb rolls out his neck, then picks up the phone. He grunts a few times, says he understands, then, "I'm glad we were able to come to an understanding. I'll have my secretary draw it up." He hangs up. "Lorraine!" he hollers.

The receptionist bounds in.

"Type this up." He hands her the bowdlerized contract, which looks like it has hardly any original text left. He turns to Dick and toasts him, "You're about to become a very wealthy man."

―――

The entire drive back to Irvine all Dick can think about is Frankie; tomorrow is Wednesday, the day Ray Hamilton is supposed to give him a lesson.

63

It's Thursday, just before noon, and Dick is back at Pentco.

"Mr. Katz," Dick says, walking into the CEO's office.

Katz sits behind a polished walnut desk, nothing on it, not a picture or a piece of paper. Behind him the Santa Ana Mountains rise majestic in the distance, their peaks encased in a shroud of clouds. Dick sets the thumb drive on the desk.

"This is everything," he says, a lump in his throat, his life's work. He hopes they do well by it and that it goes on to be the amazing medicine he dreamed it would be.

Katz gives the slightest nod, and Dick turns to leave.

"Doctor?"

Dick turns back. He's weary, so tired his bones ache. Katz's eyes hold his, studying him as if trying to figure something out.

"You could have made twenty times what you're walking away with," he says finally.

Dick shrugs, and Katz almost smiles, recognizing something in Dick like he's looking in a funhouse mirror and has just realized the distorted reflection is him by one unmistakable characteristic that links them.

"I've never been good at compromise," Dick says, offering the answer.

When Katz stands and circles the oversized desk, Dick tenses, wondering if this is the point where a team of agents or mercenaries charge in and seize him. The man extends his hand, and shaking the dry, strong palm is one of the greatest compliments of Dick's life.

64

Steve knew. He read the obituary, saw the location of the death, and knew. Ray Hamilton was a forty-two-year-old surfer with no history of heart disease but with a long history of sexual crimes against young boys. He was number eight on Steve's list of potential targets Dick might be following.

Hamilton died yesterday, and his funeral is Sunday.

Steve buys a ticket to Orange County, then calls the Huntington Beach Police Department and asks the police captain to send him a copy of the medical examiner's report and to seal off the scene of Hamilton's death until he can get there to investigate. Similar to Sheriff Barton, the captain balks at Steve sticking his nose into an open-and-shut case of a death by natural causes of a double ex-con he's probably grateful to be rid of.

He tells him to do it anyway.

He hangs up, his nerves are buzzing, the moment he's been waiting for and dreading arrived.

65

Steve is standing in front of a round bunker-type building that houses Hamilton's surfboard business, the place where he was found dead two days ago. The owner of the industrial park, a middle-aged man with a gray ponytail and tinted glasses is with him. According to the ME report, Hamilton died of a heart attack. The only anomaly was a comment about unusual swelling around Hamilton's lips.

"You think somebody might have killed him?" the building owner asks.

"I'm just looking into his death."

"Well, I think you're barking up the wrong tree. Ray didn't have enemies, a lover, not a fighter"—he chuckles and winks—"if you know what I mean."

"Thank you. I'll let you know when I'm finished."

The man leaves, and Steve steps inside the shop. Half a dozen surfboard blanks lean against a wall, and in the back are three finished boards, each like a piece of art, immaculately shaped and polished to a deep luster. The rails and backs are orange, and the fronts are white and emblazoned with an airbrushed RH logo and the words "Ray Hamilton Classic."

A half-finished board rests on sawhorses in the middle of the space, and on the floor is an airbrush and a spill of orange paint. A respirator mask with orange paint splattered on its lens sits on top of the unfinished board.

Steve bags the mask and leaves.

———

He drives to Hamilton's condo, and the property manager lets him in. The home is a mess. Soda cans, beer bottles, and food rubbish litter the living room. The kitchen looks unused. The stove has dust on it, and the fridge is empty except for half a jar of pickles well past its expiration date and a bottle of hot sauce.

He continues to the bedroom and pinches his nose against the strong odor of unwashed sheets and clothes. Though there's a dresser, it looks like every piece of clothing Hamilton owned is on the floor. Sprinkled among the clothes beside the bed are condom wrappers.

"A lover, not a fighter," Steve mutters out loud.

Hamilton was definitely getting lucky. He looks closer at the sheets. They're soiled to the point of disgusting, but he doesn't see any blood.

Movement in the front room causes Steve to turn, and he looks through the bedroom door to see a kid in his late teens with sandy, curly hair shuffling through some trash on the coffee table.

The kid sees Steve and startles.

"Looking for Ray?" Steve asks, knowing he's not but hoping to put the kid at ease.

"Ray's dead."

"I know. I just didn't know if you knew."

"I know." The kid's Adam's apple bobs as he fights back his emotions.

"Are you looking for something?" Steve asks with a glance at the coffee table.

"Who are you?"

Steve shows his identification.

"Oh."

"You don't seem surprised?"

"Ray told me his story, about how messed up he used to be."

"Bother you?"

"No. He wasn't like that anymore. Some bad stuff happened in prison that changed him."

Steve feels his own Adam's apple get stuck, thoughts of Danny momentarily blinding him.

"You two were close?" he asks.

The kid nods, shrugs, then slides his jaw forward to catch his feelings again.

"He was kind of old for you," Steve says.

"Age is irrelevant."

"He tell you that?"

"It wasn't like that." The kid looks down, and Steve feels genuine love and grief, emotion that can't be faked. "I came onto him. I knew I was gay before I met Ray, and he was the greatest guy I ever met. He never forced me into anything."

"How long were you together?"

"Since last summer."

"Was he seeing anyone else? Any other kids?"

His eyes snap up. "I told you. It wasn't like that. I'm almost eighteen."

"Okay," Steve says, backing off. "Why are you here?"

"I left some of my stuff here."

Steve follows his eye slide. Barely visible beneath the mess, under an old issue of *Surf Magazine*, the corner of a baggie sticks out. Steve hands the kid the weed.

"Thanks," he says. He starts for the door but, halfway there, reconsiders. Turning back, he asks, "Why are you here?"

"It's my job to make sure guys like Ray get a fair shake. Seemed kind of young for a heart attack."

The kid furrows his brow, considering it, then shakes his head. "No way. Everyone loved Ray."

66

The sky is mostly shadow with glints of sunlight breaking through to shine a moment before being swallowed up again by the clouds. Hundreds, maybe even a thousand mourners stand barefoot on the beach. Dick is out of place in his dark suit, navy tie, and dress shoes among the throng in their board shorts and T-shirts. Hamilton's sports agent from his competition days organized the ceremony, and the only religion among the attendees seems to be a shared reverence for the ocean and surfing.

A blue egg crate turned upside down in the sand with a microphone in front of it serves as the pulpit, and dozens step up to speak, each sharing funny, touching anecdotes that cause equal bursts of tears and laughter. Like those around him, Dick is moved by the stories and is sad things turned out the way they did. He's not sure why he is here. All he knows is, when he woke this morning, he felt compelled to be a part of it. Memorials are about the living, an opportunity to recognize the person who was lost and to draw strength from being around others who share your grief. It's about community, healing, and closure. Which he supposes explains it. He is hurting and hopes this might help.

Jason Skolnick, the kid Hamilton was having a relationship with, is the last one to speak. He hasn't shaved, and small
tufts of sandy brown fuzz pepper his face. He wears blue swim
trunks and a T-shirt emblazoned with the RH logo. His shoulders slumped and his tenor voice soft, he says, "I loved Ray."
The crowd murmurs in agreement. "He was my teacher and my
friend. Through him, I learned to embrace life and, more im-
portantly, learned to embrace myself. Ray used to say all of us
are like the waves, each of us unique in our power and design,
each of us irreplaceable, and each of us existing only for a brief
moment before returning to the sea. Ray Hamilton will forever be remembered as a great surfer, a great craftsman, a great
person, and a great friend. I will do my best to live by his example and to follow in his path." He places his fist on his heart
then lifts it to the sky. "Mahalo, brother."

The audience responds in a unified salute to the sky,
"Mahalo."

Dick punches the air with them.

There's a moment of silence, the rhythm of the ocean providing an appropriate accompaniment to the prayer.

When the moment is done, hundreds grab the surfboards
that stood sentry around the ceremony and run into the sea.
They paddle beyond the break, then turn toward the shore and
sit ready. A rolling set crests the horizon, and flank by flank, the
mourners ride to the beach, and each emerges from the water,
glistening in the shards of sunlight. When they reach the sand,
they turn to face the ocean until all of them are looking at the
lone surfer who remains.

The man bobs on the water, silhouetted by the glowing
silver horizon, and the mourners watch as a swell rolls toward
him and as, with two powerful strokes, he joins its force then
pops gracefully to his feet. From a sack slung across his body, he

pulls out a silver urn, and the crowd bows their heads as Hamilton's ashes blow out to sea.

It isn't until the ceremony ends and the crowd disperses that Dick sees him. Steve stands on the boardwalk looking back, his large frame relaxed and his hands at his sides. He wears khaki shorts and a Hawaiian shirt, and it bothers Dick that Steve knew how to dress.

"Hey, Mr. Reporter."

Dick turns to see Matt with Frankie and the skinny boy.

Dick glances back to the boardwalk, but Steve is gone.

"Are you still going to write your story?" Matt asks.

"I don't think so." Dick looks at Frankie. His eyes are the same color as Jesse's, dark like espresso, and he stands with his ankles crossed, the same way Jim often stands, and Dick feels a loosening in his chest. Turning back at Matt, he says, "You boys take care."

67

"You made a mistake," Steve says as Dick walks into the bar.

Dick nods in greeting and takes the barstool beside him. Henry-N-Harry's is quiet, he and Dick the only ones in the place beside the bartender. Country music mingles with the whoosh of the air conditioning.

His text to Dick was simple:

I need a beer.

"Good to see you too," Dick says.

Dick still wears his suit from the funeral. He stood out like the oddball he was among the surfers, holding his shoes, the cuffs of his trousers rolled up. Steve hadn't expected him to be there. It's a fallacy that criminals frequently return to the scene of the crime. Most perpetrators steer clear of anything that might implicate them. But there he was among the mourners—bowing his head, punching the air, and looking genuinely moved by the service.

"Nice suit," Steve says, unable to help himself.

Dick almost smiles but doesn't quite manage it. His eyes

are bruised with exhaustion, and his shoulders slumped. He flags down the bartender and orders the same beer as last time, Hoppy Ending.

"How'd you do it?" Steve asks.

Dick ignores him. Patiently he waits for his beer, and when it arrives, he says, "It was a nice ceremony."

"Yeah. It sounds like you murdered a great guy."

"He died of a heart attack."

Steve shakes his head and feels his blood grow warm. "You screwed up," he says.

Dick's head bobs in agreement.

"You know you screwed up?"

Dick's expression tightens, and his shoulders slump a little more, as if gravity is getting heavier and he's having a tough time staying upright.

"Actually, I don't know one way or the other," he says finally.

"Hamilton was flying straight."

"I know you want to believe that. So did I."

"But you killed him anyway."

Dick winces, and Steve feels a frisson of satisfaction knowing he landed a jab.

"Steve, how old are you?" Dick asks.

"Forty-nine."

"And in the last thirty years, since you became an adult, how many times have you had sex with a kid?"

Steve narrows his gaze, and Dick looks at him, unfazed, as if actually waiting for an answer.

"Hamilton had changed," Steve says.

"You desperately want to believe that. And like I said, so did I. But neither of us really knows, and a choice needed to be made. There was a boy, a kid, somewhere around the age of thirteen, who I believed was in danger."

Steve tries not to react but knows he did by the look on Dick's face. He thinks of Diego Ramirez. He thinks of Ally. Dick nods as if knowing his thoughts or suspecting them.

"What thirteen-year-old kid?" he says.

Dick's drops his gaze back to his beer. "Just a kid. And I tried to be sure, and I tried to figure out how to stop it or warn him, but I couldn't. And time ran out, and there was no way of knowing for certain." He stops and blows out a hard quavering breath. "And so you might be right. I might have been wrong, and I might have screwed up. But the combination of Ray Hamilton's history, along with the statistics, along with his actions were too compelling to ignore, so what it came down to was what I could live with. I don't like that Hamilton had to die, but I can live with it knowing the evil he'd already done in his life. But had I not done anything, and that boy got hurt, that would have haunted me forever."

"You're rationalizing murder," Steve says, though Ally continues to pulse unwanted behind the words.

"Maybe," Dick says. "I guess we'll never know."

"So, from here on out, this is how it's going to be? Damn the rules of evidence altogether, you're simply going to justify your actions whether you're certain of a man's guilt or not?"

Dick nods, infuriatingly agreeing with everything Steve is saying.

"You're not going to stop?" Steve clarifies.

"No. I'll stop."

"You will?"

"There won't be a choice. Eventually, my luck is going to run out. Either you'll figure out a way to arrest me; or I'll screw up, and somebody else will arrest me; or I'm going to get myself killed."

Steve stares at him. The guy is unbelievable. In his experience, murderers fall into two categories—those with motive and those who are crazy. Steve believed Dick was squarely the first but is now beginning to wonder if he's not equal parts of both.

"So what you're saying is, until you get yourself arrested or killed, you're going to keep at it?"

Dick shrugs in resignation as if there's no choice in the matter. Which is ludicrous. Of course there's a choice.

Steve tries a different approach. "Dick, think about the risk you're taking. Think about Kiley and Jim."

Dick stares into his beer. "I am thinking about them. It's all I think about."

Steve runs his hand through his hair. "This is insane. There are thousands, tens of thousands, maybe even hundreds of thousands of released sex offenders in the world. You're not going to stop them all. You're not even going to stop a fraction. So in the end, you're risking everything for what? You're not even making a difference."

Dick almost smiles as if he finds the statement is amusing. "Have you ever heard 'The Starfish Story'?"

Steve shakes his head as Dick pushes to his feet. He lays a ten on the bar. "Ask Dee to tell it to you sometime. It's always been one of her favorites."

He starts for the door.

"I'm going to stop you," Steve says to his back.

Dick doesn't turn, but he stops, and his shoulders still stooped with the weight of what he's done, he says, "I believe you. You're very good at your job. I was impressed to see you at the service this morning."

The next words catch in Steve's throat. "When I do, will I lose her?"

"I hope not," Dick says, "but I don't know."

68

Denise is so happy to see him she won't take her arms from his neck. Steve has to carry her to the steps still attached. Awkwardly, he sits with his bundle, and she kisses him full, then nuzzles into his neck. He inhales her fresh lemon scent and wishes his visit were as simple and clean, that he could simply fall into her kisses, carry her to the bedroom with her jasmine sheets, and make love to her until morning, ignoring and forgetting the real reason he's here.

"Denise, we need to talk," he says.

"Uh-oh," she says. "You know those are the four most dreaded words in any relationship." She tilts her head curiously but continues to smile, until she realizes he's serious. Untangling herself, she slides off his lap. The night is warm, the moon full. The bats serenade them, and the desert breeze carries the sweetness of last night's rain.

"It's about your brother."

"Dickie?"

Steve folds his hands, unfolds them, rubs them on his pants to wipe away the sweat. The entire drive from Irvine to Independence he thought about what he wanted to say, and after four hours, with no great epiphany, he's decided to simply tell her the truth.

"I know Dick killed Otis," he says.

Her eyes flick a millimeter left then right, but she says nothing, the lack of reaction combined with the universal tell of deceit confirming this was not a revelation.

"And since then," he goes on, "he's been stalking other released pedophiles."

Her brow furrows, and her mouth skews to the side.

"And five days ago, he killed one of them. Which is the reason I'm here in California."

She blinks then shakes her head. "What are you talking about?"

He tries to take her hand, but she pulls it away.

Steve blows out a hard breath. "I didn't see what good would come from pursuing Otis's death, and I knew Dick did it to protect you and Jesse, so I let it go."

He watches as her eyes flick again and then as she swallows.

"I figured that was the end of it. But it wasn't. Somehow, your brother has got it in his head that it's up to him to stop other guys like Otis."

She looks at him in confusion. "Dickie's a scientist."

"And a vigilante."

Her mouth tightens into a firm line, and her head shakes more forcefully, a strand of gold hair catching on her chin.

"Denise—"

"No!" she says.

"They ruled it a heart attack, but—"

"No!" she says again and stands.

"Please, Denise, hear me out—"

"I've heard enough. I get that you're grieving, and I feel bad for what happened to Danny, but not every guy who gets out of prison and then dies was murdered."

"This isn't about that—"

"I told you how I feel about whoever killed Otis. Whoever did that is my hero, and if you think it was Dickie, you should be thanking him. Because, had he not stepped in, I wouldn't be here, and you would have never met me, and we never would have . . ." The words trail off, and losing the battle with her emotions, her chin drops and tears leak from her eyes.

Steve stands and steps toward her, but she backs away.

"I'm sorry you lost your son." She sniffles to rein in her emotions, then lifts her face back to his. "But Otis wasn't Danny, and Dickie wasn't the one who killed him."

She walks into the house, and Steve watches helpless as the door to the future he dreamed of closes with a slam.

69

Dick needs to get away. Since Hamilton's death, he hasn't been able to stop thinking about it. He was honest with Steve. He made the choice he could live with, but that doesn't lessen his guilt.

Wednesday morning, he did everything in his power to find Frankie so he could warn him not to go to Hamilton's. He called every school in Huntington Beach. None would acknowledge whether or not Frankie was a student. He tried calling Zack again but got no answer.

He was parked outside Hamilton's shop, watching him work, stressed and unsure what to do as time ticked down. He had no idea if Frankie's parents were dropping him off or if he was walking to the condo or which direction he would be coming from. And once Frankie was inside, it would be too late.

At one o'clock, after nearly three hours of racking his brain, Hamilton knocked off for lunch. He pulled off the respirator mask, shook the foam from his clothes, and walked toward the sandwich shop on the corner.

As he walked, he whistled, and Dick wonders if that jaunty little tune was what ultimately tipped the scales, Hamilton in an especially good mood.

As soon as the door to the sandwich shop closed, Dick pulled on a pair of gloves and hurried into the bunker. He injected the foam rim of the mask with Cameron's Cocktail and hurried back to his car. As he carefully wiped the syringe, repacked the vial, and pulled off the gloves, he prayed the amount he used would only knock Hamilton out or possibly make him sick, buying Dick more time. The exact potency of the drug is unknown, and he also had no idea how much of the drug would evaporate from the mask in the time it took for Hamilton to finish his lunch.

The drug was originally developed as an anesthesia for horses. Its beauty was that it worked quicker than other large mammal anesthetics, thereby eliminating the stress horses suffered from fighting the effects of being induced into unconsciousness against their strong wills. FDA testing on drugs for animals is not as stringent as it is for people, and the drug, called Equine Z, had been on the market over a month before the first tragedy struck. Though at the time, no one associated the death of Cameron's lab assistant with the drug. The massive heart attack she suffered was believed to be from natural causes. It was almost two years after her death before the connection was made.

A private detective hired by the family of a woman who also died of a heart attack was the one to figure it out. The family believed the woman's husband had a hand in her death. The woman had been soaking her nails in preparation for a manicure when she died. The suspected husband was a veterinarian at a racing stable. The detective tested the drugs the husband had access to and hit pay dirt when he put a drop of Equine Z on a mouse, and within seconds, the mouse dropped dead.

Pentco assigned Dick the task of figuring out why Equine Z was lethal and how it made it to market without anyone realizing it. What Dick discovered was that the very thing that made Equine Z so effective also made it deadly. The reason the drug worked so well was its exceptionally thin viscosity, which allowed it to be absorbed quickly into a horse's bloodstream. Because of its almost vaporous liquidity, the drug evaporated very quickly when exposed to air, requiring it to be produced, stored, and administered in hermetically sealed vials. Which was the reason Cameron and the other scientists who worked on the drug never realized it was permeable to skin, making it alarmingly deadly to humans. An average horse heart weighs nine pounds, a human's only ten ounces. A few drops of Equine Z would stop any human heart cold.

A week after the discovery, Cameron resigned. Four deaths, including that of his beloved assistant, were attributed to his drug. Two weeks later, his own heart attack was reported. There was no evidence Equine Z was involved.

In an effort to put the disaster behind them, Pentco issued a recall of the drug and ordered all of it destroyed. And all of it was except the dozen vials Dick had been issued for his investigation. Dick's not sure why he kept them. Perhaps he couldn't stand the thought of destroying them. Tragic as the drug turned out to be, it was also a work of genius and Cameron's life's effort. For five years, the vials have sat in an empty Ben & Jerry's ice cream tub in his freezer. He often smiles when he sees the mint-chip carton, the same way an art collector might smile at a stunning, morbid masterpiece like Peter Paul Rubens's *Massacre of Innocents*, an exquisite revelation of the shadow side of something meant to be beautiful, whether it be religion, medicine, or people.

As Dick drove away, he passed Hamilton returning from his lunch. He carried a coffee in one hand and a donut in the other. Dick didn't think he slowed, but something made Hamilton look up. Through the open window, their eyes connected, and a flicker of recognition crossed Hamilton's face. He raised the hand with the donut in a small wave and smiled, and Dick smiled back, a moment he's relived again and again, a perpetual, exhausting reel in his mind that will not stop.

70

Dick stands in the LAX terminal, looking at the departing flights, and chooses Hawaii. Before he left for the airport, he boxed up his things. He has no idea where he will live when he gets back but knows it is time for a change. He has money now, a fact he hasn't gotten used to. Perhaps he'll buy a place, a house of his own with an extra bedroom for the kids. He misses them. Especially Kiley.

Fleetingly the remaining three Pepper files cross his mind, but the thought passes quickly. Mostly what he thinks about is sleep—dreamless, thoughtless sleep.

———

The plane sets down, and already Dick feels better. A beautiful woman drapes a purple orchid lei around his neck and wishes him "Aloha."

He drops his luggage at a resort he found on TripAdvisor that advertised peace and serenity, then heads to the beach. At the first surf shop he passes, he buys a pair of board shorts similar to what most of the mourners at Hamilton's memorial were wearing.

As he's paying, he asks the girl ringing him up, "I was wondering if you might know someone who teaches surfing."

The girl runs him over as if sizing him up for a suit and nods. "Kai would be perfect for you."

She makes a call, and half an hour later, a kid with a large smile and dark skin with indigo tribal tattoos over most of it shows up.

"D-man, nice to meet you," he says. "Ready to greet the waves?"

———

Dick learned to swim as a boy but hasn't swum much since, and he has never swum in the ocean. He's shocked by the power of it, its sheer force the most humbling thing he's ever experienced.

The salesgirl was right. Kai is the perfect instructor. Patiently and without judgment, he encourages Dick, coaxing him past his initial terror, and smiling, laughing, and reassuring him that he's doing fine, though Dick knows he's not. It takes over an hour for him to find the courage to stay on his board when a wave comes and another to convince himself to dive under one while still holding onto his board.

His heart pounds so hard the entire two hours he's in the water he's completely wiped out when Kai says, "That's it for today, D-man. Great job. You and the ocean are going to get along just fine."

Waterlogged, exhausted, and happier than Dick can remember, he staggers to the beach.

"Tomorrow, Bra," Kai says, giving him the shaka sign.

Dick gives it back. Or he thinks he does. Kai laughs, steps closer, lowers Dick's forefinger and pulls out his thumb.

"Oh," Dick says, turning it toward himself to see the difference, and another wave of pure joy washes over him.

"You're cool, man," Kai says and walks away.

Dick laughs, a playful sound that is surprising, and he realizes it's been a long time since he's felt so free.

———

Dick slept well. His night dreamless. He believes it was the ocean, the salt water a magic elixir with a lasting rhythm that lulled him unconscious and kept him that way until morning.

It's been so long since he's woken refreshed he almost doesn't recognize the feeling. He gets a warm croissant from the hotel's bistro and heads to the beach. He spent the entire previous evening reading about surfing. Dick has always found that what he lacks in athletic ability can often be compensated to some degree by understanding physics.

Kai fist-bumps him, then holds out his phone. "Check out this meme."

Dick has no idea what a meme is, but he squints at Kai's cracked iPhone and laughs at the image of a surfer flying like Superman off a humongous wave in the opposite direction of his board. The letters above and below the image read, "I MUST GO. MY PLANET NEEDS ME."

Kai tucks the phone in his backpack. "Today you surf."

He bounds toward the water, and Dick bounds after him.

"No way, man," Kai says when they reach the break with the other surfers and are sitting comfortably on their boards. "Did you practice?"

Dick feels proud. He didn't practice per se, but he did read about how the forward momentum of a surfer can propel them through even the strongest wave so long as they time the plunge correctly, piercing the water before the face of the wave reaches them and burrowing beneath it. He shrugs humbly like it's no big deal, his hands resting on his thighs like a real surfer.

Despite his studying and Kai's pronouncement that today would be the day Dick surfed, Dick doesn't manage to get to his feet. Instead, he almost drowns a few dozen times as he paddles furiously wave after wave only to get swallowed up or dumped.

"You got heart," Kai says, taking the board from Dick. "I'll give you that."

"Tomorrow?" Dick asks with more hope than expectation, thinking Kai is probably done with him.

"Tomorrow," Kai says, shaking his head and smiling. "Damn if you're not the most determined madman I've ever met." He walks away still grinning.

———

Dick stood. On a surfboard. In the ocean.

He can't stop grinning. Despite only managing it for less than a second, Kai said it counted as surfing.

Dick sits on the beach, eating a veggie wrap and beaming. Dick Raynes caught a wave and managed to get to his feet. It reminds him of the homerun he hit once. He was eleven. The feeling is the same. Only sweeter because he knows now how rare the feeling is.

He was paddling, and Kai was yelling, and suddenly he couldn't hear him anymore and he was no longer paddling, the board caught in the enormous power of the wave and Dick being carried along with it. Then in his mind, he saw Frankie and Hamilton on the beach, Hamilton demonstrating how to pop up and Frankie imitating him. And Dick did it. He braced his hands under his chest, pulled his left knee forward, and pushed himself to his feet. He was bent too far forward and tried to compensate by leaning back and flew off. But it didn't matter. All he could think about was how much he wanted to do it again.

Kai was happy as Dick, and Dick realized how hopeless Kai believed him to be. "You need me again tomorrow?" he asks.

"I don't think so," Dick said. "I think I just need to practice."

Kai gave him the shaka sign, and Dick very carefully made sure he had the correct fingering before giving it back.

"Stay cool," Kai said.

Dick laughed. "I'll try."

He sets the wrap aside and flops on his back on his towel, the heat of the sand soaking into his skin and the sun bleaching his lids, nothing in his mind but the glorious moment and the incredible feeling of being alive. He's decided surfing really is the Holy Grail, the intensity of each moment and the magnificence of the ocean allowing no thoughts beyond those of catching the next wave and trying not to drown. It's incredibly freeing, like a mental vacation from the burdens of life.

When his skin begins to fry, he sits up and pulls on his T-shirt. The wind has shifted and so have the waves, the gentle swell of the morning replaced with peaks well over the surfers' heads. Dick watches the brave surfers still in the water. One in particular catches his eye. He is patient, often falling out of the queue to pass on a wave or only riding halfway before flipping the board over the lip and paddling back out.

A swell lifts on the horizon, and the surfer swims toward it, then gracefully turns as it crests. Dick's pulse ticks up as the surfer is captured by its force then as he shoots from its cyclonic tunnel to glide magnificently across the face.

When the wave collapses to whitewater, casually, as if it's

nothing at all, he flips onto his head to ride the rest of the way to shore. He doesn't look like Hamilton. He is half his age, and his hair is not nearly as blond, but watching him causes a knot to form in Dick's chest nonetheless.

The surfer carries his board to the beach then, as if sensing something, turns. For the briefest second, his eyes connect with Dick's, and his head tilts, and the hand not holding the board lifts in a small wave.

―――

"Hi, Zack," Dick says, his eyes closed and the phone pressed tight to his ear. He is on the patio outside his hotel room. "This is the reporter from *Orange Coast Magazine*."

"Did you do your story?" Zack asks.

"No."

"Because Hamilton died?"

"Yes. Because he died. Were you at his service?"

"Why would I go to his service?"

"Because he was your teacher," Dick says, unsure what he's hoping for.

"I told you; the guy was a loser."

"Can you tell me why you hated him so much?"

"Why do you care?"

"I'm just trying to understand. He seemed well loved."

"Loved by people who don't mind fags."

The word pierces, and for a moment, Dick can't speak.

"That's why you hated him?" he manages.

"The sicko turned Jason into a homo also."

Dick doesn't say goodbye.

―――

The wet sand is cool on his feet. Dick walks with his head down and his hands in his pockets. The water laps at his toes, touching his soles and receding. He studies the shells and watches the tiny sand crabs as they are revealed by the wash then as they frantically scurry back into the earth.

How much did his first conversation with Zack weigh into his decision?

A lot. Had he not spoken to Zack, or had he understood the reason Zack disliked Hamilton, Dick would not have been so easily swayed toward the belief that Hamilton's motives were ignoble. But he was looking for Hamilton to be guilty, and Zack offered a view he was predisposed to interpret as proof of what he was already inclined to think.

Which doesn't mean Hamilton wasn't going to hurt Frankie but significantly lessens the likelihood and makes the morality of Dick's choice more questionable.

Yet, startling as the revelation is, it is not nearly as earth-shattering as Dick would have thought. Perhaps because he had already considered the possibility of being wrong. He knew when he made the decision there was a chance Hamilton was innocent. Which means, regardless of Zack, his choice would have been the same.

Again, it comes down to the math. Numbers don't lie. It's the reason he was worried about Frankie in the first place. Statistically, there was a 93 percent likelihood Frankie was in trouble and only a 7 percent chance Hamilton had changed. He tried to be certain, but sometimes . . . oftentimes . . . there is no way to be sure. He was certain about Otis. He was right about Shea. He will never know about Hamilton.

It's possible Diego Ramirez played a role as well. A young woman is dead because Dick didn't act in time. He couldn't take that chance with Frankie.

You're rationalizing murder. Steve's voice replays in his head.

Murder. The word is distinctly sour on his tongue, like when he fills out a form and, beside "Marital Status," needs to click the box for "divorced," or under family medical history, when he needs to check "asthma," "allergies," "nosebleeds," "anxiety," and "cancer."

The tide rolls out, and he bends down to pick up one of the small crabs before it can disappear. The translucent albino creature, no bigger than a raisin, darts sideways, its amoebic brain sensing danger.

Dick closes his fist around it before it can escape, tightening his hand until its desperate, frantic movement tickles his palm. For a moment he stands, face lifted toward the waning warmth of the sun, then with a deep, sorrowful breath, lays his knuckles on the sand and unfurls his fingers. And the tiny creature scurries away to burrow back to its living grave.

71

While Steve was away, summer descended on D.C., the heat and humidity grabbing the city by its throat and blowing its fetid breath into its lungs. The long, miserable days match his mood, and for a week, he's done nothing but work, sleep, and obsess over Dr. Richard Raynes.

Dick no longer works at Pentco, and Steve's efforts to discover why have been blocked at the highest level. He's more than a little curious. Dick isn't wealthy, and he has an ex-wife and two kids to support. Yet, he is not collecting unemployment and hasn't updated his LinkedIn profile, which makes Steve think he isn't actively looking for a job.

He's committed two murders in three months, and no one, other than Steve, suspects a thing. As much as Steve hates to admit it, Dick is almost the perfect criminal—ordinary as paste on the outside but with an extraordinary brain and an exceptional knowledge of chemistry. He had no association with his second victim, and there is no way to predict who he will target next.

Steve has never faced this before, certain of his suspect and that they are going to strike again, yet entirely at a loss for how to stop them. The forensic report on Hamilton's respirator mask confirmed something had dried on the frame, but they weren't able to identify it. Whatever it was had evaporated, and the thin powdery residue that remained was not in their database of known substances.

Steve closes the file, pulls out his phone, and leaves another message for Denise. His messages vacillate between desperation, anger, and apologies for his previous outbursts. This one is a combination. He tells her he loves her and that he misses her, then tells her how sorry he is for the way things ended between them. He knows she wants him to apologize for accusing her brother of what he did, and he knows it's the reason she hasn't returned his calls, but he can't do that. He doesn't believe in lying to the people you love.

He hangs up, then reaches into the back of his top desk drawer to pull out the dark blue velour box he put there the day Denise and Jesse flew home. The round diamond catches the light through the window. Only two weeks ago, he was so certain of his future, a new life with the woman he loves and a stepson he adores.

Now, he can't move forward, and he can't go back. One way or another, this thing with Dick needs to end.

72

The small cottage in San Clemente is two blocks from the ocean and twenty minutes from Irvine and the kids. A "cozy charmer" is how the real estate listing described it. He bought it the day he surfed for the first time, choosing it for its location and large backyard.

There's no picket fence, but it's the sort of house that could have one. The landscape needs work, but Dick's always wanted to try his hand at gardening. There's an old playset out back that needs to be hauled away. It would make a nice spot for a vegetable bed. He's already started looking into plants that do well in arid beach climates. Squashes and lettuces seem to be good choices. The house itself is solid and has been recently updated with new windows, wood floors, and fresh paint.

"Dee," he says from his new cellphone, in his new kitchen, in his new house, "I need your help."

"What? What's wrong?" Dee answers, her voice tight.

"Nothing," Dick says, wondering about the strange reaction. They've texted a few times, but he hasn't talked to her since he left for Hawaii, which was over five weeks ago—a glorious, rejuvenating month of surfing, lounging on the beach, and sleeping.

He had hoped Jim and Kiley might join him for some of it, but Caroline put the kibosh on the idea, claiming they were too busy.

"I bought a house," he says, "and I was thinking you and Jesse might want to come for a visit, maybe bring Janelle, and help me furnish it."

"You bought a house?" she says, relief in her voice.

"You, okay?"

"Yeah. Fine. What made you buy a house?"

"I figured it was time to get out of the apartment."

"Oh," she says flatly.

"Everything okay?"

She blows out a breath. "Steve and I broke up."

"Oh," Dick says, genuinely disappointed. Though Steve is turning out to be his nemesis, he likes him, and he especially likes him for Dee. He's the first man Dee's dated seriously since Jesse's dad left, and the first decent man she's dated since Joe.

"Where's the house?" she asks.

"San Clemente. It's nice. A beach town. You don't have to come. I can just order some things online."

"No. Of course I'll come. How about next weekend? I just need to get my shifts covered."

"Great!" he says with too much fake enthusiasm, the whole conversation off rhythm.

"Dickie?" Dee says, hesitation in her voice.

"Yeah?"

Another awkward pause until finally she says, "Nothing. Never mind. I'll see you next weekend."

———

The house is mostly empty. He has a lawn chair he bought at the drugstore, a large flatscreen TV set up on a couple cinder blocks, and a new king-size bed. Though he's not a fan of television, he keeps the set on when he's home for the noise. It reminds him of the kids. He never much cared for *SpongeBob* or *The Simpsons*, but he liked watching them watch them.

Without a job, he's horribly lonely, and it makes him miss them that much more. He needs to figure out a way to bring them back into his life. He thought the house would be a start, but when he called to tell them about it and to ask if they wanted to visit, neither was interested. Jim's in summer camp during the week and wants to hang with his friends on the weekends, and Kiley has no interest, period. Perhaps when they're older and not so much under Caroline's control, he'll be able to have more of a relationship with them, but for now, he's not sure what else to do but to continue to let them know he's here and that he loves them. Each day, he sends them each a text, often including a "meme." He likes that he knows what that is. Jim almost always emojis back a laughing face or a thumbs-up. Kiley doesn't reply.

His phone buzzes, and he looks down to see a text from Dee:

> can't come until the weekend after
> next.

He texts back a smiley face and thumbs-up, though he isn't happy at all. The isolation is getting to him.

At least, he still has his work. He is in the process of converting the third bedroom into a lab. Yesterday, the carpet was pulled up and replaced with linoleum, and today, two lab tables and twenty rodent cages are being delivered. He lied to Katz. Compound four is much closer to completion than he led him to believe. It needs a bit of fine-tuning, but the formula is solid, and it's only a matter of weeks, not years, until it will be ready for a clinical trial and then FDA approval.

It keeps him busy enough that he can mostly avoid thinking about the remaining three Pepper files. Part of him never wants to return to them again. The problem is red rose bushes. Each time he passes a red bloom, his rage returns as he recalls Cayman's post and thinks about Ingall, who his gut tells him might be the worst monster yet.

Which is why, reluctant as he is to return to that world, each morning, as he sips his coffee, he searches for Ingall's name, idly awaiting and dreading an opportunity to infiltrate his life.

73

Gus is a tall, mangy mutt without much merit other than he is quiet and housebroken. The name came with the dog, and it fits. Dick adopted him a week ago. Kiley always wanted a dog, but Caroline was adamantly against pets. Kiley actually texted, "Awww," when Dick sent her a photo of Gus. The first word she's texted or spoken to him since their disastrous dinner four months ago. Despite his repeated efforts, she has stonewalled him, pretending he doesn't exist. He won't give up. Thirteen years was given to a lie, but his love for her is real as anything in this world. He hopes someday she realizes that. Until then, his only choice is to be patient.

Having company helps. Gus follows Dick everywhere and seems sincerely interested in whatever Dick is doing, his large ears perking up when Dick bounces ideas off him and his wiry-haired head tilting thoughtfully as if giving the ideas serious consideration.

A heat wave has descended on Southern California, and the last few days have been unbearable. Even with the Pacific breeze, the cottage becomes an oven in the afternoons. Unable to take it, Dick turns to Gus and says, "Let's get out of here."

Gus lifts his head from his paws and cocks it to the left.

There's no place to go where Gus will be welcome that's not stifling other than the car, so Dick drives around aimlessly listening to jazz. Though he doesn't acknowledge it, he knows where he will end up. He has resisted the pull for days, but being in the car with nowhere to go and knowing PPR4 is so close is too compelling a combination. Now that Dick lives in San Clemente, Michael Cray, score of sixty-four, is only twenty minutes away.

One donut and two coffees after leaving the house, he finds himself pulling into a neighborhood of old ranch-style houses. Cray's house is dark brown and unremarkable except for the strange hedges, which are shaped into sharp cones with chainsawed wedges carved from them.

He continues past without stopping, his heart not in it, being here reaffirming just how much he doesn't want to start this again. He's in a good place. He's planted a garden. Dee is coming this weekend to turn his house into a home. Compound four, which he's named RepAir, is nearly ready for submittal to the FDA for human trial. Jim is texting him almost every day. And Kiley said, "Awww."

The last thing he wants is to stalk another creep and discover he is doing creepy things.

"What do you say we leave the superhero work to the superheroes?" Dick says to Gus.

Gus doesn't bother pulling his head in from the window.

Dick's halfway to the freeway when he groans and turns the car around.

He pulls to the curb, grabs one of the webcams from the glovebox, and with a sigh, steps from the car. He follows the side yard to the back of the house. All the windows have blinds except the kitchen, so he attaches the camera to the sill above the sink behind a half-dead Ficus bush. He selects the motion-sensor activation option to conserve the batteries and leaves, hoping the effort is for nothing and that Cray's life is as boring as it appears.

———

At five o'clock, the beaches open for dogs, so Dick eats his takeout Thai food with Gus on the sand as he watches the sunset and early evening surfers.

By the time he finishes, the weather has cooled, and he and Gus return home. He checks on the mice, twenty cages of four mice each. All are doing well. He's been testing four different formulas on five different allergies—pollen, peanut butter, animal hair, dust, and bee venom. The mice's immune systems are responding positively, and he estimates they should be able to be weaned from the drugs in a matter of weeks.

His laptop beeps, and he turns from the cages to see a video window open on the screen. The reception is surprisingly clear, far better than it was through Hamilton's dirty screen and window. He is looking at a kitchen with dark wood cabinets. Beyond it is a dining room with black chairs. To the left of the frame, a large bald man in what looks like a mechanic's uniform leafs through a stack of mail. He tosses it on the counter and walks out of view.

Dick watches a moment longer. With Cray out of the frame, he is able to see part of the living room—a box television on a scarred wood console and a gray couch. The house looks stuffy, hot, dark, and lonely. No ocean breeze. No Gus. A life sadder and lonelier than his own.

Cray returns, and Dick startles. He has changed out of his work clothes and now wears sweats and a T-shirt. His file said he is thirty-eight, and he looks about that, lines around his eyes and his thick brows threaded with gray. He served two sentences for identical crimes—kidnapping, rape, and sodomy with a minor. His victims were ten and eight. He was released seven months ago. His face is wide and pale, and his arms are covered with dark tattoos.

Dick doesn't know if it's the fishbowl effect of the lens, but now that Cray is in the kitchen and closer to the camera, he looks huge. Dick can't remember what the file said about his size, but on the screen, he looks large as an NBA center. His T-shirt strains against the expanse of his chest as he grabs something from the fridge.

He walks again from view, and ten minutes later, the camera switches off.

74

Dee pulls her Subaru into the driveway of Dick's cottage a little after one.

"Wow," Janelle says. "Look how cute it is."

Dee agrees. The house is gray shingled with white trim and a bright red door. The earth has been freshly turned beside the brick path, and there are plastic containers with peonies ready to be planted beside it. They grab their bags from the trunk and walk inside without knocking.

Dick comes out from a room at the end of the hall and closes and locks the door behind him. "You made it!" he says, a crooked proud smile on his face.

His appearance is as surprising as the charming home he bought. The board shorts, T-shirt, and flip-flops are shocking, but it isn't his clothes that make her smile. Her brother is tan, and his hair is lighter and longer than she's ever seen it. He's also fit, thin and sinewy like he was in college without an ounce of paunch around his middle.

"Wow, you look great," Janelle says, beating her to the punch.

"Thanks. So what do you think of the place?" He waves his hand around the living room.

"This is amazing," Dee says.

"It needs your magic, but—" He is interrupted by a skinny, mangy dog bounding in from the kitchen.

"Cool, a dog!" Jesse says as the animal greets them with jumps and licks.

"You got a dog?" Dee says, her mind trying to catch up with all the sudden changes.

"This is Gus."

"You're allergic," Dee says.

"Not anymore."

She's about to ask how that's possible when Jesse says, "Whoa, whose surfboard?"

Dee turns, and sure enough, propped in the corner of the living room beside the fireplace is a large red surfboard.

"Mine," Dick says.

"Yours?" *Who are you? And what have you done with my brother?*

"On my vacation, I learned how to surf. It's why I bought this house. I can walk to the beach, and there's a great surf break less than a mile from here."

"Can I go?" Jesse asks Dick while looking at Dee.

"Absolutely," Dick says. "There's a surf shop nearby that rents boards and wetsuits. If the waves are good, we'll go tomorrow. You girls should try it as well. It's amazing."

Dee shakes her head, mostly in disbelief but also because she has no intention of swimming into the Pacific and purposely trying to get a wave to sweep her up and try and drown her while she attempts to stay afloat.

"Not me," says Janelle. "The closest I get to the ocean is a seaweed facial."

"Dee?" Dickie asks as Jesse says, "Mom?"

She stops shaking her head and looks back and forth between

them, knowing this is her moment to be a cool mom or a wimp. Desperately she wants to choose wimp.

"Sure, I'll give it a try," she says, and both boys light up. She might drown, but it's worth it.

"I'm so glad you're here," Dick says, his excitement bubbling over in a way she simply can't remember. "Do you think you can fix the place up?"

"Depends. What's my budget?"

"Unlimited."

"Unlimited?" Janelle chirps. "Greatest word in the human language when it comes to money. What are you, like Mr. Moneybags suddenly?"

Dee has the same question. Since his divorce, Dick's been stretched thin. "Did you get a raise because of Freeway?" she asks.

"Actually, I quit my job."

Okay, she's getting the hang of this. Whatever she expects, Dick is going to say the opposite.

"Good for you," Janelle pipes in. "That stupid company never appreciated you."

Dee shoots her a look. Pentco has been good to her brother. A lot of companies would have fired him after a fiasco like Freeway. And his work is the one thing her brother has always cared about. For him, being a chemist isn't just a job, it's an identity.

"So, what are you doing?" she asks, straining to keep her voice light as her last conversation with Steve buzzes in her brain.

Dick smiles the crooked smile again. "I'm living. I finally figured out what it's like to be living."

75

Dick is in the cottage alone. Dee, Jesse, and Janelle are shopping. It's their last day in San Clemente before they return home, and Dee is on a mission to get everything ordered so it will be here when she returns in a couple of weeks. The mice have been under treatment for two complete cycles with perfect results, and it's time to make the call.

"Doctor, what a surprise. Calling to extort more money?" Katz says, his voice smooth as ever.

"Actually, yes."

Katz chuckles.

Dick explains what he's been working on and how it's progressing. "So, you see, the research and development of compound four progressed much quicker than I anticipated and is almost ready to be submitted for clinical trial."

"And this involves Pentco how?"

"I want you to buy it from me and produce it."

"But we don't want to pursue compound four. We've been through this."

"That was before, when you thought you could go to market with Freeway ahead of a cure and secure a foothold, but if compound four goes to a competitor, they'll bring it to market at almost the same time as Freeway, completely negating it."

There's a long silence. "This was your plan all along?"

"Actually, Mr. Katz, my plan was to do my job and for you to do yours. We got into this business to create medicines that help people. This is my life's work, and I couldn't let you bury it so Pentco could make a profit off people's chronic suffering."

"You don't know you can cure them," he says. "It's still just a theory. If I recall, your first premature theory nearly destroyed your career."

Dick closes his eyes, the regret of his earlier mistake still sharp.

"Did you know I got myself a dog?" he says.

"Good for you."

"It's the first dog I've ever owned." Dick looks at Gus, who is flopped on the floor just inside the door where the light slants through the window.

Katz remains silent.

"Until a few weeks ago," Dick goes on, "I never considered having a pet. It wasn't an option because I've always been too allergic." Dick feels a knot of emotion in his chest. As a boy, it was his strongest wish. "His name is Gus."

Katz laughs. "That's a terrible name."

"He's a terrible dog."

Another dry chuckle, then silence.

Dick waits him out.

"So let me get this straight. You want me to buy the product I didn't want and ditch the product I just spent three million dollars on?"

"Yes. I want you to do what's right."

"And what's right just happens to benefit you enormously. How much do you want for us to *do what's right*?"

"Royalties only. Two percent."

"Scientists get half a percent."

"Scientists who work for you get half a percent. I'm a consultant. I want two."

The silence lasts well over a minute, Dick's heart pounding with the seconds. If this works, his legacy will be assured, as well as the financial future for Jim, Kiley, Dee, and Jesse. His initial payout ensures he can continue to help at the same level he has, but if Katz agrees to this, it will ensure this generation's financial future along with the next.

"One percent," Katz says finally. "And the only way I agree to it is if you're reinstated as an employee so Pentco gets the patent and is credited with its development."

"You want me to come back?" Dick says, his voice breaking in surprise.

"*Want* would be a strong word, but it's the only way I see this working. No one, except you and I, ever finds out about this deal, and once the IND is submitted for the clinical trial, you resign."

Dick thinks about it and is impressed by how much sense it makes. Dick will work out the protocol for the trial, and the patent will belong to Pentco.

"I think that will work," he says, trying not to show his eagerness. "I'll have my attorney draw up the papers."

"I've heard about your attorney," Katz says, sarcasm bleeding through his words.

"He's good."

"Yeah. I wish he was on my side." He guffaws, then says, "I underestimated you, Doctor. All these years you worked for me, and I never even knew who you were."

Neither did I, Dick thinks, smiling as he hangs up the phone.

76

Like clockwork, Dick's computer beeps. Cray is a creature of habit, and each day, his routine is the same. He returns at six, gets changed, takes a beer from the refrigerator, then after an hour or so, makes himself dinner.

He is an impressive cook. Tonight he is making pasta with a mushroom sauce accompanied by a tomato salad drizzled with oil. Dick watches while eating a burrito from Del Taco. Dick can't hear what's going on in Cray's house but can tell music is playing by the way Cray bobs and dances as he cooks. After he eats, always in front of the television watching what looks mostly like zombie movies and thrillers, he cleans up. Around nine, he turns off the television and heads to bed.

A lonely life.

77

Dick has been back at Pentco almost a week, and progress on the submittal for the clinical trial is going well. As he makes the twenty-minute drive home, he listens to jazz and whistles along. Dee, Janelle, and Jesse arrived yesterday and are waiting at the cottage, and he thinks how nice it is to be going home to someone.

His first clue that something has changed is the door. In the center is a pretty wreath with flags and stars for Labor Day, which is a couple weeks away.

"Surprise!"

He falls back as his three ambushers whoop and clap and as Gus leaps around excitedly.

"Wow!" he says, as he takes in the living room, which no longer looks anything like the barren room he left this morning.

"Do you like it?" Dee asks, her hands clasped in prayer fashion in front of her.

It looks like a photo from a magazine. Two overstuffed denim chairs and a sofa in white and blue pinstripe surround a large wood table with shells and candles on it. The highlight of the room, however, is mounted over the fireplace, and Dick can't take his eyes off it. Suspended in the center of the wall and spanning almost its entire width is a Tom Blake wooden longboard with his trademark squid design emblazoned in red and green on its glossy cedar deck. Dick told Dee about the surfing pioneer and his amazing innovations in surfboards, and she must have remembered and somehow got her hands on one of his reproductions.

"I love it," he says, eyes still on the board.

———

To celebrate the completion of the first room, Dick treats everyone to dinner at Tommy's, a local diner walking distance from the house.

"Anyone up for a stroll on the beach?" Janelle asks when they walk from the restaurant, fat on burgers and fries.

"I'm beat, and this one needs to go to bed," Dee says, tousling Jesse's hair.

"I'll walk with you," Dick offers.

Dee and Jesse turn one way, and he and Janelle go the other. He startles at how quickly the energy transforms, the strange molecular rearrangement that happens when a man and woman are alone together, regardless of species. And immediately, he feels the old awkwardness he always suffers around women he finds attractive.

"This place is beautiful," Janelle says, taking a deep inhale of the cool salt air.

She looks especially lovely tonight. She is wearing the white zodiac halter top she bought on their shopping trip with a pair of tight jeans. Her blond curls are piled on top of her head, and her gold hoop earrings sparkle in the moonlight.

He considers telling her but, instead, like an idiot, blurts, "Richard Nixon used to have a vacation house here. It's called the Western White House."

"Oh," Janelle says.

They reach the beach, and Janelle braces herself on Dick's shoulder as she slips off her shoes, the touch sending an electric buzz down his spine. Then, as if it's the most natural thing in the world, she takes his hand, and they continue to walk toward the shore.

Arousal and confusion overwhelm him, and he's transported back in time to twenty years earlier when, out of extraordinary pity and compassion, Janelle gave him his first kiss.

"Let's go up," Janelle says, gesturing to a closed-up lifeguard tower.

Dick follows her up, his brain seizing in a dozen different directions. He and Caroline have been divorced two and a half years, but it's been several years longer since he's been with a woman. And while the notion seems preposterous, he thinks there's a chance Janelle is seducing him.

Janelle dangles her legs off the edge of the platform and retakes his hand, and for a while they look at the ocean as Janelle prattles on about everything and nothing. She is the easiest person in the world to be around. She likes to chatter and can create conversation out of anything—songs she likes, movies she's seen, why purple is magic and blue is sorrow. She talks a little about Dee and Jesse and a lot about Otis and how scary it was when he came back.

"I know it's a sin," she says, crossing herself then looking up at the heavens, "but I'm glad he's dead."

Dick nods and tries not to react beyond that.

"God finally weighing in on things, if you want my opinion." She sighs and leans her head on Dick's shoulder. She smells like gardenias, and somehow their hands are now on her thigh, though he hasn't a clue how they got there. She's saying something about maple syrup and agave, but Dick can't concentrate, the heat of her skin through the denim, several degrees warmer than the air, making it impossible to think about anything else.

As if knowing his thoughts, she lifts her face and giggles, and his face flames. Then she is kissing him, her soft lips pressed to his paralyzed ones.

"Relax," she says, pulling back and smiling.

He tries. Closing his eyes, he listens to the ocean, focusing on its rhythm and strength, and when she kisses him again, he falls into it, his lips molding to hers and heat filling him.

She puts her palms on his chest, then slides them up his neck.

"I like the way you smell," he mumbles.

Her smile causes their lips to break apart, and she looks at him with pure mischief in her eyes. Then she is fumbling with the buttons of his shirt. Unable to get them undone, she says, "Screw it," and yanks the shirt over his head.

He takes it from her and lays it on the plywood deck before lowering her onto it, the cool Pacific breeze rushing over his skin, and his mind on fire.

———

Janelle pecks him on the nose, then bounces to her feet. "Brrr," she says as she tosses Dick his pants, then grabs her own shirt from the deck and quickly pulls it on.

When they're clothed, they sit again on the edge.

"I like this new you," she says.

"Obviously," he answers with a blush.

She giggles. "Yeah, I guess I wouldn't have done that with the old you. But, the thing is, the old you never would have done that."

Dick smiles at the thought. She's right. Five months ago, none of this would have had the remotest chance of happening.

"Though I suppose," Janelle goes on, "it's not really a new you, it's just that you're finally letting this part of you out." She shivers as she says it, and he realizes she's cold.

He stands and helps her to her feet, and they climb down. He wraps his arm around her as they walk back across the beach toward the street.

"I suppose all of us have that," Janelle goes on. "Different parts of our personalities, but we only reveal certain ones."

Dick wonders about that. He's always considered himself an open book. One look and you know exactly who he is: awkward science nerd.

"Do you have a different personality?" he asks. Janelle's always seemed like an open book as well—sunshine and sass with a heart of gold.

"Secretly," she whispers, her eyes darting around furtively, "I'm a double agent for the CIA investigating cybercrimes."

He laughs, and she nudges him.

"Nope. I'm just me."

"Well, thank you for being just you," he says, then suddenly feeling like he should say something else, adds, "About tonight—"

She turns and puts her fingers to his lips. "Tonight was fun. It's a beautiful night, I had a couple of glasses of wine, and I find you attractive. Don't blow it and stop being cool now."

He laughs. He's not cool. Having sex leaves him feeling exactly as it always has—self-conscious, guilty, and incredibly grateful.

78

Dee tucks Jesse in on the air mattress in the bedroom and sits on the pretty couch she bought from Restoration Hardware. She's proud of the front room. The surfboard makes her smile. Her brother, a surfer? Life is strange.

She considers turning on the television, but she doesn't want to watch TV. She hasn't wanted to do much of anything since Steve left. The constant ache of missing him makes her restless at night and hollowed out during the day. He called as they were leaving Independence. She reached to answer it, then pulled her hand away as she's done every time for the last countless times. The message he left said, "I wish you'd talk to me. I love you, and I miss you."

What bothers her is her patheticness. Before Steve came into her life, she was happy. Not euphoric over-the-moon giddy, but fine. She had Jesse, Janelle, her friends, her job. Why can't she get back to that place of contentedness?

She looks at the closed door to the third bedroom. Dick's made it clear the room is off-limits. He said it's his lab and that it's to remain locked. She stares a minute longer, then pushes to her feet, grabs his keys on the counter, and hurries down the hall.

It's a lab. Exactly as Dick said. Sterile and white with the faint smell of a zoo from the mice that lived here until a week ago.

Dick's laptop beeps, startling her, and she walks to the table to look at the screen. A small window pops up within the larger one. The image is dark, and it takes a minute for her to recognize what she's looking at—a large bald guy with tattoos in a kitchen. He switches off the light, and the screen turns to shadow.

Her heart pounds, and she races from the room, hoping to forget what she saw.

79

A smile curls Steve's lips as he looks at the single line in Dick's latest Mastercard statement. Dr. Richard Raynes is going to a party. Two days ago, he paid two thousand dollars to the Ingall Foundation.

Grayson Ingall, a.k.a. Irving Grayson Ingberg III, is at the top of Steve's list of prospective ex-felons Dick might be watching. Ingall is a grade-A deviant with a lot of money, which in Steve's experience is a dangerous combination.

Steve pulls up the foundation's home page. The Ingall Foundation annual fundraiser is being held at the benefactor's home in Anaheim Hills a week from Saturday. The tickets are a thousand dollars apiece, which means Dick is bringing a guest. His heart tightens with the thought that it could be Denise.

"I never received your transfer request."

Steve looks up to see Gelson in his doorway.

"I've decided to stay," Steve says.

The lines around Gelson's mouth tighten. "You have?"

"Yep. You'll be happy to know I'm not going anywhere."

Not much is sweet about Steve's current situation, but watching Gelson squirm gives him a distinct sense of satisfaction.

"If this is about what I said about getting rid of your position—"

"It's not," Steve says. "I've decided not to transfer, though it does look like I will need to go to California next week."

"You do understand you only get three weeks vacation a year?"

"It's not a vacation."

"It's business?"

Steve considers this. "Business and personal," he says.

Dick—*business*. Denise—*personal*. It's been two months since things ended with Denise. He called her last night and left another message. It's pathetic, but he can't help himself. He hates how they left things. Every other thought is about her, and at least once a week, he breaks down and calls to tell her he still loves her and that he misses her.

Gelson narrows his ferret eyes but wisely chooses to let it go. With a military heel turn, he pivots and marches away, and Steve looks again at the screen and the glitzy page for the Ingall Foundation's fundraiser. Things have been eerily quiet since Hamilton, an ominous, foreboding calm. Steve senses it, something about to happen, and Steve intends to be there when it does.

80

Dick feels bad that Dee is upset because he invited Janelle to the fundraiser instead of her. She pouted as they got ready and made it clear how unfair it was. Dick promised to make it up to her. He chose Janelle because she's less curious and observant, as well as less likely to care if he wanders off and leaves her alone.

Dick is grateful Janelle didn't kiss and tell. He doesn't know how Dee would feel about what happened between them and doesn't know how to explain it, except to blame it on the moon and stars, that it was one of those mystical, magical moments that comes along incredibly rarely and entirely defies logic and reason. Janelle hasn't brought it up, and neither has he, their relationship returned to its easy natural state of sweet platonic love.

"I feel like a princess," she says as Dick drives through the iron gates. "I think I should have a fancier name, like Catherine or Elizabeth."

"Your name is fine," Dick says, not really listening.

For three months, he has waited for an opportunity to infiltrate Ingall's life, and if he blows this, he doubts he'll get another. Unlike Hamilton, Dick has no reservations when it comes to Ingall. All it took was for him to pull up an aerial view of Ingall's property on Google Maps to see the evidence of his guilt. Red-flowered bushes surrounded the perimeter, walkways, and house.

"Fine," Janelle says. "Janelle it is. But can I at least say I do something more interesting than working as an order clerk at the quarry?"

"What would you like to do?"

"I'm a singer."

"And what if they ask you to sing?"

Her brow crinkles, but she has no time to come up with an alternative cover because a valet is opening her door. Another valet frowns as he takes the Volvo's keys from Dick.

"Wow!" Janelle says, goggling Ingall's home.

Dick agrees it's impressive. The brick horseshoe driveway fronts a white-columned portico, and through a pair of grand doors, a marble-floored entry teaming with tuxedo-clad people is lit by a crystal chandelier the size of a Volkswagen.

Janelle stops in her tracks. "No way!" she says, yanking him back. "Do you know who that is?"

He follows her eyes to a tall, gaunt woman across the room with silky black hair chopped severely at her chin and a pop-your-eyes-out green dress. Dick has no idea who she is but knows she is important by the air she exudes that says "you will look at me while I refuse to look at you."

"That's Theresa Webb," Janelle hisses. "The evil matriarch in *Devastation*."

Dick looks at her blankly, and she rolls her eyes. "It's only like the number one show on Netflix."

Dick doesn't have Netflix. He barely knows what Netflix is.

"I'm going to say hi," Janelle squeals mischievously, like the idea is a dare both brilliant and scandalous. Dick thinks the woman might like if someone says hello. She looks a bit bored.

Janelle hurries off, and he scans the room. His greatest fear when he bought the outrageously expensive tickets was that it might tip Steve off. Though Dick hasn't heard from him since their beer after Hamilton's service, he knows he's keeping tabs. He can feel it, a tingly sense, constant and certain.

Relieved to see that everyone is a stranger except Janelle, who is now laughing with Theresa Webb like they are old friends, Dick turns into a parlor on the right. In the center, a grand piano is being played by a brilliant pianist. Dick walks behind the guests gathered around it to a hall that leads to a back staircase. Earlier in the week, he spent several hours at the Anaheim Hills city hall, studying and memorizing the house's building plans.

He takes the stairs two at a time, his heart pounding so loudly it drowns out the music. What he is about to do requires far more courage than what he did with Otis or Hamilton. At least two hundred people are only a floor below, and there would be no explaining his actions if he is caught.

A step from the landing, he stops and takes several deep breaths to calm his nerves, then pulls on a pair of white cotton gloves and continues quickly down the hall to Ingall's private suite.

The room is the size of a small apartment, with a sitting area, desk, and four-poster king bed. On the nightstand closest to him, two thorny branches poke out from a small terracotta pot.

Dick's blood grows hot knowing what the seedling symbolizes, and he continues to the fireplace to set to work. The plan is simple. Check that the damper is closed. Snuff out the pilot. Turn on the gas. Earlier this afternoon, he turned off the main at the street, and tomorrow night he will return to turn it back on.

He hit pay dirt when he was studying the plans and realized that, thanks to a remodel done ten years ago, the house has two gas lines, one that services the water heater, kitchen, and furnace, and a more recent one that services the pool and fireplaces.

Thanks, Dad, he thinks and smiles softly knowing it's because of his dad, jack-of-all-trades at the hatchery, that he knows
about gas lines and the danger of gas leaks and carbon monoxide poisoning.

He holds his lighter over the burners to confirm the gas is
off. So long as Ingall doesn't decide to enjoy a fire on this warm
August night, he shouldn't notice anything is amiss. The plan
isn't foolproof. Carbon monoxide poisoning takes hours, and
there's a chance Ingall could wake and save himself, but it's the
only idea Dick could come up with where the death would
appear accidental.

He puts the lighter back in his pocket, pushes to his feet,
and pans the room to be sure there's nothing he's missed. His
eyes catch on a smoke and carbon monoxide detector on the
ceiling, and his heart skips at least two beats as he realizes how
close he came to missing it and blowing the whole thing.

Using a chair from the sitting area, he climbs up to remove
the batteries, and it screeches in protest. His brain seizes as he
yanks out the battery. It stops, and he slams the case shut, leaps
to the floor, shoves the chair back in its place, and races from
the room.

Halfway down the stairs, he stops and bends over his knees,
his beath coming in gulps. He focuses on pulling air through
his nose and counting until finally his heart resumes its rhythm.

Straightening, he pulls off the gloves and returns to the
party.

"Where have you been?" Janelle says when he finds her.
"You missed the magic show."

"There was a magic show?" Dick says.

"You okay? You're sweating."

She hands him her cocktail napkin, and he blots his forehead.

"It was amazing. I got to pick a card, and I picked the four of spades, and then the magician touched my head, and wham, just like that, he totally read my mind and said, 'four of spades,' and there was no way he could have known."

Dick smiles at her astonishment.

"We should go outside," she says, her brow wrinkled with concern. "You look like you're about to pass out."

He forces a reassuring smile. Theresa Webb toasts Janelle with her martini as they walk toward the open patio doors.

A waiter passes with a tray of wine, and Dick grabs a glass and gulps half of it down as he follows Janelle outside into a yard the size of a football field, with a glowing pool and so many rose bushes the entire landscape is bursting with ruptures of red.

"Wow. It's like a fairytale," Janelle says as Dick thinks the opposite.

A twelve-piece orchestra plays on a stage, and a million twinkling lights sparkle around them.

"Ooh, and there's a band," Janelle says.

"Maybe they'll ask you to sing with them," he says with a wink.

She lights up, and he can almost imagine her joining them just for the dare of it.

The cool air and wine are helping, and his pulse has begun to slow.

He lifts his glass to take another sip when Grayson Ingall appears. Flanked by two older bejeweled women, he walks king-like through the doors. Over six feet tall, with silver-white hair and intense blue eyes, he is even more distinguished in person than in his photos.

Janelle prattles about another magic trick she saw, while Dick listens to another conversation altogether.

"I only grow Ora Kingsleys," Ingall says.

He and the ladies stand a few feet away beside a hedge of roses.

"Why's that?" one of the women asks as she bends to smell a bud.

"Because they're always in bloom. I couldn't bear to see my bushes dormant."

"You have so many."

"A hundred and twenty-three."

Dick chokes on his wine, and Janelle stops what she is saying to pat his back.

When he recovers, she grabs his hand. "Let's dance."

She leads him to the dance floor, and as they sway to the music, he glances again at Grayson Ingall—dignified, handsome, charming—and Dick is reminded of Shakespeare's *Hamlet* and of how difficult it was for the young prince to believe his uncle could be guilty of poisoning his father even though his father's ghost told him it was so. One hundred and twenty-three rose bushes—it's almost impossible to believe.

81

"Sorry, sir," the field agent says. "The only thing the target was guilty of tonight is bad dancing."

Steve doesn't laugh. He doesn't even smile. He asked for two agents, but the LA field office was stretched thin and could only spare one. The event ended an hour ago, and he and Agent Myers, a middle-aged man innocuous as rain, are at a nearby Denny's for the debriefing.

"You had eyes on him the whole time?"

"Except the first ten minutes," Myers confirms.

The lapse wasn't the agent's fault. There was a magician at the event, and the show blocked the entry to the foyer. Steve doubts it's relevant. Ingall was with the agent watching the magician perform, so he wasn't in danger during that time.

"He looked like a guy at a party having a good time," Myers says. "And his date was a hoot. And *she* knew how to dance. No crime there."

Steve checks his reaction. Myers doesn't know this is personal or that Janelle is someone Steve cares about.

"So he never got close to Ingall?"

"There were a few minutes when they were both outside together, but your man barely glanced at Ingall."

Steve thanks the agent and Myers leaves.

Steve stays in the booth, sipping his coffee and looking out the window at the pitch-black sky as he tries to puzzle it out. Ingall is the target, and tonight was about something. What is Dick up to?

82

It's Sunday evening, and Dee, Jesse, and Janelle have gone to a movie.

Dick stayed behind to finish his notes for the clinical trial. His tenure with Pentco ended Friday, but there are still a few protocols he wants to pass on to the chemist who is taking over the project. He offered to stay on, but Katz categorically declined.

"I would thank you for your service, Dr. Raynes, but I wouldn't mean it. Enjoy your newfound wealth, and I hope to never see you again."

He yawns and stretches his arms over his head. He and Janelle didn't get back last night until after midnight, and this morning, Gus woke him at dawn to remind him it was time to go for their run.

He looks at the clock in the corner of his screen, surprised to see it's nearly seven. His stomach rumbles, and he wonders where Cray is. Typically they eat dinner together around six thirty. Over the past month, Dick's become accustomed to his routine.

He returns to his notes, and at seven fifteen, the screen opens, and Dick looks up to see Cray entering from the garage as he always does. But this time, he walks backward, dragging . . . no struggling . . . with something through the door.

Dick freezes, his eyes fixed on the screen as his throat closes and his brain seizes.

He leaps from his chair and races for the door.

From the prepaid cellphone he keeps in his glove box, he dials 9-1-1. The call might be traced back to him, but he doesn't worry about that, no thought in his brain other than the ice-white panic that he won't get there in time.

"2190 Solanto Drive in Lake Forest!" he barks when the operator answers.

"Sir, slow down. What's your emergency?"

"A boy's been abducted, and I believe he is going to be raped."

He repeats the address, hangs up, and slams down on the accelerator. The Volvo groans in protest then reluctantly obeys, revving to sixty then seventy. He whips onto the on-ramp, then slams on the brakes, stopping an inch from the car in front of him.

The freeway is bumper-to-bumper traffic. He runs his hand hard through his hair, then pulls onto the shoulder and ekes his way to the next exit as horns blare.

He rides the off-ramp, then the on-ramp, then does it again, praying the seconds will help.

He gets stuck behind a big rig he can't maneuver around, and his chest tightens as his fingers start to tingle. He can't have a panic attack. Not now.

Sing. It's a trick he learned in graduate school. Singing relaxes the larynx and opens the lungs.

The only song Dick can think of is "Take Me Out to the Ballgame." So, loud as he can, he belts it out, pushing the words through his constricted throat. He looks like a madman, but it works, his lungs opening and mercifully drawing air.

Finally he reaches the exit and races the remaining three blocks to Cray's house. Grabbing Lucille from the trunk, he runs for the door. His only plan: *Stop him!*

Music blares from behind the wood as he hammers his fist against it. It's the kind of noxious noise Jim and his friends listen to. "Justice is lost, justice is raped, justice is gone . . ."

He runs around the side of the garage and, using the barrel end of Lucille, breaks the glass of the door. His forearm tears on a shard as he reaches for the lock, but he barely notices as he turns the bolt and charges inside.

The music is deafening, the volume so loud he knows it's to cover the screams. His momentum never slows as he scans the familiar interior, panic propeling him forward and down the hall where he saw Cray dragging the boy. Through an open door at the end, Cray stands naked in front of a bed, a large crucifix with Jesus draped on its transom tattooed on his enormous back.

Adrenaline makes Dick's brain work faster, absorbing all the details at once. Two thin pale legs drape over the end of the mattress between Cray's hairy ones. Cray's hands move in circles in front of him in a bizarre dance that doesn't match the music. His face is tilted toward the ceiling. The Mother Mary with a gold halo stares from the wall above the headrest. From somewhere beyond, incense burns.

Cray lifts his left arm, and Dick catches a glimpse of the boy—straight dark brown hair and duct tape over his mouth. He sees Dick, and his eyes widen. Cray, noticing, starts to turn.

All of it happens incredibly fast yet in time-warped slow motion. Lucille rising in Dick's hands as he continues to charge. Cray's arm swinging around as the bat comes down on his back and across the chest of Jesus.

Cray flails as he staggers to regain his balance, and the bat rises then smashes down again, this time with a sickening thud, a melon splitting open, as the wood strikes Cray's head. He tee-ters, then falls, his hands shooting out to catch himself on the mattress on either side of the boy. His feet slip out from under him, and he collapses.

Dick steps forward to help pull the boy free, but at that exact moment, the music pauses, a breath between notes, and in that small rest, Dick hears the faint howl of sirens. Whirl-ing, he races back the way he came, down the hall, through the living room, and past the kitchen to the garage.

He runs to his car, peels from the curb, then forces his foot to lighten its pressure on the gas. The first police car passes as he reaches the stop sign at the end of Cray's street. Four more pass before he reaches the freeway.

It isn't until he's nearly home that he realizes he is bleeding. Body trembling, he looks down to see blood leaking from his forearm onto his pants. He pulls to the side of the road, takes off his dress shirt, and wraps it around the gash. Dropping his head to the steering wheel, he sucks air through his nose as his body continues to quake.

Things were starting to go so well.

83

Dee knows before she enters the house something is wrong. The front door is unlocked, and the door to the lab is open.

Gus jumps up to greet them, but she ignores him.

"Dickie?" she hollers.

No answer.

"Where is he?" Janelle asks, walking in behind her.

"Janelle, take Jesse and wait outside."

"Where's Dickie?"

"Janelle, go!"

Janelle flinches, then wraps her arm around Jesse's shoulder and leads him away.

Dee walks into the lab, Gus on her heels. The laptop is open, and the screen shows the same kitchen from before. The house is empty, but she is compelled to stare.

"Everything okay?"

"Janelle, I told you, stay with Jesse!"

"I just—"

"Janelle!"

"Okay."

"No, wait," Dee says.

Janelle's blue eyes brim with tears.

"Take Jesse and go," Dee says.

"Go? Go where?"

"Home."

"Now?"

"Yes."

"I'll get our stuff."

"No. I'll get your stuff."

"But how will you get back?"

"I'll figure it out." Dee's heart races, and it takes all her will to keep her emotions in check so as not to freak Janelle out any more than she already has. "Please. I need you to take Jesse and go."

Janelle's eyes scatter around the lab before she nods and hurries away.

Dee turns back to the screen.

She sits on Dick's stool at the exact moment the door to the house on the monitor slams open.

Two police officers, a man and a woman, enter in a crouch, their weapons drawn. The woman disappears out of view, down what looks like a hallway, while the man turns left and walks past the camera.

He's gone only a few seconds before he races back in the direction of his partner.

A minute later, they return together, the man carrying something in his arms.

He sets it on the couch, and Dee's eyes fill as her fingers go to her mouth. She can only see the back of the boy's head and his thin shoulders, but she sees he is shirtless, and thoughts of Ed flood her mind as sickness rises in her throat.

The woman officer gently pries what looks like duct tape from the boy's mouth. The man drapes what looks like a throw over him.

Dee is staring so hard she doesn't hear the front door open, and only realizes she's not alone when Gus leaps up. She lifts her face to see Dick in the doorway, his face pale and his nose opening and closing with his breaths.

"Dickie," she croaks, looking from him to the screen then back again, unable to say more, a lump like a fist lodged in her throat.

He steps up behind her and places a hand on her shoulder, and she places hers over it. Together they watch as more people arrive—paramedics, more police, others in suits and regular clothes. The boy pulls on his clothes that the woman police officer has brought him, and Dee looks back at Dick. He's in his T-shirt, and his dress shirt is wrapped around his arm.

"You're hurt," she says.

He looks down, and only after scanning his body does he seem to notice the makeshift bandage and blood that seeps through the cloth.

84

"I'm sorry," Dick says.

He is sitting on the toilet as Dee kneels in front of him, cleaning the cut.

"I think you might need stitches," she says.

"Dee—"

"You saved that little boy." She shakes her head as tears brim in her eyes.

She dabs at the wound with iodine, and he winces. The gash is an inch long and slices clean through the skin, and he thinks she might be right about the stitches. Around the wound, his arm is splattered with blood. Cray's blood. And seeing it causes bile to rise in his throat.

"I'm sorry," he mumbles, the words a confession, and this time, she nods in understanding.

She places a bandage over the cut and wraps a strip of gauze around it.

When she is done, she pushes to her feet, and Dick stands with her. She washes her hands as he pulls on a fresh shirt.

Her back to him, she dries her hand on a towel and says, "Steve knows what you're doing."

"I know."

"You do?"

He buttons the last button. "He's very good at what he does."

She turns, her green eyes so sad it hurts to look at them.

"It's why I need to go."

"Go? Where?"

"I'm not exactly sure."

"Dickie—"

"Don't."

She stops, and her eyes drop to the floor between them, her chin trembling, as bravely she fights to keep her emotions at bay.

"I need a favor," he says. "Actually, several favors. I need you to look after things. Greg Larson is in charge of my estate—"

"Estate!" she yelps, her face snapping to his, and he realizes it was the wrong choice of word.

"My finances," he corrects. "I've set money aside for Jim and Kiley, and there's a college fund for each of the kids, including Jesse—"

"College funds!"

He gives her a minute to catch up. He killed a man. He won't be coming back.

The tears she's been fighting escape, and it's almost more than he can take.

"I need you to look after this place," he manages, "and Gus."

On hearing his name, Gus thumps his tail.

"And I need you to check in on Jim and Kiley from time to time to make sure they're okay." His voice catches. "Make sure they know I didn't abandon them and that I love them."

Her hand goes to her mouth as the tears continue to leak, but she manages to nod.

"Thank you," he says, then leads the way out of the bathroom and through his very cool living room, with the Tom Blake surf-board, out the door to his car.

When they reach it, he turns to her and says, "He's a good man."

"He's trying to arrest you."

"He's doing what he believes is right."

"But it's not."

"Who's to say?"

"Dickie—"

"Dee, he believes in something and is willing to sacrifice for it."

She takes a shuddering breath. "Everyone I love gets destroyed."

"The opposite."

She looks up through her teary lashes. She has the prettiest eyes, and looking at them, he realizes they're the exact color of the ocean when you first jump on your board and can look through the water and still see the sand.

"You saved me," he says. "More than once, you saved me."

A car pulls onto the street, startling them. It's a false alarm, only a minivan on its way to a driveway a few houses away but warning enough for them to finish their goodbye. He hugs her tight then climbs in his car and, eyes on the rearview mirror, drives away, watching his sister, his house, and his dog until the road turns and they disappear from sight.

———

Dick knew this day was coming. He just didn't think it would come so soon.

As he drives to Anaheim Hills, he thinks about all the things he still wanted to do. Mostly he thinks about the kids and the time he is going to miss with them, and he tries not to feel sorry for himself, but finds it impossible.

It's nearly nine when he pulls to a stop beside Ingall's estate. With barely a thought, he climbs from the car and turns the second gas main back on, then drives back the way he came.

85

Michael Cray was sixteenth on Steve's list. Steve was on his way to number nine, a man by the name of Kristian Knott who lives in Cypress, when over the police scanner, he heard the call about a child abduction at the home of one of the other names on his list.

He walks toward the house as a tall man in a gray sports jacket and maroon tie walks from the front door. The reporters turn and swarm him like pigeons to a picnic, microphones thrust forward like bobbing heads and questions slung at the man like squawks.

"Detective, can you tell us what happened?"

"Has the victim been identified?"

"Do you know who saved him?"

The detective lifts his hand to settle them. His face is set in an expression of cool detachment, though Steve can tell he is amped. This is probably the biggest professional moment of his life. The story has national sensation written all over it—mystery hero swoops in to save a young boy and kills his attacker. He can see the *Lifetime* based-on-a-true-story movie now.

The man waits for the cacophony to die down and, when

he has the stage, begins, "A young boy was very lucky this evening. Michael Cray, a man with two prior convictions for child molestation and who was released from prison seven months ago, abducted the nine-year-old from El Toro Park while his mother was in the restroom. He brought him here, where fortunately the crime was interrupted by an unidentified assailant. Cray was killed during the altercation, and the assailant fled. We do not have any suspects at this time, but we are investigating. That's all."

"Suspects?" a reporter yells out. "Does that mean you think the act of saving the boy was criminal?"

"Whenever there's a death of this nature, we need to look into it. I have no comment as to whether it was criminal or not."

Another smattering of questions is thrown at the detective, but each time, his only response is, "That's all."

The detective returns into the house, and Steve waits several minutes for the hubbub to die down before following.

He finds the detective in the kitchen. "Steve Patterson, FBI?" He extends his hand, but the detective doesn't take it.

"This isn't federal," he says.

"No." Steve conceals his irritated sigh. "But I have an interest because of who the victim was."

"The boy is being taken care of."

"Not the boy," Steve says. "Cray."

The man squints, and Steve pulls out a business card and hands it to him.

"Federal Special Investigator for Crimes Against Sex Offenders," he reads out loud, then guffaws like the idea of Steve's job is a joke. He looks up and squints again, his dark eyes slits of distrust. "And you just happened to be in the neighborhood?"

Ignoring the question, Steve says, "I'd like to take a look around."

The detective's eyes flit side to side, and Steve knows he's trying to think of a way to say no. But whether he likes it or not, Fed trumps local, so after a few seconds and no great idea, begrudgingly he nods.

Steve returns to the living room and, standing near the front door, takes in the house. It's a typical tract home, single story with a pitched ceiling and large brick fireplace. It's dingy and rundown, coated with dust and age, and the only thing of value he can see is an expensive stereo system with enormous box speakers.

He knows Cray's body is in the main bedroom down the hall, but he turns the opposite way toward the garage, knowing it's where the crime began.

He sets his hand on the hood of a white Chevy van. The metal is slightly warmer than room temperature, and he thinks there should be a law against windowless vans and sex offenders.

He's about to return to the house when he feels a slight shift in the air and follows it to the door that leads outside. The bottom pane is broken, allowing a small breeze. Shards protrude from the frame, and the tip of one, in the bottom right corner, is slightly discolored. After a quick glance over his shoulder to be sure he's alone, he shoots a photo with his phone, then pries it loose with a tissue. Carefully he wraps it and tucks it in his pocket.

Turning, he follows the crime forward. Dick, somehow knowing what was happening, broke into the garage to get in the house. He killed Cray, stopping him from molesting the boy, then fled before the police arrived.

Adrenaline courses through his veins as he follows the path through the garage, past the kitchen, and down the hall to the main bedroom.

He stops outside the door. Just inside, Cray lies dead, his upper body collapsed on the bed, and his splayed legs still bracing him. A photographer circles, documenting the body and the scene. Left of the bed, the detective and medical examiner talk.

"A bat?" the ME says, though he's nodding as if it makes sense.

"That's what the boy said," the detective answers. "He said the guy was skinny and hit him with a bat."

"Speak softly and carry a big stick," Steve says almost to himself, quoting Theodore Roosevelt.

"*Walking Tall*," the ME says, looking up. "Loved that movie."

The reference to the iconic movie sends a tremor down Steve's spine at the idea of Dick being hailed as a modern-day Sheriff Buford Pusser, avenger of evil and beacon of good.

"Did the guy say anything to the kid?" Steve asks.

The ME looks with Steve at the detective, also curious, and reluctantly, the detective answers, "Nope, not a word. My guess is he didn't want to stick around for our arrival. We got here within minutes of the call."

"Call?" Steve asks. "You got the call before the guy was dead?"

The detective's eyes connect with Steve's as he realizes the significance. "You think the perp called it in?"

Steve doesn't answer. He doesn't need to, the answer obvious. Dick called 9-1-1 before he got to the house, even though he knew the danger it put him in.

Leaving the detective and ME, he returns outside and, for a long time, stands in the driveway looking at the house. Dick knew the boy was in trouble. *But how?* Cray abducted the boy from a park, but Dick didn't react until the boy was here.

He thinks about Dick's new home and the time it would take to drive here. The timing makes sense. He was home when he realized what was happening, raced here, calling 9-1-1 on his way, and knowing there was no time to wait for the police, broke in and saved the boy himself.

Despite himself, Steve feels a well of respect for Dick's bravery. It's no small thing to race head on into danger for another.

This wasn't like the others—Parsons, Shea, Hamilton . . . Ingall? Careful, premeditated, methodical. This was harried and panicked. Dick wasn't expecting it.

86

Dick sits in his cubicle staring at the "BREAKING NEWS" on his computer. In front of him are his last-minute notes for the clinical trial, shorthand he knows Graham will be able to decipher. He won't be here for RepAir's success, a loss nearly as devastating at everything else he's giving up, but he hopes to leave it with its best chance for success.

A detective stands on the steps of Cray's house, a tall man in a gray jacket with a reassuring, calm manner. He nods somberly. "The boy is okay. He has been reunited with his family and, I am pleased to say, released from the hospital."

Dick's emotions flood into his eyes, a tidal wave that takes enormous effort to contain.

"The family has asked me to convey how grateful they are to the police, the paramedics, and the community. And of course to the Good Samaritan who intervened and stopped this from becoming a much worse crime than it was. They also ask that you respect their privacy during this difficult time. Thank you."

The reporters scream questions, but the man ignores them and returns into the house. The camera pans back to the reporter, and that's when Dick sees him, Steve standing in the driveway, his hands loose at his sides and his head cocked left as he looks at the house.

Dick blinks several times in surprise, wondering how he got there so fast. But he knows. Steve was already here. He was at the fundraiser last night. Dick just didn't see him.

Steve being here changes things. He glances at the clock then returns to his work.

Time is running out.

87

Steve returns inside and follows the crime again.

On the second pass, he sees it, a reflection within the reflection of the kitchen window, almost invisible except for the faint outline of the lens concealed in the leaves of a bush. He smiles and points his finger, his thumb up. As he pulls the trigger, he mouths the words, "Got you," and hopes Dick is watching.

At that exact moment, his phone buzzes with a text. He pulls it out and, slightly stunned by the timing, reads Dick's message:

> Impressive. I suppose I always knew
> I was outmatched. I thought about
> heading to Mexico. There's an artist
> I'm trying to track down. But I assume
> you have the borders covered. So
> instead, I will be waiting for YOU at
> Pentco, where I have another loose
> end to tie up.

Steve stares at the words, trying to decide whether or not to trust it. Constantly Dick has been two steps ahead, yet something about the veiled reference to Diego Ramirez along with the "you" convinces him. Irreverent of the law as Dick is, he has also proven to be honorable. So without a word to the detective, he leaves Cray's house and drives to Pentco alone.

The bored night security guard tells him Dick is on the roof.

Steve climbs the three flights and pauses on the landing to catch his breath before pushing open the door.

Dick sits on the parapet, legs dangling over the edge and the tip of a cigarette glowing.

On hearing the door, he looks over his shoulder. "You got my message."

"I did," Steve says, stopping several yards from where Dick sits, his precarious perch concerning. "You left a bit of a mess at Cray's place."

"Not my best work."

Dick flicks ash from his cigarette, and it flutters like snow toward the ground.

"I thought you quit?"

"I started again."

"Can you get down from there so we can talk?"

"I prefer it up here."

"Please."

Dick swivels around with such recklessness Steve misinterprets it. "No—"

"Scare you?" Dick asks with a cockeyed grin.

Steve swallows, and Dick looks away. His feet are now on the tar roof, his back to the three-story drop. He takes another drag and holds it in his lungs before blowing a stream of smoke upward. The night is cool, but Dick wears only a dress shirt, and through the thin cotton, Steve is able to make out a strip of white around his forearm and assumes it's a bandage over the cut he got at the scene, and he wonders who wrapped it. Janelle? Denise?

"Tonight wasn't planned," Dick says.

Steve nods. "If you turn yourself in, it will go better."

Dick levels his eyes on Steve's. "I'm afraid I can't do that."

"Of course you can. You turn yourself in. You're hailed a hero. And if it goes to court, which is unlikely, it will be impossible to find a jury willing to convict, and that will be the end of it."

"It won't be the end of it, and you know it," he says plainly. "Which is why, if I'm arrested, I'll plead guilty. But we both know it's better if that doesn't happen."

Steve's nerves buzz with concern. Dick is looking at him so calmly, entirely serene and composed as he sits on the edge of a thirty-foot drop he openly intends to take. Over the years, Steve has seen his share of people teetering on the edge. He has felt their desperation along with their silent plea for help. This isn't that. This Steve has never seen. Rationally and lucidly, Dick sits between the choice of turning himself in or leaving this world, and clearly, the latter is winning. An emotionless, thoughtful calculation has been made, and its conclusion, at least in Dick's mind, logical and certain.

"The best scenario is that what happened tonight appears random," he goes on, "a chance intervention by an accidental passerby who happened upon a crime, stopped it, then fled because he didn't want to be involved."

Desperately, Steve wishes that was the case, a little boy saved by a good person stopping a bad person from doing something bad.

"Otherwise," Dick says, "as you said, I will be hailed a hero. My face will be plastered all over the news, and it will only be a matter of time before the connections are made to Otis and Hamilton."

It was Steve's exact thought when the ME mentioned *Walking Tall*.

"Which will lead back to you," Dick continues. "And Dee. Possibly even Sheriff Barton. Things would spiral, and ultimately my actions would be revered. Which as you've pointed out, would be catastrophic. Rogue justice, if celebrated, or even tolerated, will lead to copycats and anarchy, and would undermine the foundation on which our justice system was built."

Steve's mind spirals wildly to come up with an argument to his own convictions, and he thinks it's good most criminals' IQs hover in the lower range. If they were all like Dick, cops wouldn't stand a chance.

With a hard breath of frustration, he says, "Either way, the connection's going to be made. You made the 9-1-1 call, and your blood was at the scene."

"I don't think so."

Steve's not sure but thinks he detects the twitch of a smile.

"You came here alone," Dick says. "If you had shown up with a legion of cops, then yes, my fate would have been sealed."

Checkmate, Steve thinks, the reason for the twitch. Steve came alone and played right into Dick's hand.

"I was trying to do you a favor," Steve says.

"No," Dick says. "You came alone because you also recognized that it's better if this doesn't get out, so you chose to protect me."

The shard of glass in Steve's pocket grows warm.

He runs his hand hard through his hair. "This is ridiculous. I'm not going to let you kill yourself."

Dick leans back slightly, his brows arching as he drives home the point that the choice isn't up to him.

"Fine," Steve says. "You win. It's over. Tonight you were lucky, and that boy was lucky. Tell me this is where it ends, and I'll see to it that the case goes cold."

Dick takes a drag and blows the smoke out slowly before saying, "I'm afraid I can't do that."

"Are you kidding?" Steve spins and punches the air in frustration. "What part of 'tonight you were lucky' didn't you understand?"

"I won't make a promise I don't intend to keep. As you said, tonight I was lucky and so was that boy. Which means, if I don't die, there will be no choice but to continue to prevail."

"That's stupid. If you die, it's over."

"Yep."

"That doesn't make a goddamn bit of sense!" But even as he says it, he knows that it does. Dick doesn't want to die, yet he will not compromise who he is to save himself.

His frustration at critical mass, Steve says, "You know I can't just continue to let you keep doing what you've been doing."

Dick nods. "Hence, our spectral gap."

Steve has no idea what that is.

Dick helps him out. "A problem that is unsolvable." He snuffs the cigarette on the parapet. "Steve, it's okay. I've said my goodbyes and made my peace. All I want now are a few minutes alone to say my final prayers and smoke one last cigarette."

Steve considers tackling him off the wall but knows there's more chance of sending them both over the edge than saving him. He tries a Hail Mary pass.

"You know, you might not die. People have been known to survive greater falls."

"Let's hope I get lucky," Dick answers, unconcerned, then with a sad smile, adds, "It's a beautiful night." He nods at the clear starlit sky. "And I'm as good as I'll ever be. I have something worth giving up and something worth saving. How many can say that, then choose their final moment of destiny?"

The words pierce. Steve has seen it in war, brave soldiers,

usually damaged, who have seen a lot of death and decide they've had enough. Looking at a future they don't want, they decide instead to face their maker on their terms. Some choose to go out in a blaze of glory. Others opt for noble self-destruction with a purpose. Seppuku is what the Samurai call it, a death of honor.

A lump forms hard in his throat. While he doesn't want Dick to die, he also doesn't want to mess up his death.

Dick, perceiving the change, says, "Thank you," and the tightness in the words belies the veneer of calm Dick has maintained throughout the exchange.

Steve holds Dick eyes for another second, the color the same remarkable green as Denise's, then with the smallest nod, forces himself to turn and walk away.

When he reaches the door, he stops.

Turning back, he says, "I wish it could have been different. I love your sister, and she loves you. I want you to know, I intend to win her back and to take good care of them."

He continues through the door and doesn't see Dick nod or his shoulders heave.

88

Steve's body is revolting. Two years ago, he swore off hard alcohol, but last night, he needed to disappear. The half-empty bottle of Jack Daniels blurs into focus, and he groans as he sits up, head throbbing.

Wobbling as he stands, he realizes he's still a little drunk and considers taking a swig to restore his equilibrium, then pushes the thought away. It's a slippery slope, one he slid down for over a year after Danny's death.

Dick is dead. The thought brings a new level of pain and nausea.

The morning light through the windows works like daggers on his brain as he stutter-walks to the bathroom. He downs two Advil, splashes his face with cold water, then returns to the front room to check his phone for messages. There are several, but only the last one, left at 4:58, matters.

We all make our choices. Thank you for allowing me to make mine.

Now it's your turn.

You know the address: 12541 Rockingham. The

house is lined with red roses, each bush planted in honor of a boy. There are a few new seedlings that have only just begun to sprout. Others have been there for decades.

The gas began to seep in around nine last night. If you get there before seven, you might still have time to save him. If not, your conscience will be spared.

Take care of my sister and nephew.

Steve looks at his watch, 6:02.

His hangover combined with the surge of adrenaline makes the air thick and his body clunky as he races from the hotel to his borrowed agency car. He considers calling for backup, but something stops him. Two moves ahead. Whatever Dick's up to, Steve isn't certain he wants anyone else involved.

The email arrived a little over an hour ago, which means Dick didn't jump. Steve wishes his brain was working better. None of it makes sense.

If he wanted to run, why the scene on the roof?

———

There is no traffic, and he reaches Ingall's house in record time. His hangover has really heated up now and pulses behind his eyes as he pulls to a stop in front of the monogrammed gate. When the buzzer isn't answered, he uses the hood of his car to scale it and runs up the drive. He bangs on the door, then rings the bell.

He waits a full minute, timing it on his watch, then tries the door.

Finding it locked, he runs the perimeter, looking for another way in. Sweat drips beneath his shirt as he tries to each window, his skin and clothes tearing on the bramble of rose bushes that line the house, each with large red blooms and wicked long thorns.

The third patio door is unlatched, and he yanks it open and races inside. His watch says 6:43.

He allows a small sniff and smells nothing but lemon wax. Returning outside, he takes a deep gulp of air, then charges back in, up the sweeping staircase, and straight for the double doors at the end of the hall.

The smell of gas hits him as he bursts into the room, and his head snaps to the source, a marble fireplace with the gas key cranked right.

Grayson Ingall lies on the bed across from it, the covers pulled to his chest.

Steve moves closer, wondering if he's too late.

He touches the man's wrist, and his fingers register a slight pulse. He runs to the window, wrenches it open, and sticks his head through. His intention was to grab a breath of air then haul the dying man down the stairs to safety, but the perfume stops him.

He stares. The rose bushes are planted not only around the house but around the sweeping green yard as well . . . *each bush planted in honor of a boy. There are a few new seedlings that have just begun to sprout, others have been there for decades.*

There must be hundreds. From below, it looked like dozens. But from here, Steve can see the true expanse, morning dew glistening like diamonds on the red felt petals. His throat closes, and emotions rise in his eyes. He thinks of that boy last night. And of Jesse. He thinks of Danny as a boy. He thinks of Ally and of Diego Ramirez. He thinks of Shea and Memphs and all their victims who the system failed to protect.

Dick once told Steve that he was the checks and balances,

the one to decide if the law is at odds with what is right. And now, in this final chess move, he has laid down the gauntlet, challenging him to make a choice. His heart pounds, and he wonders if it is possible to do both: serve the law and also serve justice when that same law fails.

A truck labors up the hill, and a moment later, a crow flies overhead and lands on one of the spearheads of the iron fence.

His heartbeat slowing, he turns back to look at the man on the edge of death. On the bedside table is a pot, two thorny branches sticking out at odd angles. He moves closer. In careful cursive around the rim of the terra cotta, a single word: Phillip.

Turning back to the window, he lowers the pane, then using his sleeve, wipes it clean and returns downstairs.

89

Steve leans back on his elbows and watches Jesse surf. Denise lies beside him, her slightly rounded belly protruding over her bikini. Today is their six-month anniversary.

The third bedroom of Dick's cottage is in the process of being converted into a nursery, and Janelle's coming next weekend to help Denise pick out the furniture.

Jesse bounds from the water, Gus by his side—a mangy, uncoordinated mutt Steve's taken an extreme fondness to. Jesse's surfboard is under his right arm, and in his left hand is something Steve can't make out.

"Look what I found. Mom, will you keep it for me?"

"Sure, honey." Denise takes the starfish and sets it on the towel beside her.

Jesse sprints back into the water.

After Steve left Ingall's house, he drove to Pentco to discover Dick had left moments after Steve the night before. No suicide. No forwarding address. Outwitted, outplayed. He imagines Dick went to Mexico as he insinuated in the text he sent the night of Cray's death. Dick versus Diego, two brilliant minds at odds. He has his money and hope on Dick.

After Steve realized he'd been duped, he drove to Dick's new house. He didn't know what he expected to find, but when Denise opened the door, she fell into his arms, and all that day and night, that was where she remained.

They never talked about the night of Cray's death or what happened to Dick. The boy who was rescued, Mark Adams, has become a celebrity. Constantly, he and his mom are being interviewed, the story of his ordeal and his amazing rescue dissected again and again. The police concluded there was not enough evidence to identify the man who saved him, and the mystery of the anonymous hero has grown to epic proportions.

Steve looks at the starfish on the towel. "What's the starfish story?" he asks.

Denise cocks her head. "The starfish story?"

"Dick said it was one of your favorites."

"He told you that?" she says with a smile.

"I told you we talked about you," he says, rolling sideways to caress her arm.

"'The Tale of the Starfish,'" she says with a contented sigh that sounds like a purr.

She props herself on her elbow and brushes a strand of hair from her face, making Steve almost forget he'd asked a question.

That's the thing with second chances; they're sweeter than first chances. Nothing taken for granted. How beautiful his wife is. How much he loves the way she sweeps tendrils of loose gold from her eyes. A stepson he adores, and a daughter on the way. A home that smells like jasmine and fresh baked cookies. A mangy dog that reminds him of his wife's brother and constantly brings a smile.

"Once upon a time," Denise starts, "there was an old man who used to walk on the beach each morning before he went to work. Early one day, he was walking along the shore after a terrible storm and found it littered with starfish far as the eye could see."

She sweeps her free hand toward the ocean.

"In the distance, he noticed a boy walking toward him." She nods her chin toward Jesse. "As the boy walked, he paused every so often to bend down, pick something up, and throw it into the sea."

She gestures like she is flicking something away.

"Time and again, he stopped, bent down, and did it again."

She flicks her wrist again and again.

"When the boy got closer, the old man called out, 'Good morning. May I ask what you are doing?'" Denise deepened her voice in imitation of an old man.

"The boy paused, looked up, and answered, 'Throwing starfish into the ocean. The tide has washed them onto the sand, and if they don't return to the water, they'll die.'

"The old man nodded thoughtfully then said, 'But there must be tens of thousands of starfish on this beach. You can't possibly believe you are making a difference.'

"The boy smiled politely, bent down, picked up another small starfish at his feet, and threw it into the surf. Then he turned to the man and said, 'Made a difference to that one.'"

Steve notices as she says it, she sounds a little like Dick.

"I forgot how much I love that story," she says and lies back down, a smile on her face, and Steve rolls onto his stomach and places his hand on his wife's swollen belly, then closes his eyes and reminds himself that tomorrow he needs to drive to Cypress. It will be stifling hot, but the batteries in the webcam need to be changed.

AUTHOR'S NOTE

Dear Reader:

Two Good Men was the second novel I ever wrote. The first version was written over sixteen years ago and had the working title *Average Dick*. The name was terrible, and I knew it would never make it to print, but it made me smile. I've always loved double entendres, and the concept was to take an average guy named Dick (of the phrase "every Tom, Dick, and Harry") and, through a remarkable set of circumstances, turn him into an unlikely defender of children against perverted dicks (both possible meanings apply) and have him pursued by a heroic but down-on-his-luck detective, also known as a dick. Thus, four "average dicks" and a quadruple entendre! Voilà!

Despite its awful starting moniker, the concept worked. When I was in middle school, I had a teacher who was more poet than educator. Looking back, I think he hated his job, but at the age of twelve, I didn't recognize that. All I saw was a tall, skinny guy standing at the chalkboard day after day, his posture stooped as he recited whatever lesson he was supposed to be teaching to a bunch of disinterested kids. His eyes slid to the clock often, and every once in a while, as time was ticking down, he would segue into something that had nothing to do with what he was teaching. Once, he nodded out the window toward an oriole in a tree, then spoke for several minutes about birds and the powerful pull of place from thousands of miles away that caused their yearly migration. Another time, he recited a poem about a bottle in a field, then asked if we thought the bottle made the place significant because it gave it a focal point or denigrated it because it was trash. "But is it trash to an ant or a marvelous glass cathedral?" No one answered.

The digression I remember most was a story he told of a man who stood outside the Pearly Gates of Heaven. His whole life, the man had been a history buff, so when asked by God if he had any questions, he said, "Tell me, Heavenly Father, who was the greatest hero to ever live?" God parted the clouds, turned back the hands of time, and pointed down to a man outside Grand Central Station shining shoes. The history buff was baffled. He'd been thinking of Pericles or Joan of Arc or Alexander the Great. God smiled. "Had there been a war during his time, he'd have been the greatest hero to ever live."

The story made an impression. It's hard to know the greatness we possess until it is tested. Who knows who any of us might be if our circumstances were different? From that point on, I looked at greatness through an altered lens, giving as much credence to the context as the heroism—appreciating the story that allowed the greatness to shine—and always imagining who the hero might have been had things not unfolded as they did.

I bet that teacher has no idea the effect he had on me. I was the kid in the back of the class with the notebook full of doodles who never looked up and certainly never raised a hand. I probably appeared more bored and disinterested than anyone in the room. But I heard every word, and many of those melancholy introspective moments stayed with me and, ultimately, more than twenty years later, his morsel about heroes inspired this story. I have no idea what the teacher's name was, but the middle school was Neeta School in Medford Lakes, New Jersey, and the year was 1978. So if you were a tall, skinny, brooding teacher of prepubescent ingrates that year in the piney backwoods of the Garden State with a penchant for imparting wistful wisdom, thank you. You and the typing teacher from that same year are the reason this book exists.

We never know all the people we affect or how our ripples rearrange the world.

Best,

S. E. Redfearn

ACKNOWLEDGMENTS

This book would not have been possible without the following people:

For reading this story before it was pretty, I thank my daughter Halle, my husband Cary, and my good friend Glenn Rogers.

Thank you to my agent extraordinaire, Gordon Warnock, who resurrected this story from the archives and believed it could make it into the world.

Thank you to the amazing crew at Blackstone Publishing, which includes Addi Wright, Josie Woodbridge, Lysa Williams, Celia Johnson, Daniel Ehrenhaft, Levi Coren, Alenka Linaschke, Nicole Sklitsis, Rebecca Malzahn, and Rachel Sanders. Your guidance and input were invaluable, and each of you was a joy to work with.

DISCUSSION QUESTIONS

1. What would you have done had you been in Dick's position when Otis returned? How do you feel about him killing Otis? Do you think it was justified? If caught and sentenced, Dick would have served twenty-five years to life. Do you think the cost still would have been worth it? Was Steve right to bury the evidence and not charge Dick with murder?

2. Graham poses the question of whether it is ethical to alter personality traits to cure obesity. How do you feel about that sort of genetic meddling?

3. Donald Memphs and Otis Parsons, dangerous felons who have served their time, need to live somewhere. Do you think our current system of requiring them to register on a database but live where they please is the right one?

4. Dick has a conversation with Joanne where he wonders why most of us never become the heroes we believed we were going to be when we were kids. Do you think as we get older, we lose some of our idealism to change the world? Did you used to dream of saving the pandas or

discovering a cure? What was your big-picture dream?

5. How do you feel about Dick stalking released felons? Is it over the line? A violation of their rights? How about Captain Goh? Should the police be allowed to keep tabs on felons who they believe pose a danger?

6. What do you think Ally should have done once Diego was released? Moved? Changed her identity? What would you have done?

7. Pentco doesn't want to pursue protocol four because a cure would ultimately hurt profits. Do you think companies should be held accountable for unconscionable actions that put profits over people? Is it criminal?

8. Do you think there should be a position like the one Steve created (which is fictional), a person or department dedicated to defending the rights of released felons?

9. Dick kills Hamilton even though he is not entirely sure of his guilt. Should he have waited? Would the risk to Frankie have been worth the certainty?

10. Do you think, if the public learned what Dick had done, he would have been hailed a hero? And, if so, would it have had repercussions such as vigilante copycats taking it upon themselves to hunt ex-felons?

11. How do you imagine the future unfolding for the characters?

12. Who was your favorite character? Why?

13. Movie time: Who would you like to see play each part?